THE RED STAR™

The son of an American doctor, ARTHUR BYRON COVER was born in the upper tundra of Siberia on January 14, 1950. He attended a Clarion Science Fiction Writers' Workshop in 1971, where he made his first professional sale, to Harlan Ellison's *Last Dangerous Visions*. Cover migrated to Los Angeles in 1972. He has published a slew of short stories, in *Infinity Five*, *The Alien Condition*, *Heavy Metal*, *Weird Tales*, *Year's Best Horror Stories*, and elsewhere. He has also written several SF books, including *Autumn Angels* (a Nebula Award nominee for "Best Novel"), *The Platypus of Doom*, *The Sound of Winter*, *An East Wind Coming*, *Isaac Asimov's Robot City 2* (with William F. Wu), *Buffy the Vampire Slayer: Night of the Living Rerun*, and two bestselling novelizations of the comic book series *J. Michael Straczynski's Rising Stars*. Additionally, he has written scripts for issues of the comic books *Daredevil* and *Firestorm*, as well as the graphic novel *Space Clusters*.

SCIENCE FICTION UNIVERSES

published by ibooks, inc.:

THE RED STAR™

ARTHUR BYRON COVER

BASED ON THE SERIES
CREATED BY CHRISTIAN GOSSETT
AND WRITTEN BY BRADLEY KAYL

ibooks

new york
www.ibooks.net

DISTRIBUTED BY SIMON & SCHUSTER, INC.

An Original Publication of ibooks, inc.

The Red Star and all related characters
are TM and © 2002 Christian Gossett
ALL RIGHTS RESERVED.

An ibooks, inc. Book

ibooks, inc.
24 West 25th Street
New York, NY 10010

The ibooks World Wide Web Site Address is:
http://www.ibooks.net

The Archangel Studios World Wide Web Site Address is:
http://www.theredstar.com

ISBN 0-7434-7532-1
First ibooks, inc. printing November 2003
10 9 8 7 6 5 4 3 2 1

Special thanks to Team Red Star

Cover art by Christian Gossett

Printed in the U.S.A.

PROLOGUE: 1242

With the coming of the spring, Lake Vevad had thawed, and the bloated corpses of the Teutonic Knights and their horses had begun to float to the surface and drift to the shore, where they tended to pile up in the reedy marshes. Alexander Nevskii, the young prince whose army had defeated the Crusaders who had wanted to embrace the unwilling city of Gorodnov in their religious fervor, had slipped away from his encampment at dawn. He needed time away from his entourage and his bishop, his family, and his armies; he needed time alone so he could ponder his future, which was inexorably tied up with that of the loose network of city-states he was attempting to forge into a nation. But at the moment he most needed to get away from the riverbanks, away from the mighty smell that seemed powerful enough to permeate the entire Motherland.

For a while he allowed his horse to guide him. Alexander was still a young man, not quite twenty-five, though he was well aware that God could strike down the healthy as easily and as capriciously as the feeble and the sick, and that His hand was stayed no less in times of peace than in those of war. His dress was modest; his iron-ringed armor and pointed helmet matched those of the common foot soldier, while most of his finery was confined to his horse's saddle. He would be seen as a boyar, or a commander, but certainly not one of the importance he in fact was. As to why he had decided to roam the countryside without the safety and support of company, he had no idea. It had been a whim, and an illadvised one at that. There were still powerful families in the land whose patriarchs would not shed a tear if he were struck down by "thieves."

He came upon a modest cottage near the marsh. Smoke rose from a hole in the roof, and there was much chopped wood lying about in huge piles. A child could be heard crying inside. A baby.

As Alexander dismounted, a woman with a haggard face, long white hair that reached to her knees, and a frock—embroidered with patterns he associated more with the women of the Eastern hordes than the women of the Motherland—came to the doorway and demanded to know his business.

"I mean you no harm," he said, not unkindly, even though he was used to being treated with far more deference. "I have an appetite, and was merely wondering if I, a lonely traveler, might take advantage of your hospitality."

"You are lying," answered the woman. "You have come to have your fortune read."

"I was not lying. I am lonely and I have been traveling."

"But not for long," she said.

"That is true," he said, tethering his horse to a tree. She impressed him as being a woman of power and mystery. "I have never had my fortune read. What may I give you in return for such a service?"

"Merely being in the presence of a man who has released so many souls into the air we breathe is reward enough," said the woman. Her eyes flashed a crimson light that he could not assume was merely a reflection from the sun.

"You are a sorceress," said Alexander.

"And you are Alexander Nevskii," she said. "But I am afraid I am no sorceress—not a true one, in any case. I am a mere fortuneteller—nothing more, nothing less. Please, do me the honor of entering."

For a woman of such modest living conditions, she was gracious; her manners were those of the court, rather than of the humble sort who lived on and worked the land. Alexander took off his helmet and bowed.

The interior was modest, a few pieces of furniture, a place to skin animals, and a place to build a fire. Yet despite the hole in the roof that permitted the smoke to escape, the place was very warm.

"Please, sit," said the woman.

Alexander did so. "If I known such things were possible, I might have had my fortune read before the battle."

"It would not have made a difference," said the woman. "That is the strange thing about man's fate. He encounters the one he is meant to have, whether or not he is aware of his final destination."

"Then what is the point of this service?" he asked, in a light tone of voice.

The woman replied, "Because you are curious. All men are curious, but especially powerful men." Her child—a boy—began to cry again, and she picked him up and gave him her breast, which he ardently suckled.

"So," said Alexander, "just how does one read another's fortune? I have heard that in the West they use a pack of cards."

3

"Such systems are complicated and unnecessary," said the woman. She sat down at the opposite side of the small table between her and Alexander. She carefully gave him a blackened saucer. "Please hold this on the bottom."

He did as she asked, and then returned it to her. She showed him the bottom; on it his fingertips were plainly visible. She examined the fingerprints carefully, for many minutes, while Alexander sat in uncomfortable silence.

"The Goddess of Truth is pleased with you," she said finally. "Your fidelity to the truth shall be your greatest weapon, for your time of battle is past."

"But how can that be?" asked Alexander, thinking of the extreme threat of the hordes on horseback from the East. They brought bloodshed and death on a scale unprecedented in the histories written of in the Chronicles, and those peoples who defied them became the recipients of unspeakable cruelty, followed by certain death.

"Truth shall protect you, if you use it wisely, and do not seek to contradict it," said the haggard woman. "If the Goddess of Truth tells you that to fight is to lose, find a way to win without fighting, whatever the cost." She set down the bowl. "That is your fortune, Alexander Nevskii."

"I am not sure I comprehend it," he replied, "but I shall think of it."

"Think well, and it shall serve you well."

He stood. "I fear I must leave. My entourage is apt to be getting very nervous by now. They cannot act wisely in my absence, it seems."

"A problem that has plagued rulers since the dawn of eternity," said the woman, stroking the cheek of her suckling son.

"That is a fine, strong lad," said Alexander, "who shall surely grow to be a fine, strong man."

"Indeed. He was weak and sick before the battle, but since then he has drank deep from the wells of the souls released from their mortal prisons."

Alexander wasn't sure he knew what that meant, but it stood to reason that a fortune teller would speak in riddles. "What is his name?"

"Imbohl. He shall live a very long time. Of that I am certain."

Alexander smiled. He enjoyed the company of babies, of their innocence. But when he leaned closer to this Imbohl and looked into his eyes, a chill ran through him. He could not help but frown. "And have you seen his destiny?" he asked the woman.

"Alas, I cannot. I can only see that alone among us, my Imbohl has the gift of choice. But the nature of that choice, whether it be good or evil... I do not know."

"Then I pray he chooses wisely," said Alexander, and took his leave.

CHAPTER ONE

The pre-recorded music of the Transnationalist nemesis blared from the cabaret speakers. It celebrated materialism and youthful exuberance, but the mix was bad, and the bass was turned way up even though the corner speaker to Alexandra Goncharova's left handled it with more of a thud than a tone. Well, that was the Motherland's technology for you. Still at the analog stage, trying to play music intended for Transnationalist digital. Nevertheless, Alexandra enjoyed it as a guilty, almost illicit pleasure, as did, presumably, the other hundred or so fellow citizens already in attendance here at The Pravda Hollow.

Alexandra was a strong, slender woman of medium height. Her dark hair was styled long at the top but shaved at the neck, like a cadet's. Her smile could be broad and easy, even when her jaw was set hard. Her straight posture and determined gait was an accurate indication of her character: brash but not arrogant, the sort of Krawl Captain who could walk into a collective as if she owned the place, yet be agreeable about it. Her uniform was literally an old suit of clothes, though on her it radiated strength and an aura of beauty one might well associate with a forewoman's work overalls. She had come to The Pravda Hollow because she was lonely and at loose ends. She was hoping to find someone. At the moment, she had no idea who, but she was certain they would know one another.

The cabaret, a popular nightspot among soldiers and well-heeled party members, had a rustic motif, intended to evoke the feeling of a small ravine. The floor was painted gray, brown, and moss green, like a river bed, while on the ceiling and walls a phantasmagoric panorama depicted, to Alex's left, a brilliant sunny morning on the great steppe; in the center, noon in the forest; and to her right, a starry night in the snow-capped Caucasian mountains. The panorama was supposed to be realistic in approach, but its brilliance was more in intent than in execution. On the other hand, beneath the noon sun was rendered, with some degree of success, a bear and a pack of wolves, ignoring one another as they drank from opposite sides of the river. Perhaps the scene was symbolic of the current standoff between the URRS and the Transnationalists, but Alex doubted the artist's intentions were so perceptive.

She stood at the top of the winding staircase leading to the tables and dance floor below and wondered: should she go toward the night, the noon, or the dawn? It was a question she often asked after entering in—though she always regarded any answer she received as a direct result of her decision as precognitively insignificant.

Tonight the tables near the stage and the dawn were mainly occupied by party members, young civilians in fashionable, occasionally provocative or dashing office wardrobes. She knew their class well. Their day jobs usually involved the glacial movements of the Citadel bureaucracy. How they performed their jobs, and their devotion to the Internationalist Cause, determined whether their assignment would lead to an eternal dead end or to a more productive, personally rewarding calling. Tonight's crop of party civilians was especially young and energetic. The dancers danced as if earthquakes were going off in their feet, and a number of the tables were crowded with almost as many empty wine bottles as there were people gathered around to drink from them. Alex perceived tonight's crowd as too boisterous for her taste, but in truth, she envied them. She might have been one of their group herself, if she hadn't felt the calling to be a soldier. And if she hadn't fudged on her aptitude exams, just to ensure she got on the job track she wanted.

Beneath the noonday sun, between the bear and the wolves, were the brightest lights and the people who loved to stand beneath them. They included a wide cross-section of young Citadel society: non-coms and officers, artists and workers, party members and political conscientious objectors all mingled freely, all on the same endless quest for love or oblivion. Alex knew from bittersweet experience that an added goal was to impress their importance upon everyone. Her immediate impression was that this bunch was trying too hard: to be important, attractive, available and/or intelligent.

Tonight Alex felt much too old for that game. She had had a hard day. Most of it spent sleeping, but that was precisely the problem. Alex's dreams had been especially disturbing and vivid of late, populated by too many ghosts. Since waking she'd felt like she'd been walking in a shadow.

The canned music changed: an electronic trance effort backed by strings, and with a passionate Mid-East male/female duet. The singers' successful illusion of unlimited, untamed devotion touched a chord in Alex's heart. She glanced toward the starry end of the room, where the soldiers had discretely gathered.

Even from a distance she could tell they were relaxed. It was a tradition in the Red Army that certain locations, such as cabarets, were free zones, where non-coms and commissioned officers alike could forget the duties and restrictions of rank and regard one another as equals. The higher-ups didn't like it, which is why they usually weren't found in the Pravda. Alex was ranked about as high as they came.

But as soon as she'd passed through the doors, her rank had ceased to matter; belatedly she noticed a weight had been lifted from her soul. Before she knew it, she'd navigated through a sudden flurry of bustling waiters and was approaching a table populated mostly by young soldiers—and, most significantly, a buxom young female private with big blonde braids, her uniform unbuttoned practically to her navel. She had muscular arms—she looked like she could handle a blast furnace as easily as a general—and was holding court with the confidence of the socially adept.

Alex recognized neither the woman nor the others, but that didn't stop her from sticking her head between the shoulders of two men and saying, "Good evening, comrades. Salutations."

Such had been Alex's contributions to the patriotic cause in battle that she fully expected to be recognized. Much to a strange mixture of amusement and dismay, however, her greeting was met with a tableful of blank stares. The aroma of the various forms of alcohol, not to mention that of the half-eaten cuisine—lobster, caviar, cheese and crackers, pretzels, and Transnational beef patties—assailed her senses. She suddenly realized she was famished and weak with hunger. She had not eaten all day and now she was becoming unsteady.

A strong hand gripped her elbow. It belonged to one of the men who had been sitting down. He had black hair and dark brown eyes. The tattoo on his right temple indicated he'd seen combat in sunny Southern Africana. He guided her to his seat.

Alex gasped with gratitude. So much for her imperious air. "Thank you, sir." Actually, he was only a sergeant, but cabaret protocol required her to call him "sir" just as a five-star general would be obligated to call her "ma'am." Anything else would be a social faux pas that would require, at the very least, several rounds of drinks paid by the offender.

"I know you," said the sergeant. z DEMYANYCH. "Did I not see you during the Public Service Hour on URRS Channel Five recently, extorting the masses to support charities for veterans maimed in battle?" He reconsidered. "No, wait! It was workers maimed in industrial accidents!"

Alex blushed. Now it would truly be bad form to mention her exploits on the battlefield. Not that she minded, by this point. Her exploits all involved blood and death, the tragic waste of good patriots, and the necessary waste of misguided foes fighting for unworthy causes. That was merely her rationalization, however. The truth is, no one hates war more than a soldier who has seen combat, and Alex had seen more than her fair share.

"I have no idea who you mean," Alex said to Demyanych, answering truthfully.

"I know you!" said the buxom blonde. She pointed her forefinger, not impolitely, at Alex. Half the finger was missing. "I used to see you at The Beloved Revolutionary Sweetheart!"

"No," said Alexandra, firmly but with a smile.

"Hey, let me be your beloved revolutionary sweetheart," said a non-com sitting beside the blonde. He'd put his arm around her, but she was pointedly ignoring his familiarity. Indeed, he had an eager air. He wasn't bad looking, so it was possible he would find company tonight, but not if he kept his aim focused on the blonde.

"Then who are you?" asked a stout woman in the Medical Corps, probably a surgeon who'd saved many lives on the battlefield, judging from the array of medals on her uniform.

Alex introduced herself demurely, omitting rank, exploits, everything but her name.

"I don't recognize your name, but I do recognize you," said the stout woman. "Are you a movie star?"

A freckled-faced rube, whose accent indicated he was from the marsh country and who was depending on a friend to stand up straight, said, "Well, if you've come to research a part, you've come to the wrong place. Between us we've fought a hundred battles, but none of us can agree on anything—especially what it means!" He belched. Loudly.

"My name is Varya," said a woman whose soft peaked cap was tipped too far to the left and too close to her eyes to meet the dress code. She wore her bright red hair in a bun. And though she stood uncertainly and revealed herself to be slightly tipsy when she leaned over to shake Alex's hand, her grip was strong and bold. The respect in her voice came through quite clearly as she said, "And I do know you, Alexandra Goncharova."

Alex felt her chest swell, involuntarily, with pride—at last she was recognized by one of her peers in the manner to which she'd become accustomed. She knew the sword of pride was double-edged. Pride motivated the individual to do her best, yet at the same time pride tempted one to put their interests above those of the team—or worse, those of the state. In Alex, this temptation was always present, though she believed, and her record proved, she had succeeded in keeping the temptation in check. What is more, she decided instantly that she liked this Varya.

"Among those of us stationed in the Balkan Fortress, you are well known as the best friend of Sorceress-Major Maya Antares."

Alex's ego instantly deflated. She'd hoped this evening would ultimately be all about her. Despite her disappointment, she found herself blushing. "Well, I am her friend. And I am proud to say she is mine."

A man put his arm over her shoulder. She quickly noted his breath reeked of vodka, he had laughing eyes, and he outranked her. "Alexandra Goncharova! It is an honor to make your acquaintance. Any comrade of the great and renowned Sorceress of Kar Dathra's Gate is obviously a comrade of mine!"

"Thank you," said Alex, politely pulling away. "But as Sorceress-Major Antares would be the first to tell you, she was but one of five hundred Comrade Sorceresses. She fought no more bravely than they, gave no more nor less than they, and the sacrifices they made were often many times greater than any she might have made for the Motherland."

"True," said Varya. "But Comrade Antares is as famous for her steadfastness and her beauty as she is for the example she set for us all with her courage. Few people know when to defy orders and still be a heroine."

"Mainly I think she is famous for her sublime beauty," said the man, a major. He put his arm around her shoulder again, as if he was fitting a piece of plumbing beneath the kitchen sink. "And, as her sidekick, you are in the best position to tell me and the other unattached officers here what exactly she is like."

"A sidekick!" Alex, slinked out from under the man's arm and out of her chair, grabbed the man by the lips and pressed them together as one would an unruly child. "I can show you my kick. Should I begin now?" She smiled when she said that, to let him know she was in jest.

"Not a sidekick!" said the man with a bow. Alex realized there was humor, and friendship, in his voice. "But a comrade. I am honored. My name is Vladimir!"

"My name is Mymrina," said the buxom blonde bombshell. That opened the floodgates, and everyone who had yet to introduce themselves did, seemingly all at once.

So many names, Alex thought, *and so little reason to remember them.* Yet she was gratified by their hospitality. Even their over-familiarity was simply a form of friendly hazing, a rite of passage.

"So tell me," said Demyanych, "my friend wants to know—" he indicated Mymrina "—has Major Antares put her grief behind her yet?"

The blonde blushed and jabbed Demyanych in the ribs with her elbow. The blow was harder than she'd probably expected to deliver, and certainly harder than he'd expected to receive.

"She has not. She is temperamentally incapable of it." Alex smiled slyly. "So trust me, should one of you be so honored to meet her, you wouldn't stand a chance."

"I was afraid of that," said Vladimir.

"Well, I can dream," said a corporal whose name Alex hadn't caught.

: us if our trifling stirred up the badger in you,"
1 eating a series of pretzel sticks, one by one,
with the precision of a robot arm in an assembly. "I was
wondering if you would honor us by telling us what it
is like basking in the mammoth personal aura of so
august a sorceress."

Alex couldn't resist laughing. "I am sorry, forgive me,"
she said hastily, when she noticed the man's crestfallen
face. "I truly don't think of my relationship with Maya—I
mean, Comrade Antares—in such epic terms."

"Then how *do* you think of it?" asked Vladimir.

Alex sighed. She knew when she was beaten. "Perhaps
I can be persuaded to elucidate, if you people would be
so kind as to buy me a few drinks. Starting with a
straight Steel. *This* tall." She paused as her audience
nodded as one. "The first thing you must remember about
Comrade Antares is that, all evidence to the contrary,
she is just as human as any of us. She has always stood
by me whenever I have needed her. I remember..."

And then she was off, narrating stories of Maya's
inherent kindness and courage, her determination and
reason, but mostly her capacity to love all mankind and
her devotion to the Internationalist cause. Utopia wasn't
just an idealistic dream to Maya Antares, it was the very
embodiment of absolute possibility. World peace wasn't
just a children's fantasy, faith wasn't just another word
for an irrational belief, and true love wasn't just an
excuse for desire. Maya didn't waste time articulating
her ethics, her social standards, her innate gentility; she
lived her principles, steadfastly, exclusively, passionately.
Yet Alex strove to be clear: Maya wasn't a humorless
embodiment of a socialist cog from the early decades of
the Revolution. She laughed easily, and her conversation
possessed a delicious sense of irony. She had clear ideas

of right and wrong. She would not have participated in a purge or tolerated the starving of millions or assisted in the execution of freedom fighters because they might have posed a threat to the cause in the future. Woe to the dictator or minion who might have given her such an order! (Of course, woe to Maya if she had defied such orders during the Patriotic War, when the Committees had possessed the unwavering devotion of many powerful sorceresses. But the point was, Maya would have gladly taken on the burden of that woe.)

As Alex spoke, the music changed, from one form of Transnationalist dance tune to another, and the Steels came and emptied until she felt the room spin. Rather than dampening her perceptions, however, the alcoholic haze magnified the intensity of her feelings for her friend. She realized she had been wrong to be disappointed that the source of her fame among these good people had been her connection to Maya rather than her own heroism. Maya was indeed a special person, whose very presence was a blessing to the world. Even the coldest hearts of the Revolutionary Stalwarts of the Golden Age might been humanized if they could have stepped into her aura, though the chances were not even Maya could have diminished the collective ruthlessness of their actions.

One thing you could say about the current crop of Red leaders: they were ruthless, but they were not insane. Misguided and confused perhaps, but not insane. And they had recognized the contributions Maya had made to the Motherland simply by remaining true to herself, and they had subtly contributed to and profited from her fame.

Alex noticed a significant development during her talk: the attention of a young man who had been sitting quietly at a spot at the table where he had initially been hidden in shadow. But as her talk wore on, he leaned forward into the pool of light, his eyes fixed upon her, and she began to perceive signals that he was interested in her. He wasn't bad looking, either. His body was slender but strong. He wore civvies but he also wore a kepi, the flat-topped hat with a visor that indicated he was part of the Internationalist Air Force. Indeed, he had the ruddy complexion of a man who'd spent a great deal of time on a skyfurnace. Soon, Alex was finding it difficult not to stare at him, and she knew it wouldn't be long before she was asking him to escort her home.

Suddenly, she gasped as a familiar face loomed over the table. It was a handsome face, a typical Antares face, strong and straight, with direct eyes and a square chin, but it was not quite as handsome as some Antares faces Alex had known. She also perceived that the Antares in question was thoroughly inebriated.

"So, you know Maya Antares, eh?," said the man with the face. "Well, I know her, too, and I think she's a fake. I don't even think she's much of a goddamned sorceress. Overrated in the extreme, if you ask me. I should know! And as for that much-vaunted idealism, I think it's just an excuse to keep from getting drunk, like me!"

"Urik!" Alex exclaimed, standing.

"The one, the only," said Urik Antares—Maya's brother-in-law. He meant only to belch, but then he turned away from the table and leaned over, just in time.

The people Alex had labored so hard to impress wavered between being amused and being disgusted.

Infuriated, she was tempted to deliver to Urik the swift kick to the rear she'd felt he'd deserved for nearly a decade, but instead she found herself at his side, holding him steady. "Look at you. I swear by Great Ivan's ghost you're a mess. And your uniform! It looks like you bought it at a pawn shop. What the hell's the matter with you?"

"I'm drunk. What do you think?"

I think you've derailed what would have been a successful evening, Alex thought. But she only said, "Let's get you out of here."

"I didn't mean what I said earlier about Maya. What *did* I say, anyway?"

"Nothing," said Alex sharply.

They had walked in mutual silence for the past kilometer and a half, and were now walking past St. Basil's Cathedral. Alex was exhausted. She had spent most of the walk supporting Urik, but since he'd opened his fur-lined overcoat and relieved himself on the rear wall of one of the eight churches that comprised the cathedral, he'd been able to stand on his own. She was still smarting from embarrassment at his vulgar behavior in public; she was certain the constable standing beneath the blue spruce had seen them—Urik had been standing smack in the glow of a street lamp—and had only refrained from taking action because it was clear the perpetrator was a man in uniform, and hence was deserving of a slight amount of slack. Usually she was of the opinion that off-duty soldiers should have a minimum of social privileges, that they should be treated just like ordinary citizens. As things were, soldiers like Urik tended to lose perspective.

Of course, she remembered, he'd lost perspective nine years ago.

They began walking across the Crimson Plaza. It was practically deserted, save for a lonely automobile spewing exhaust, a few couples wandering and holding hands, and a pneumatic tank standing guard near Gorkovsky's

Tomb. The bricks that covered the open space were slippery and glistened from the snow that had melted that afternoon.

"Let's go to the Tomb," said Urik. "I have something to say to His Worship."

The last thing Alex wanted to see was Gorkovsky's waxen mummy face, and she certainly didn't want to hear whatever it was Urik might have to say to the dead founder of the modern Mother State—chances were it could get them arrested, if overheard—but she consented nonetheless. She knew Urik well enough to know that he would go with or without her, and this way she might encourage him to hold his voice down to a whisper, if nothing else.

The cathedral domes and other landmarks on the borders of the square were illuminated, but in such a way that they minimized the "light pollution," so the stars above were very clear, considering that she was viewing them in an urban environment. Alex sighed. By now there were at least 150 known planets outside the solar system, probably all gas giants many times the size of Jupiter, and recently the Red scientists had announced the discovery of a ring of several billion stars circling the Milky Way. Her own personal problems were as insignificant as a lonely atom compared to the vastness of the universe, and perhaps the same might be said of the entire human race. Yet the knowledge made her problems no less difficult to deal with. If only her spirit could somehow vault up into those unknown realms, explore them and gain wisdom, then perhaps the Earth might somehow be infused with the love she believed lay dormant and unfulfilled in her breast.

At that moment her ideals seemed futile. Not much blood, proportionately speaking, had been spilled on the

Crimson Plaza during its existence, but those who had marched here every May Day, those Czars and Commissars who had stood on the platforms to view their salutes, and goodness knows how many jackals and murderers who had watched from sidelines—they'd spilled rivers of blood both innocent and misled. She had spilled quite a bit herself. Her soul felt it was being swept along in rapids of that blood, rushing downstream toward an ignoble destination.

Alex shrugged off the feeling with an effort. Given her preference, she would die an old lady, via a heart attack induced by the passion of a young man, but she knew that hardly ever happened to someone with her salary. She was a soldier. And given what was happening in the world, she would most likely die a soldier.

While the stars looked down, indifferently.

Seven soldiers stood guard at the entrance to Gorkovsky's Tomb. The current President of the URRS, Vladimir Moszkowski, had recently decreed the shrine open to the public, in order to boost morale, and to send a signal to the nation's enemies that the people were unwavering. As an unintended consequence, the shrine had become a preferred target of terrorists whose objectives were symbolic rather than military. The guards looked up at Alex and Urik as they walked inside, then promptly returned to the games and movies on their hand-helds. The music of Anatasia Romanoff's *Romeo and Juliet* emanated from one hand-held, and a hummable song from another. Alex approved that the guards' pastimes were not totally devoid of culture, but she wished they hadn't been so immediately accepting of the late night visitors' uniforms. If she were a terrorist, she would have...

Never mind. Such thoughts were sacrilege, especially

here. She knew this place was nothing more than a glorified mausoleum, but the cold pale light and the perfectly preserved corpse of the great man himself stirred her devotion to comrade and country nonetheless. Indeed, how could it have been otherwise? Gorkovsky's face was peaceful and composed, yet such was the illusion of life—of sleep—that it seemed he was on the verge of awakening, and his jaw would once again be set with determination, his eyes afire with a vision of the future that could be compassionate or ruthless, depending on the obstacle of the moment.

"Nice suit," said Urik.

"Urik!" Alex hissed, *sotto voce*.

"Nice shoes, too," he said, running his fingers over the top of the symbol of a hammer and sickle in a pentagram etched on the foot of the monument. "A little out of style. Have you ever noticed how world leaders—Internationalist, Transnationalist, or otherwise—are always so immaculately dressed? Especially those who claim to be of the people. The people aren't so well-dressed. Look at me, for instance."

"A trip to the cleaners would fix you up nicely," said Alex, who wore her uniform proudly, despite its age. Her mind, however, was not on her charge. She found herself staring intently at Gorkovsky's folded hands, with their manicured fingernails and hairless wrists, the fingers intertwined so naturally on his chest. Wrapped around two of the fingers was a small gold chain, at the end of which was a small rock. He had regarded it as a good luck charm; rumor had it it was a piece of a meteor, but no one had ever been allowed to study it. It was sacred.

"I think he's starting to decompose," said Urik.

"Don't say that!" Alex replied, shocked.

"Look at that eyebrow. See?" He was insistent. "The hair is all screwed up."

"It looks as real as mine," said Alex bravely. She was reluctant to take too close a look, for fear Urik might be right. He occasionally was.

"You know, come to think of it, I have hair just like it, too," he said, "only not on top of my head." He turned to her and smiled. "So, what are the odds I'm going to get lucky tonight?"

"The odds are better that you'll get castrated."

"We'll see about that." He took a satellite phone from his pocket and said, "Dial Noémie Chérnega, please."

Alex felt her face turning beet red. She had assumed he had meant her, like most sane men would at this point. Of course, she would have said no, a thousand times no, and would have meant it, but that didn't stop her from resenting the fact that he had given up so easily. Perhaps that castration remark had been a little harsh...

Listening to him squire a name from his cell phone while standing in Gorkovsky's tomb, however, boded ill, in her opinion, for the future of the Motherland. And to think, once Urik had been as strong and focused as his brother.

She wondered, was the Motherland capable of producing men like Marcus Antares anymore?

CHAPTER TWO

T HE YOUTH OF TODAY ARE THE FUTURE OF TOMORROW! So read the sign on the huge billboard nailed to the barb-wired posts that stood in the trenches between the highway and the grassy tract that separated the Gorky Youth Encampment from the rest of the world. On the billboard were painted three young people: a teen-aged girl and two boys. Their eyes were fixed on the sky, and a soft light shone on their handsome, determined faces. Maya could tell the painting was recent because the girl's earring was in the shape of the modern cyber-sickle all the kids had been wearing two or three years ago, and one of the boys had a dark complexion and high, noble cheekbones meant to invoke an Islamic heritage. The implication being that all the citizens of the URRS, former and otherwise, belonged together, were destined to work together, and would one day be forged into a community that neither misfortune nor prosperity could rip asunder.

The chauffeured station wagon made the turn toward the Encampment front gate. Sitting in the back seat, lost in her thoughts, Sorceress-Major Maya Antares sighed wistfully and recalled the teen-aged girl of spirit and spunk she had once been: an idealistic lass totally receptive to the billboard's message. Indeed, a part of her still believed in the message, and what's more, clung to its ideals with ferocious tenacity. Maya believed her faith in the dream was greater than that of the leaders whose responsibility was making the dream a reality. And although she was too modest to say so, others who had noted the trait were of the opinion she nurtured this faith with the utmost humility.

Sitting next to her in the back seat was Kyuzo. Kyuzo was a Hailer. A Hailer's sole assignment was to protect a sorceress regardless of the circumstances, regardless of the cost. In the west such an individual was known simply as an escort, or a bodyguard, but beneath the Red flag they were named after the heavy-caliber weapons attached to their shoulders and right arms. Every .hailer weighed thirty pounds, and with the assistance of the proper protocols could fire seventy rounds a second. Kyuzo seemed to barely notice the weight, or the weight of the rest of his weaponry. May knew the only burden he noticed was that of his duty, and that consisted solely of protecting the Sorceress-Major.

Kyuzo was uncomfortable in the wagon, not only because he was a big man, but because the proximity of the Sorceress-Major induced it. Besides, he would have felt better if he'd been allowed to ride on a motorcycle alongside the station wagon, to better protect the Major in the event of an incident. But it had been cold this morning, and the Major had insisted he enjoy the comfort of the vehicle's heat.

The driver was listening to the radio, a classical piece. It had been playing for nearly half an hour, and seemed to be reaching its climax. Although he knew it was *de rigueur* for Red soldiers to appreciate the finer things in life, Kyuzo had difficulty relating to classical music. He much preferred traditional folk and dance music.

Yet he watched the Sorceress-Major's concentration with interest. Often she closed her eyes and waved her left hand as if she was conducting. During the low tempo sections where the strings came in too heavily for Kyuzo's taste, she held her breath, and her eyes appeared dreamily fixed on a distant plane. He decided there must be something to this classical music after all, if it could help the Sorceress-Major forget her troubles for a time.

"Do you know this work?" she asked him.

That took him off-guard. Usually she did not ask his opinion on anything. She merely went about her business.

Kyuzo cleared his throat. Nervously. "No. I do not know music."

"But you listen, do you not?"

Kyuzo shrugged. "I am here, am I not?"

She smiled. She clearly knew he was not being sarcastic or rude, that he was only stating what was, for him, a simple fact. "What do you think of the music?"

Kyuzo hesitated. "It very much embodies the crimson spirit—briskly, and tunefully. Yet not without pathos, and certainly not without struggle."

"It is by Kalinnikov," said the driver, an old man who was trying to be helpful. "He died young, at the turn of the century."

"That is true," said the Major. "This is his Second Symphony. I think of his music as being similar to that of the romantic Petyr Krylov, only without the wringing of the tears."

"Or perhaps like Radishchev, but without so much melancholy," put in the driver.

"This Kalinnikov—he died young?" asked Kyuzo.

24

"Of tuberculosis," said Maya.

Kyuzo pondered this. "I see. Obviously he was a man of talent, who could have been of some use to the new state after the Revolution. It is a shame the health care for the intellectuals was as bad as it was for the masses during those dark times, otherwise this Kalinnikov might have lived to write many more symphonies."

The Major nodded in approval. "Funny. I was thinking much the same thing."

The symphony had reached its triumphant conclusion as the driver braked and the wagon stopped. A sentry who could not have been shaving very long stepped out of the gatehouse and inspected the driver's ID. He looked at the passengers and saluted the Sorceress-Major. He said he was honored to meet her, then asked Kyuzo to step outside.

In a combat situation, Kyuzo moved like a panther, but in more peaceful circumstances he tended to be slightly awkward. Getting out of the wagon, he bumped his forehead and struck his shoulder. A lesser man would have seen stars, but Kyuzo was merely embarrassed. He did note, with some gratitude, the Major pretending not to notice.

Kyuzo folded his arms across his chest and loomed over the sentry. "I take it you wish to inspect me?" His voice was a Siberian chill.

The sentry blanched. "You have weapons."

"So do you." Kyuzo pointed at the rifles being carried by an approaching trio of sentries.

"They don't have firing pins."

"Not much use in a situation then, are they?"

The sentry cleared his throat. "This is a Youth Encampment. We are not yet officially soldiers."

"I can see that."

"Kyuzo." The Major's tone was neutral, which was all it needed to be.

Now it was Kyuzo's turn to blanch. The mere possibility that he might annoy or offend the Major was enough to make him behave. He detached his .hailer and unceremoniously dropped it into the young man's arms. The sentry nearly fell over. Kyuzo pretended not to notice and slowly removed the remainder of his weaponry.

"Do not worry, Kyuzo," said the Major from the vehicle. "The only mortal danger you'll face at Gorky is the number of schoolgirls who'll undoubtedly develop crushes on you."

The driver laughed. Kyuzo grunted; the prospect lacked appeal.

Maya, meanwhile, blushed. She believed her words were inadvertently inappropriate, that perhaps she should not have mocked her Hailer, however slightly. After all, the schoolgirls of today were the women of tomorrow, and perhaps by then Kyuzo would have put aside his singular devotion to his duty and let a little happiness into his life.

"Should we go inside?" the driver asked her.

"Please," said Kyuzo. "I am not yet done." Indeed, he had loaded down another cadet and was still handing guns, knives, and various other concealed devices to a third. "I will catch up with you."

Maya nodded, and the driver took her into the school. The Gorky Encampment resembled all such establishments: Gray stone buildings. An administrative section that overlooked a drill field and a small stand of bleachers. On the field was a slew of sharp-looking youngsters, laughing, saluting, practicing their rifle routines, and running laps. The encampment Maya had attended had the exact same feel; so had all of them. These places were like idyllic purgatories where the students changed, but time never passed.

A statue of Gorkovsky and President Moszkowski standing shoulder-to-shoulder had been erected before the administrative headquarters. Lost pondering whether Moszkowski really believed the fantasy propaganda that cast him as the spiritual heir to Gorkovsky, she hadn't noticed the station wagon had stopped until the driver opened the door for her. She got out, thanked him, and took the steps two at a time. She saluted the sentries at the front, and without hesitation—she remembered the way from her previous visits—walked directly into Commandant Kuchar's office.

An orderly sitting at a desk snapped to attention and saluted her.

"At ease, youngster," said Maya, taking off her gloves. "I am—"

"I know," said the young lady, breathlessly. "Shall I tell Commandant Kuchar you have arrived?"

"Please."

But Kuchar already knew. He had been informed by the sentries at the gate. He chose that moment to step into the waiting room. He beamed and opened his arms for a friendly embrace.

Major Antares snapped her heels together and greeted him with a polite salute. Kuchar cleared his throat. He should have known. This woman was as distant as she was beautiful.

And Kuchar believed if Major Antares were any more beautiful, her distance from humanity would take her off the planet. Kuchar was a late-middle-aged, round man with white hair and a bold white moustache. He believed himself to be of some importance in the party structure, the sort of person even a sorceress-major might want to cultivate favor with. He was completely wrong, of course, and was fortunate indeed that his life would never depend on Maya Antares' estimation of him. But it was beauty that addled his mind—the beauty of her oval face, her porcelain skin, and her silky blonde hair, always tied so neatly in that long braid.

The overcoats of a red uniform tended to obscure the figure of a woman, but such was not the case with Maya Antares. He had the feeling he had already seen her shape, on an armless staue of an ancient beauty displayed in a Europa museum. Custom, duty, and manners demanded that he not regard her as the object of a fantasy merely because she was a woman, and her cool demeanor certainly did not encourage it.

However, the commandant had seen sorceresses in action before, working their protocols in the great airships. Suspended in mid-air, their uniforms skin-tight, their faces glistening with perspiration, their energies filling the hollows of the great vessels with pulsating magnetic fields. The kind of man who did not feel excited at the notion of being intimate with one of those women was not the kind of man who was welcome in the Red Army.

Kuchar had deluded himself into believing he was a practical dreamer. True, a marriage of romance was out of the question, but an alliance between an older man of the world and a woman of beauty and intelligence had been known to happen, making it at least within the realms of possibility. So he took her distance in stride, beamed beatifically as he offered her coffee, biscuits, and other hospitalities, and attempted to make small talk. "Come into my office, please. Sit. Yes, sit, make yourself comfortable. Do not worry, your Hailer will be made comfortable outside, when he arrives. I would like to speak with you, to get to know you. I mean, I feel as if I already do, but I would like to get to know you better."

Maya did as she was asked, and even answered a few of his questions in honest ways that divulged as little information as possible, but the commandant would have been disappointed to know that while speaking to him, she did not think of him at all. She noted with passing interest the party awards and declarations posted on the walls of his office, the magnificent view of the encamp-ment training fields afforded by the frosty picture win-dow behind his desk, and the collection of vintage toy soldiers and war artifacts on proud display in a glass case. This Kuchar was a good educator in the ways of war, she suspected, but he did not know war itself. Oth-erwise he would not have enthusiastically collected so many of war's heirlooms.

"So tell me," he asked, "what is the subject of your speech to the cadets today?"

Maya blushed. "I have some notes. I hope they aren't expecting too much."

"Just the fact they are hearing the words of the heroine of the battle of Kar Dathra's Gate will be enough," Kuchar replied with sincerity.

Maya smiled at him. "I appreciate the sentiment, but please, I am no heroine."

"But you are!" he exclaimed. Perhaps a little too emphatically, but he had been taken off-guard by the honesty of her reaction, and a little disappointed, too. If truth and sincerity were the only way to get this sorceress to notice him, then truly he had no chance with her. He went on to explain that the cadets had spoken of nothing else since her appearance had been announced, but inwardly he was already plotting the next move in his social life. There was a meeting in Citadel next week: the widows and widowers of veterans were plotting how to increase their benefits. Prominent widows would undoubtedly be in attendance, and it wouldn't hurt for some of the cadets to think he was fighting for the social well-being of their surviving parent.

The orderly knocked on the door. "Madam Antares? Your Hailer has arrived."

"Send him in," said Maya, knowing that Kyuzo's presence would put a stop to the commandant's small talk while they waited for the call to assembly. Even now cadets finding seats in the bleachers could be seen through the picture window. Maya regarded the coming speech with nervousness and a sense of responsibility, but at the moment she was distracted and amused at the young orderly's wide, eager eyes as they followed Kyuzo striding in.

Kyuzo, naturally, did not notice. His mind was obviously on other matters. Without so much as a word of greeting, and only the most perfunctory salute, he said, "Comrade Commandant, I fear I must report to you it took three cadets to carry my weaponry to the armory. I fear their upper body strength is inadequate."

Maya had invited Kyuzo to sit next to her on the wooden stage that had been erected in the center of the athletic field, but he preferred to wander among the cadets standing in the field and sitting in the bleachers. This wasn't a formal affair; attendance was voluntary, and the cadets weren't required to stand in formation. Nor were they all required to be in dress uniform; boys and girls alike often wore fatigues or their gym outfits. Unofficial rallies were a frequent occurrence at encampments—they kept up student morale, and were especially helpful in keeping the students focused during times of political uncertainty.

Kyuzo was not a sentimental man. A soldier could not afford to be overtly emotional in the modern world. Due to the fact that his grandfather had disgraced the family by becoming a counter-revolutionary, Kyuzo had not been privileged to attain an encampment; his education had been on the collective, on the wrestling mat, and in boot camp. Yet he did not envision his young self as having been substantially different than these children. These were all innocent, strong, idealistic youth, brimming with piss and vinegar. He prayed that when they reached his age, they would have retained more of their idealism than he had.

Though when it came to piss and vinegar, he yielded to no pup. He was not obvious or aggressive about it, but he was firm; to a person, the young made way for him as he wandered back and forth on the field. Furthermore, he knew they ceded their position, however temporarily, not merely because he was a massive hunk with a brooding, fear-inducing appearance, but because they did not wish their attention to be diverted from the Sorceress-Major sitting so demurely, yet so loftily to the left of the podium on the stage.

Knees together, hands folded on her lap, Maya had fixed her eyes just above the heads of the crowd. She had buttoned her great coat so as not to draw attention to her inherent femininity, yet the curve of her single golden braid lying down her right breast provided the hint of unobtainable promise that had been the secret fountainhead of Kyuzo's devotion.

At the podium stood Commandant Kuchar, speaking into a microphone with a short somewhere in the wire, so his voice kept cutting out through the speakers. Four other uniformed adults—staff and teachers, probably—sat on the stage as well. They attempted to face front, but their eyes constantly strayed to the Major, who while not exactly ignoring them, managed to remain shielded in the wall of her own aura.

Kuchar was the sort of speaker who wanted to be forceful while gaining the respect of his audience, yet he lacked the talent for it. He succeeded mainly in haranguing the students. However, his sentiments were noble enough. "You will be the URRS future because you are the future—I am your Commandant, but I am only the trustee of youth. You belong to the nation. When you grow up, you will look back in pride and say, 'I was a lad or a lass when a new URRS was born!'"

Kyuzo remembered with fondness that he'd once wanted to hear someone speak those words to him. No one ever had, unless you counted his wrestling coach. The children of today had no idea how lucky they were, for when Kyuzo was young, the State had not always appreciated what youth had to offer, or how important the strength of the young would be in the future. Once upon a time the State had trained only young bodies; today the State, despite all the setbacks of the Internationalist cause, trained young minds, hearts, and souls as well. Kyuzo realized his attitude toward these children was undergoing a transition: rather than feeling his condescension toward them was justified, he felt he had erred. Grievously. Men such as he and women such as the Sorceress-Major could not carry on the burden forever—one day they would be forced to relinquish the yoke of freedom, and it would be up to these children to take it. Looking at their determined faces, he knew they would be ready.

The applause, cheers, and sloganeering following the climax of Kuchar's little talk were politely enthusiastic, but nothing like the response that greeted Sorceress-Major Antares as she stepped up to the podium. She stood at the podium and acknowledged the applause with a nod for a minute or so, then held up her palm, silently asking the students to cease.

"Thank you," she said, and that was as far as she got when the microphone conked out again. She smiled, raised a forefinger, and waved it three times. A yellow light emanated from her finger and coalesced in a circle around the microphone, where it remained, continuing to exist, neither growing brighter, nor diminishing.

"There. That should be better," she said.

Indeed, it was. Her voice echoed from the buildings like a birdsong in a canyon. She spoke softly, clearly, vibrantly. Kyuzo had heard her speak many times before, and though this time the subject matter and the presentation were no different, he found himself listening attentively, as always.

And he was, as usual, extremely moved by her story. How could it be otherwise? Maya had been orphaned when her parents were killed in a terrorist action carried out by the Transnationalist lackeys in the Middle East. The State cared for her, fed her, and clothed her, until she could be reunited with her aunt and uncle in Siberia. Her relatives had encouraged her intellectual development at some risk to their relatively comfortable existence in that harsh environment, for celebrating the freedoms the young took for granted today often landed good citizens in serious trouble. But that had been before the advent of the policies of openness that had proven necessary if society was ever to achieve genuine socialism. The State graciously recognized Maya's devotion to the cause and

33

the power she could contribute, and overlooked what was then considered an improper curiosity about the emotional and decadent literature of the west. Upon her admittance to the Academy, the depth and extent of her sorceress abilities revealed themselves. As usual, Maya's speech did not leave out the comic aside that highlighted her humility and humanity: the story of how she accidentally exploded a latrine.

Kyuzo expected the tale to lead into the usual homilies about devotion to the cause, the need for sacrifice, the glories of the future, of how the youth of today would be instrumental in bringing the fruits of their labors to their grandchildren. That sort of thing. The traditional thing.

Today, she surprised Kyuzo.

"I do not believe I have found happiness," she said, "though I pray I have found satisfaction. Remember, I am one of you. Probably you shall not find happiness, but if you are fortunate you shall find satisfaction. What the Motherland will require of us in the future will undoubtedly be difficult, and it will probably be heartbreaking. In that regard what befalls us will be no different than what befell our ancestors. The history of our land is one of misfortune. Geographical misfortune—for once we were a primitive people caught between the pull of mighty empires, vast and slow—but misfortune nonetheless. Bearing it stoically, with quiet pride, has become something of a tradition for our people, and I do not predict a change for the foreseeable future.

"But I have confidence we shall live up to the standards of our ancestors, that we shall meet the expectations of the ghosts that hover over our great Motherland. I have confidence because what we do is not as unique as it seems, that it is, in truth, a fundamental component of human nature. There is a Transnationalist scientifiction writer by the name of Anson MacDonald. I read his books when it was illegal for a student of the Academy to do so, though it is legal now, and I encourage you to read them. Their philosophy is an interesting combination of personal liberty and social responsibility. One of his books is a collection of stories and essays, a book called *Expanding Quasars*. One of those essays contains a parable, the recounting of an incident which he claims is absolute truth, though I have not made an effort to research the matter." She smiled. "You remember what the great leader Uncle Petrel said about the Transnationals: *Trust, but verify*. In any case, it is the principle of the story that is instructive.

"According to Mr. MacDonald, this happened when he was a young man growing up during the Great Depression that nearly wiped out the faith and trust the common man placed in the capitalist hierarchy. A homeless man who had taken to traveling by hitching unauthorized rides on the trains that crisscrossed the plains came upon a young couple who were well-known in Mr. MacDonald's community. Normally, the couple might not have acknowledged him, or if they had, they would have urged him to hurry on his way. But today they had need of this man who had been tossed away and forgotten by society, for the woman had gotten her foot stuck between the railroad tracks, and her husband was unable to extricate it.

"The homeless man, though he had never seen these two before in his life and had no reason to expect any reciprocal kindness from them, commenced to assist the man. Things did not go well, and they grew worse when they heard the sound of an approaching train. The husband continued the struggle to free his wife, unsuccessfully. The homeless man struggled as well. He would not leave this man to try to save his wife alone.

"Presumably, the engineer noticed the presence of this trio on the tracks, but he was not able to stop in time. All three died instantly, literally crushed to bloody pulps beneath the wheels of industry.

"As Mr. MacDonald pointed out, it was the honor and the duty of the husband to die for his woman."

The hall was silent. Kyuzo had imagined a humorous coda to the tale, not a brutal conclusion. Looking at the stunned expressions of the assemblage, it was clear they were of the same mind.

"But what of the homeless one?" Maya continued. " Surely no one would have thought ill of him had he fled. As it was, no one ever knew his name, or why he had become homeless, or where he might have been going. And no one knew why he had chosen to sacrifice himself for two people he had never met.

"There is one possible reason: To aid others, despite the considerable cost it might inflict on the individual, is simply a fundamental part of human nature. By sacrificing himself for strangers, the homeless man was being true both to himself and to the highest ideals of socialist mankind. That is all we shall ever know of him. That is all we shall ever need to know."

She stopped talking—it was unclear whether she had merely paused or if the speech was over. She smiled enigmatically. The adults on the podium looked at one another in confusion, and the cadets simply stared at her. Kyuzo knew what they were thinking; he was wondering the same thing: Would he make the ultimate sacrifice for a faceless capitalist simply because it was the noble thing to do?

That was leaving aside the question of whether it was the right thing to do, or the intelligent thing.

Kyuzo felt a curious tingling on the back of his neck. During Maya's pause—the prelude to more words or to a bow, that part was still unclear—his perception of time altered. The duration of a second stretched into a highly personal time zone when a thousand observations and details became prominent all at once. Most of them weren't important: the shadow of a female cadet's hair on her uniform; the peach fuzz on a lad's face; the whistling of the wind between the distant buildings; the odor of the perspiration emanating from a contingent of gymnasts who had not had a chance to shower before coming outside. But they were all incredibly vivid, and during that protracted nuance of time he had to parse through them in order to focus on the detail that had aroused his instincts for danger.

That detail was simply the young female cadet sitting on the far right corner of the bottom row of the bleachers.

She had not been present earlier. Kyuzo would have dismissed her as merely a late arrival, save for the fact that she did not look as sharp, as young, or as innocent as the other cadets. Indeed, there was a weathered severity to her face, and her jaw was set with grim determination.

Before he knew what he was doing, he was pointing at her. Before he knew what he was saying, he had already spoken: "BOMB!"

He was already cursing the Gorky Encampment regulations that had prevented him from carrying his cache of weaponry. Because if he had been armed, she would already be dead before she could do what she was doing:

springing up and pressing the control hidden beneath her bogus uniform.

Kyuzo dashed toward her, but he knew he would be too late.

Most of the cadets in the general vicinity were doing the only intelligent thing under the circumstances: trying to get far away or find cover. They would not succeed. A few had evidently taken Major Antares' speech to heart, and were diving for the suicide bomber.

But it was clear to Kyuzo and anyone watching that they would not have the opportunity to smother the blast, to sacrifice themselves but save others in the process. Already he could envision the blood, the gore. He had seen much in his day, had believed himself inured to it. But this he thought would be more terrible than he could stand.

The bomber opened her mouth to make one final scream of defiance at her enemy. It never materialized.

The bomb exploded.

Time slowed still more; each nanosecond seemed like an eternity.

But the flash was dampened, the sound muzzled.

Two of the cadets got within only a few feet of her—then they slammed against an invisible barrier.

A barrier that contained the blast.

The bomber bore the full impact of the explosion, liquefying in an instant, spraying the interior of the barrier evenly, exposing its hidden shape.

A bell jar.

The cadets who had bounced off the barrier stared at one another, amazed to still be alive. No more or less amazed than the other cadets, or Kyuzo, but he was the first to realize what had happened.

Sorceress-Major Antares stood on the stage with her

arms extended, the gesture of a powerful magical protocol successfully concluded.

The invisible bell jar disappeared, and the skin, blood, and body parts of the suicide bomber slid to the ground.

Kyuzo fell to his knees. The cadets were in a totally understandable emotional state that bordered on hysteria. The adults were attempting to induce calm and order even though they were surely just as upset. Yet Kyuzo felt a powerful peace and an overwhelming sense of relief, greater than any he had ever known. He thanked Gorkovsky for the promise of these youngsters, and he praised his ancestors that there would be no Russian ghosts born today.

Now that the situation was over, time ceased to have meaning. He had no idea how long he stayed there on his knees—probably a minute, perhaps more. Time only resumed its normal flow when a soft hand laid itself on his shoulder.

He looked up into the serene face of the Sorceress-Major. Despite his emotional exhaustion, Kyuzo was elated. She had come to him! She was paler than usual, but her smile was warm.

"You did well today," was all she said. It was more than enough.

CHAPTER THREE

The names on the red-starred tombstones in the Citadel National Cemetery are written in an identical style in small, carved letters on the left edge of the top of the square stones. There are over ten million graves in the cemetery. They are spaced five meters apart, in even rows ten meters apart, without exception. That way every corpse has its equal space, and no one can ever say that one soldier died more gloriously than another, or made a greater sacrifice. MIAs and those whose bodies were blown or torn to bits are afforded space equal to those whose corpses were returned reasonably intact. Death in the name of the Motherland is truly the great leveler.

There are no roads or sidewalks in the CNC, only well-worn paths. Visitors are transported to various stops via passenger cars suspended from a monorail, its chain of steel girders rising up from the ground like skeletal arms. The grounds are always well maintained but are like the steppes, in that no trees or shrubs break up the monotony. When the skies are clear, the passenger cars and all that support them cast long shadows across the rows and rows of graves. And when snow covers the ground, as it did on the day Sorceress-Major Maya Antares sat

in a car and composed a letter she intended to leave at
a gravesite, the shadows of the girders are like the many
fingers of God, stretched over a plane where nothing
ever happens.

Maya wrote the letter in a traditional method, with
paper and pencil. But the paper floated in the air, and
she had no need to touch the pencil.

Beloved Marcus,

*Today is the ninth anniversary of our
nation's defeat at Kar Dathra's Gate. The day
that would prove an omen of catastrophe. How
could we have known then, as we marched
onto the battlefield, the pride of the Red Fleet,
that losing the war of Al'istaan would mean
the end of our country itself?*

*Such fools we were, to believe ourselves
invincible. To allow military parades and patriotic slogans to convince us that triumph was
guaranteed, victory our destiny. Destiny does
not speak in slogans, but in cruelties. The
United Republics of the Red Star are no more.
Lost forever. All of our sacrifices powerless to
stop their collapse.*

*Still, I shed no tears for their passing.
What was taken from me at Kar Dathra's Gate
was far more precious than the ambitions of
any government. I would watch the decay of
a Thousand Empires for one moment spent in
the warmth of your arms, one more taste of
your kiss. Our people lost a war. I lost you.
My Marcus. My Love.*

*I no longer fight against the memories of
you. They have become my treasures. In this*

shattered place that was our homeland, all we
have left are ghosts.

For Eternity,
MAYA

The letter completed, she folded it, kissed it, and carefully placed it in a bouquet of red roses. She tenderly placed the bouquet on her lap.

"Excuse me, Comrade Sorceress," said the white-haired veteran sharing the car with her. "I didn't want to intrude until you'd finished your letter."

She smiled at him. The car had a sign reading SILENCE EQUALS RESPECT, but the State was always trying to encourage people to act in such a way that they would not inadvertently offend another with an opinion. The most popular offensive opinion was that the sacrifices of war had been in vain, that war had been waged merely for the status and power of the government, and not, as they had been told, for the good of all mankind. Once upon a time the State had not needed signs—it had used laws and harsh punishment instead.

"Back in the Great Patriotic War, we farmboy soldiers always considered it good luck to have a sorceress light our cigarettes." The old veteran, whose overcoat was worn from age and use, happened to be holding a cigarette in his single, gloved hand. The sleeve where the other arm should have been was folded and stapled. "Could you be so kind?"

"Of course, Comrade Corporal," Maya replied at once. She actually disapproved of smoking, but refusing the man's request was not an option. Much of the Great Patriotic War was fought on Russian soil, against Fascist Europa invaders who detested Trans and Internationalists equally, who sought to conquer not for the good of mankind, as had Gorkovsky and Petrel, but simply to cleanse the species of perceived impurities and make the survivors submit to the jackboot heel of authority. Thus an unlikely alliance had been born, for a few years, during the fourth decade of the last century, as Trans and Interns worked together to crush their common foe.

However, the war was not fought on Transnationalist soil, but on Europa and Red soil. The Internationalists bore an inequitable amount of death, and their suffering was compounded by Petrel's ongoing paranoia. Many a freedom fighter was forced to lay down his arms and submit to exile or worse after the war was successfully concluded. For all Maya knew, this man might have suffered horribly, beyond the probability that he'd lost his arm in battle, merely because he had answered the call of the Motherland. Besides, if smoking hadn't killed him yet, at his advanced age, a few more cigarettes weren't going to make a difference, one way or the other.

Holding the bouquet tightly, to insure it would not fall, she leaned over and reached out, palm upwards. The veteran leaned over, put the cigarette in his mouth, and held the tip over her empty hand.

A flicker of flame arose from her palm.

"Thank you, Comrade-Sorceress," he said, taking a deep drag.

"It's an easy thing to give, sir. Please, call me Maya."

"Very well. I am Vanya," said the man pleasantly. The car made a turn, and for a moment the sun shone through the window at the right angle for the array of medals on Vanya's uniform to reflect the sunlight, so brightly that Maya blinked. The colors of the medals told a story of heroism and service. He had won the Red Cross, the Blue Star, the Nevksy Medallion, the Molotov Wreath, the Gold Ribbon, the Cross of St. Peter, and many others. It made Maya wonder:

"Your record of service is so distinguished, yet you are only a corporal. If you don't mind my asking..."

Vanya chuckled. "Ah, if my dear departed wife were here today, she would tell you that I have a loose tongue."

Maya smiled. "And *you* would say...?"

"I do not suffer fools gladly. I have encountered so many in the Red Army. I have a feeling about you, though. Perhaps I am just an old man struck by your beauty and demeanor—but wait. Surely I am not the first."

Maya felt herself blush. "No."

"Sorry. I only meant to say I have the feeling that you are the kind of woman we who fought in the Great Patriot War hoped would inherit the responsibility of steering the Motherland into the future."

"It is very kind of you to say so, but it is my humble opinion that you represent the greatest generation."

"That is nonsense. We merely did what we had to do. And besides, every generation has its own call to greatness. I suspect you have answered yours with truth and vigor."

"Who do you visit here today?" Maya inquired.

A flicker of sadness passed over the old man's eyes, yet he smiled and answered easily, "Too many to mention, my dear, too many to mention. If not for the cemetery railcars, I would have had a heart attack years ago just trying to visit them all." He paused. "And you?"

Maya had expected that question; after all, she had begun the line of conversation. Yet suddenly her years of grieving might well have begun yesterday. Her answer was but a whisper. "My husband."

"Your first husband?"

She shook her head. "My only husband."

"I'm sorry," said Vanya with much kindness. "Al'istaan?"

"Yes. Nine years ago today. At the battle of Kar Dathra's Gate."

"Ah." Vanya nodded in that knowing way all veterans have—an understanding of the cruelties of war that could be shared only by other warriors. He regarded her for a moment. "Would you care to talk about it?"

Maya hesitated. The weight of the years, of the loss, had always been heavy on her shoulders, but she had borne it with the sort of lonely dignity expected of her station—as a sorceress-major, as a war widow. Not even her closest friends—Alexandra Goncharova among them—could begin to imagine the irreparable damage done to her soul on that night a lifetime ago. It was an injury that refused to heal, a piece of her heart forever torn away. Nine years later, and it was still difficult for her to discuss her husband's final moments without feeling that wound reopen.

And yet, there was something about this war-weary soldier, this man who had seen far more tragedy in his lifetime than she, that brought a sense of calm to her troubled heart. Perhaps it was his easy smile, or the glow of his soul that her heightened vision could detect, even without the aid of a sorcerous protocol. No—it was the eyes. Their corners shone with the light of a good life lived, of battles won and victories celebrated. But their pupils were dark with the shadow of great loss, hardened by the forges of war, haunted by the specter of death.

The same sort of eyes that continued to stare back at her for close to a decade, every time she gazed into a mirror.

"Al'istaan," she said slowly. The corners of her mouth dimpled with an unaccustomed smile—the first real smile in... she couldn't remember how long. "When I was a schoolgirl reading underground romance novels, it was the country next door, where young Reds in love fled so they could live happily ever after..."

Al'istaan. The escape valve for the intelligentsia. The country where the dissidents and freethinkers fled to their little villages, where they tried to blend in with the local populace. A rugged man with a modest income could live like a warlord among the poor Al'istaanis. And a member of the black market could amass a fortune in no time, provided he bribed the proper *real* warlords.

It was an exotic country where the women wore veils and were not allowed to fight, and men warred among themselves not for ideological reasons, but for those of territory, personal honor, and commerce. Al'istaan. Whose mountainous terrain had once been the redoubt for a mighty civilization. Whose people had once fought off the lackeys of an imperialist Transnational empire. And whose people resisted the Internationalist call to rise above the anarchy that had unfortunately befallen them since the days of the imperialist invasions. Twenty-five years ago, Premier Kolujinsky had ordered the formal acquisition of Al'istaan. Her people were to be given a choice: cooperate with the impending forces of utopia, or suffer the consequences of the renegade.

Much to the surprise of good Russian citizens such as myself, the Al'istaani people chose the latter.

Citizens of the URRS who, as they say, had "gone native," becoming farmers or religious thinkers or pillars of the local communities, chose to assist the resistance.

The Transnationals chose to support the resistance by

providing them with training, weapons, and other forms of aid. This was their way of fighting a war without it costing them any bloodshed. And while I would like to believe it was a dastardly technique, fit only for cowards who lacked the backbone to stand up for their principles, I am compelled to admit the very technique worked for the Internationalist cause in the past, when our diplomatic and military strategy successfully drew the Transnationalists into the cobwebs of a proxy war. I always thought it supremely ironic that Premier Kolujinski fell into the exact same trap, only without the active participation of the Transnationals. He had done it all on his own, and his people were to pay a heavy price.

The indigenous soldiers used the mountainous terrain, with its complex network of caves and narrow valleys, the way a fox on the run uses a thick forest to hide from its pursuers. They would hide for days or weeks and then suddenly attack, striking a column or stronghold of Red Forces, inflict some damage, and then slip back into the mountains. They would attack a village of "collaborators," kill as many of the elders as possible—that is, if they weren't distracted by the opportunity to kill the warlord of a rival tribal faction—instill terror in the survivors, and then slip back into the mountains. They were always slipping into the mountains. Our aerial reconnaissance was not up to the job. They blended into the terrain like chameleons. The Transnationalists jammed our satellite spying capability (their diplomats always professed innocence, and blamed sunspots which our scientists could never verify), and our skyfurnaces were vulnerable to the handheld surface-to-air missiles when the "freedom fighters" desired to stand their ground.

There were many battles. The indigenous forces could not hide forever, nor did they desire it. Their sorceresses possessed a bloodthirsty lust for battle that was both intimidating and legendary. Their infantry fought brutally, mercilessly. They gave no quarter and asked none. Their treatment of prisoners was unspeakable. Their tactics were uncivilized, without precedent or honor. We obviously had no choice but to respond in kind.

After Premier Kolujinksi died, his successor, Premier Zarudnov, decided the Al'istaani rebellion had claimed enough lives, had drained more than enough resources, and had distracted the true believers long enough. He ordered a slash-and-burn march on the rebel villages and cities located on the major tributaries and rivers. We later learned his generals and advisors had warned him of the possible dire consequences of such a scheme. Zarudnov chose to ignore their advice and ordered the implementation of the plan to be accelerated.

Many of our ground forces were sickened by what they had to do. The mental wards are full of veterans, and many more wander the streets or, if they are able to maintain their status as contributory citizens, do so only with the assistance of heavy medication, most of it pilfered from the patents of Trans pharmaceutical companies. The State would have you believe they live full lives, but that has not been my impression.

There has never been an accurate estimate, to my knowledge, of how many non-combatants the Red forces slaughtered the first few weeks of the campaign. I do believe, to this day, the Trans media estimates are skewed to favor their ideological perspective. I simply cannot accept that the common Red soldier would be so brutal, above and beyond the call of duty.

Premier Zarudnov was mistaken about many things during his tenure. I do not believe it is unpatriotic for me to state that—it is merely a fact. But he was correct in the assumption that his plan would draw out the enemy combatants. Al'istaani forces converged on the approaching Red army. They would have been as weak as water, ripe for conquest, had not the warlords risen to a new level of treachery and cooperated with one another, choosing and following the command of a single leader and attacking en masse as a disciplined unit.

They met us at the pass known as Kar Dathra's Gate, in the southern region of Al'istaan. The pass was named after one of the Al'istaani heroes: a holy man, a great defender of his country.

It seems impossible this was the last time the Red Fleet would be so mighty an armada. We were the most feared military force in the world—at the time.

None of us dared admit the futility of our task.

You can vanquish an army, you can subjugate a people, but you can never defeat an idea.

We, who so revere Alexander Nevskii, should have taken the hint from the very name of the place.

Kar Dathra's Gate was the most sacred ground in the Nistaani region. Beneath its rock and dust were buried the bones and artifacts of failed invaders dating back to the dawn of history. The people drew strength from this ground. Here the indigenous fighters felt closest to their god.

For them, this was holy war.

They could never accept surrender, only victory or utter destruction.

Central Command did not listen to such nonsense. They could only conceive of the people's victory, and could not imagine anything else.

They ordered us onward.

We were to do no less than destroy the Nistaani resistance. Our force was so large, there was no use trying to conceal our position or intent.

I shudder to think what we were supposed to do after we achieved victory. The great city of Khan'dahar was only fifty kilometers downstream. It had a population of nearly fifteen thousand.

At first the indigenous forces did not put up much of a fight. Their front lines withered quickly beneath the twin onslaught of the skyfurnace protocols and the regulars—of whom my Marcus was one—who came down on the flying barges and took their positions in the rugged mountains.

The magic on both sides was powerful, savage. The Red magic was particularly potent that day. Vast numbers of the enemy fell, more quickly than we Reds, and still they came: The Nistaani hordes and their holy men, wave after wave, the rage of their angry god burning in their blood.

Sometime during the day, slowly at first, but gradually becoming clearer, it became evident to even our obstinate commanders: we were losing ground. We were being beaten back.

And because it was happening on their watch, they were going to be noticed—by the media, and by history; by their superior officers and party officials—but, most significantly of all, by Premier Zarudnov.

His judgment was regarded as somewhat definitive in matters of victory and defeat. It was also swift. The kind of judgment that, once enacted, made it difficult to rectify an error.

A last push was ordered. And Marcus's unit, which had been held back, presumably to execute a coup de grâce, was dispatched into Hell. Dropped from a low-flying barge smack into the middle of indigenous troops.

The fighting was too close and too frantic for the Hailers of either side to get a good bead on a foe—you'd just as likely hit one of your own men. So the fighting was predominantly hand-to-hand. Such a tactic would have been suicide for any company in another country's army. Marcus' unit was comprised of the best in mind, spirit, and bulk the URRS could offer. Not to mention the most skilled. On the ground, fighting hand-to-hand, they had a better chance than most.

As for me, I was stationed on board a skyfurnace—the *Konstantinov*. I was only a lieutenant then, and my entire unit was on isolator duty.

After all my years in the Corps, the first thing I always recall about isolator duty is that only one sorceress in every thirty endures to the end of a typical battle. To train a sorceress is expensive, and sorceress power is not a commodity to be wasted capriciously. Not that that ever stopped the Commanders before, especially during the heat of battle.

At the moment the Commanders decided to use me, I was hanging in the chamber as if I was being drawn and quartered. Or crucified, depending on your point of view. My chains were made of light, powered by the electrical harnessing of a protocol. They sent energy coursing through me, and they sucked it out of me. I felt like a human whirlpool.

"BLAST CONTROL TO ISOLATOR CHAMBER TWENTY-THREE. APPROACHING THIRTY SECONDS TO TRANSFORMATION PROTOCOL."

"Affirmative, Control," I said. And so said, I am sure, the other nine sorceress who formed the array I was part of. An array can be anywhere from ten to fifteen chambers. Forged from an alloy of the most durable metals, my chamber was a cylinder twenty meters in diameter and thirty meters long. While it was closed, the air smelled like being smothered in a gasoline blanket.

Then there was that coolant. After three hours in battle the chemical scent of the coolant fluids is at its worst. Of course, if not for the coolant, you would bake like a sausage on a spit from the heat in the chamber, so nobody complains.

The hybrid generators—so called because they work on both scientific and magical principles—started to hum.

"TARGETING ENEMY MARK AT COORDINATES ZERO-ZERO-NINE. CHECK HUDs FOR CONFIRMATION."

Several of the chamber plates shifted. I shifted too, like a gear in a melting clock. They never tell you what the targets are. It doesn't really matter. You are going to shoot *when* they tell you to, *where* they tell you to; at *what* is inconsequential.

"FIFTEEN SECONDS, MAYA! DO YOU READ?"

"Yes, Captain, I'm here," I replied, perhaps a little too testily.

"YOUR HEART RATE IS UP TOO HIGH. WE'RE GOING TO HAVE TO ADJUST YOUR CARDIO."

The deck kasters in blast control monitor everything. They've hooked into all vital systems and do not hesitate to pull your strings. Heart rate too high? They zap you to bring it to safe levels. Body temperature unstable? They'll set one for you and make sure you stay there. Never mind those ripping sensations in your brain! Never mind their lack of interest in what's happening to all your *non*-vital systems.

"TEN SECONDS. OPENING ISOLATORS PREPARE TO FIRE!"

And if that wasn't bad enough, when the caps fall and the chamber opens to the outside world, your stomach drops like an anvil. The sorceress engineers never quite learned to control that feeling.

"CONFIRM CAPS DROPPED ON ALL PORT ISOLATORS."

Then it begins: the transformation protocols. The hell of all this is, regardless of your physical pain and acute mental agony, you still have to think. You still have to rearrange matter and fold space in your head. And all of it must take place on the molecular level too; any plane larger and dire consequences in the time/space continuum theoretically could result. I say theoretically because no one who has ever effected change on the incorrect plane has survived to inform the scientist-mages if they ever glimpsed the creation of a parallel world.

After several transformation protocols, your nervous tension is gone. No wringing of the hands, no involuntary movement in your legs. The last few seconds feel like one unbearable moment.

"PREPARE TO FIRE IN THREE..."

Your body is dead weight, but your mind screams at you.

"TWO..."

Will I kast the protocol correctly? you wonder. Will the isolator chamber function properly upon my return? Will the coolant spray, or will I suffocate in the darkness?

"ONE ..."

Then, thankfully, the mind is silenced.

"FIRE!"

Transformation. No thought. No consciousness. I am the heat of my nation's anger. I am the burning will of the State. An inferno, clearing the path of those who resist.

More prosaically, my life-force merged with those of the other sorceresses in the array. The lights, the chambers, our magic were suddenly focused into a single purpose, a blind discorporate entity that converged into three beams of blue death outside the skyfurnace to strike an enemy barge.

Not just strike it, though. Not just penetrate it. Our combined energy pushed everything in its path through the hole we bored into the enemy barge. Any soldier standing directly in the path of that light was instantly obliterated.

The other sorceresses and I had no idea what was happening, if our "aim" was accurate or not. That was all up to Control. All we could perceive was our brief foray into the intricacies of a group mind on a higher plane of existence.

Occasionally, when a shot is particularly well-aimed, we can glimpse the souls of our victims, wailing as they are snapped up into purgatory. I glimpsed many souls, that day. Later, I learned the barge we had fired upon had plummeted like a great stone onto the ground, killing all those on board who had managed to survive the sorceress volley.

Twenty-seven million calculations performed in less than a second, and then my scattered atoms were teleported back into the isolation chamber. The first sense to return is smell, and then taste. The coolant is thick but you smile anyway, because you survived.

The transformation completes its cycle, assembling your genetic code as you drop into the energy harness. The sensation of the fastening against your arms and legs tells you that no part of you was left out there at the point of impact.

At least no part that could be seen.

"THIS IS BLAST CONTROL TO BATTERY SIX. GOOD WORK, SISTERS. TARGET VESSEL DESTROYED. NEXT TRANSFORMATION IN SIXTY SECONDS. REPEAT: THIS IS BLAST CONTROL TO ALL

ISOLATORS IN BATTERY SIX. APPROXIMATELY SIXTY SECONDS
TO TRANSFORMATION PROTOCOL..."

Together my comrade sisters and I were successful. For
the next five hours we tore up the enemy barge fleet like
confetti, and all it took was being torn apart and put
back together a hundred different ways. All of them quite
painful.

We endured numerable glimpses of nirvana, a thousand points of hell. I just wanted the pain to stop. So did
all the sisters who died that day, I'm certain.

Meanwhile, the Commanders were elated. They had
overcome their fear of personal disgrace and risen like
a phoenix from the ashes of defeat. They had destroyed
the Nistaani barge fleet and stymied the waves of enemy
soldiers hitting the men on the field.

One final step to victory, Commander Brusilov must
have thought as he held his binoculars to his eyes and
watched, grimly satisfied, as yet another barge was
inundated in blue light and sent plummeting.

Beside him stood my brother-in-law, Commander Urik
Antares, the second-finest man I ever met, next to my
husband. He told me he could appreciate Brusilov's ela-
tion, but could not share it. For if Urik has a flaw as a
Commander, it is that he cares too much for the fate of
his crew and comrades; he does not view them strictly
as fodder that must be spent if one is to climb the ladder
of promotion. During the battle he knew many were still
in great danger of losing life and limb, and they included
his brother and his sister-in-law. Don't get me wrong.
Urik was no less focused on victory than the other aerial
officers—he was simply not as detached about his fellow
soldiers.

He had the suspicion, however, that his priorities and

those of his superior aerial officers would soon converge. He maneuvered through the shifting winds on the upper deck, snapped his heels together, and saluted smartly.

"Commander Brusilov," he said, "The *Solaris* has reported in. They are in position and awaiting further orders."

"And the *Aurora*?" demanded Brusilov.

"She has dispatched the last Nistaani barges and will be entering into position momentarily."

"Good."

The plan had been daring and simple: force the Nistaani troops into a narrow valley, then clear the sky of their ships for the final move. Or so we had hoped. And at the moment, it looked like that was happening.

"Urik," said Brusilov, "patch me through to all sky-furnaces."

Urik still had misgivings—the plan was notably devoid of the assumption that one's enemy would inevitably respond to an offensive move—but he gave the order enthusiastically: "Lieutenant, open a channel to all furnaces!"

His words were captured in the mental net of a sorceress in the communications room. She wore a listening device, a microphone shaped like a chip, and an eye shield devoid of openings—but those were merely props to help her focus. "Secure channel to all furnaces open," she said. "Go ahead, Commander."

"This is Commander Brusilov. Prepare to evacuate all reactor crews to blast chambers!"

A hundred thousand hearts skipped a beat the moment Brusilov gave that order. Everyone knew what to do; they had performed it in surprise practice drills at least once a week. But to actually go through with the task was not something to be done lightly. So many things could go wrong, and the consequences were dire at best. The fact that so many skyfurnace crews would have to perform the task in synchronization only added to the pressure.

I know Urik was thinking of me, but mostly he was thinking of his brother, still fighting hand-to-hand below. He could only hope Marcus got the proper order in time, because the coming attack wouldn't distinguish between friend and foe.

I could hear the loudspeakers in the corridor outside through the chamber walls, so I was able to listen as Urik gave the series of orders that led to deployment. I remember wondering why Command was always so worried about secure channels when they habitually kept shouting their orders loud enough to be heard on Saturn.

The orders kept rolling out. I had seen the drill so many times before I knew exactly what was happening, on each and every skyfurnace. Judging from the sound of things, the synchronization was happening perfectly.

The fans of the coolant water were switched off.

The carbon dioxide coolant was induced to break down.

Control rods were automatically withdrawn.

The flow of spent fuel was diverted. The drains in the tanks holding spent fuel were opened, and the fuel flowed like ectoplasmic lava throughout the bowels of the sky-furnaces. With luck, the crew had all evacuated those sections by this point. The fuel was forged of both scientific and magical elements, its temperature a mere 150 degrees. The structure and machinery had been built to withstand that heat, as had the protective suits. But the suits were notoriously unreliable; even the Party had to admit that. So best to have the contaminated areas evacuated.

Orders of sergeants, ensuring each step of the process was taken properly, were audible through the chamber walls as well. It wasn't long before all was quiet. As was customary, the officers were the last to reach their stations, either on the bridge or at a strategic point where it was important for someone to be available to take personal responsibility for potential accidents. They were also the last to suit up.

The call came down from on high and was taken up by a chorus of lesser voices: "COORDINATE FULL VENTRAL IMMOLATION—NOW!"

An average skyfurnace has seven vats, and the *Konstantinov* was in a fleet of one hundred and sixteen ships. At the flip of a switch on the bridge of each vessel, the bottom of the vats dilated open and pointed the discharge directly toward the ground. That's how we got maximum burn.

Even deep within an isolator tunnel you can feel it when the ventral furnaces blast. First you hear the distant rumble, like an earthquake. Then it becomes more definite, more inescapable. Your teeth start to rattle. This time it was so bad I bit my tongue. I was unable to feel the pain, and only noticed it because I happened to look down and spotted a big red stain expanding ever outward on my jumpsuit. I spat out the blood. It struck the floor and hissed into reddish steam.

Meanwhile, the steel began to cry and the bolts creaked. The entire ship moaned in protest at the crew's efforts to hold the *Konstantinov* in place and prevent what would be in effect a second-stage liftoff.

Hunkered down in the bridge of the *Konstantinov*, one eye on the gauges and the other on the windows, which had been known to shatter from the stress of immolation, Urik was praying as well. He knew that Commander

Brusilov had only given a cursory glance at the battle-ground below, that they had not been one hundred per-cent certain the Red ground troops were all in place before the order for maximum burn was given.

The plan on the ground was simple, though knowing Marcus as I did, he surely resented the order for his units to engage the enemy, to draw them onto the plateau, and then pretend to suffer a rout, breaking through the enemy horde and scattering to the hills. The idea was that the Nistaani would be so intoxicated with the notion of victory that they wouldn't suspect anything was amiss when 116 skyfurnaces passed overhead.

We of the crew all knew the possibilities—that if a blast tank ruptured, the ship would be our coffin; that if it did not, if all went well, then we would live to fight and perhaps die another day. Those below, those caught in the blast, would not be so fortunate.

When I was in the infantry, during basic training, I had an opportunity to witness a burn at ground level. We were brave and foolish, like all recruits. We dared one another to see who would stand the closest to the perimeter, the absolute edge between safety and fate.

I almost came too close. Another few steps and I would have crossed the line.

The first thing to hit you is a wave of heat and smoke. It is as if you were standing on the brink of Hell itself. Indeed, at that moment I actually began to believe maybe the ancients were not so fuzzy in their metaphysics after all, that maybe Hell really had a physical location, where the evil and sinful were punished. Then comes the stench. The smell of ashes and accelerant is not something you easily forget.

Anything that happens to be within the brunt of the blast is instantly obliterated—including human beings.

THE RED STAR

At Kar Dathra's Gate, the power of the coordinated furnace blast was stronger than we had imagined. The heat had become so great that clique after clique of desert sand was fused into thick white glass.

The fallen Nistaani had been felled in an instant by the power the State had trained us to wield. Even the hardest of us gave in to the moment of joy and relief. We were not children—we knew we were disposable in the eyes of the Motherland. We had cursed Central Command for every moment of the damnation that was the war of Al'istaan. But in an instant, that bitterness dissolved. For a beautiful moment, we believed perhaps we had won the war. Perhaps there would be a parade in Red Square in our honor. Perhaps we had removed a major obstacle to a world socialist movement and would be able to live out the rest of our lives in a measure of peace.

And perhaps I could be in Marcus' arms for as long as we wished, knowing we were both safe.

Perhaps, perhaps, perhaps. How foolish we had been, even if but for a moment. We had actually believed our victory, once won, was inevitable.

I learned a valuable lesson that day. In war, nothing is inevitable. Our moment of collective celebration was not to last.

When the blast died down, Marcus and his men lowered their weapons, listening to the winds die into soft breezes that dissipated the dust and smoke and stench of burned meat. They truly believed they were standing on the vanguard of history—but instead they were standing on the precipice.

For through the dust and smoke and flame, across the glass-like terrain, death strode toward them.

I was not there, so I can only imagine that, for the

first time that day, my husband felt fear. A soldier can control his emotions when he knows what to expect, and what is expected of him. But no amount of self-control could have prepared Marcus and his men for the sight of three men, walking through the flames.

No, not walking through the flames, but bringing the flames behind them the way a vampire in my grandmother's folk tales would bring the fog. The edges of their long, flowing mantles rising and flickering from the hot air, two of the men walked a respectful distance behind the man in the center. His greater height and aura unmistakably denoted him as the most powerful.

It is easy for me to surmise how Marcus responded to the sudden presence of these beings. Marcus was brave, and would have sought a deeper strength within himself, even though conventional wisdom would dictate he accept defeat. Most of his men, I am certain, reacted likewise. Determined to persevere, they raised their binoculars and tried to look at the faces of their new enemy—and saw nothing. The strangers wore kaffiyehs—large square handkerchiefs—over their heads and shoulders, the fabric tucked in their collars. The fabric was old and dusty. It evoked the bandages of ripened dead lepers and implied there was not a face beneath the kaffiyehs, but an abyss.

The desert was already waist deep in the ashes of dead men, but the battle had only begun. The furnace blast was supposed to be our checkmate, but we had forgotten yet another fundamental rule of warfare: do not assume the enemy cannot play chess as well as you. The Nistaani priests were not fools. Their sorcery had done its work. They had sacrificed entire legions to the furnaces for a single purpose: To summon the ancient defender of their land.

Kar Dathra the Eternal.

Legend has it that Kar Dathra had once been a man, but that he had tricked an ancient djinn into giving him all his power. Whatever his origin, an entity named Kar Dathra has always had an undeniable, indelible historical presence in the land now known as Al'istaan. Thus had it been ever since Byzantine invaders were defeated by nomads under his leadership, soon after the fall of the Western part of the early European Empire. Whispers that his existence continued to this day were always suppressed by Central Command as nonsense or religious superstition.

Yet there he was, flanked by his honor guard: two swordsmen who, legend has it, betrayed him during the Mongol invasion, and whose punishment was to stand always by his side—neither dead nor alive, but always at his service.

Still several hundred meters away from the stunned army under Marcus' command, Kar Dathra stopped and raised his staff to the sky. The crescent moon at the top of the staff glistened with the reflection of the unholy fires the ancient priest and his honor guard had brought with them.

With a gesture of his hand, the sky went black.

And from the darkness a million soldiers seemed to boil upward from the sand. Some of them had been mere ashes moments ago; many more were much older. Some had turned to dust long before the nascent stirrings of the industrial age.

We had committed everything. We had been only a few moments away from total victory. But when Kar Dathra appeared before us, we knew that moment would never come.

CHAPTER FOUR

I t was not the memory of the horror of that day that
gripped Sorceress-Major Maya Antares so much as
the sadness she had endured as a result. Riding the
car above the Citadel National Cemetery, telling her story
to the kindly old soldier Vanya, she realized her people
had not taken much stock in such soft-headed Transnational concepts as post-traumatic stress syndrome or
bipolar disorder, but just because you ignore a thing, or
shut it out from your worldview, does not negate its
existence. And it seemed not just she, not just her generation, but all the generations of the Motherland since
the time of Ivan the Cruel were suffering severe psychological damage that both the people and the State had
been unwilling even to name, much less cope with.

The train had made an entire pass around the Cemetery
since Maya had begun her story, but she and Vanya still
shared the car alone. Visitors to the Cemetery generally
preferred solitude, and tended to enter empty cars if
available. Yet Vanya, for his part, was not anxious to
leave and pay his respects to his fallen comrades. He had
paid his respects so many times before; if his comrades'
ghosts did not recognize his veneration by now, then
eternity itself wasn't long enough for it to happen.

As for Maya, sitting in the car or standing alone at the tombstone honoring Marcus' missing body, it was all the same. Right now her grief was as fresh and inflamed as if it had begun yesterday. "I had what so few people ever experience," she said. "The love of another who is as thankful for your life as you are for theirs. I don't know if it's possible to ever be free of such love, once you've lived it. Even when that love is stolen from you by the hand of death.

"Death ends life, but it does not stop the minds of the living from reaching into the darkness of the afterworld and searching for the spirit of our beloved. To somehow recapture the moment of the joy we shared. To remember his scent upon your body. To mourn for the dreams of what might have been.

"I can no longer count how many times I've visited his grave. Yet this day, the anniversary of his death, is the most difficult. This is the ninth anniversary. For each year, I add a rose to a bouquet, one for each year I have lived without him. Perhaps one day I will no longer bear the weight of them."

What this woman needs is the love of a good man. Truly, if only I were forty years younger, thought Vanya as he hid his red-faced discomfort at the notion by lighting a fresh cigarette from the butt of an old one. He respected this woman. He respected her patriotism, her power, her love for her slain mate, her devotion to his memory. But her love for this Marcus impressed him as a cold flame. An eternal flame, but cold nonetheless. Love was best an inferno blazing with red coals.

"I want to thank you for listening to me," Maya continued, staring at the seemingly endless rows of tombstones on the snowy ground. "I don't usually speak of such things to anyone. It means more to me than I could have realized."

Vanya nodded. "Roses. I never did bring roses to Citadel. Cigarettes, yes, roses, no. Yours are quite beautiful. There is no need to thank an old man for listening, Maya Antares. If only our bullheaded people would pay more attention to our past, then perhaps we—ah, well, do not let me go to bitterness. I will say this, child. We are soldiers. We know what war is. We can only share it with each other. In battle, we keep each other alive. After the years have passed and the weapons are cold, it is our duty, still, to help each other survive. So tell me of this man of yours. This Marcus. To have earned such devotion from a woman like yourself, I am sure he is worth the tribute. Not to mention, after reading the State's 'official' version of the war, it would be nice to hear the truth this time."

Maya sighed. She had relived those terrible events so many times in her mind, but rarely had she spoken of them. Rarely had she so much as alluded to them. But today she felt the need to unburden her soul. "Very well then..."

The skyfurnaces had scorched the battleground. We had turned the Nistaani desert into a valley of ashes.

But this did nothing to stop them.

There must have been tens of thousands of them, coming from all sides at once.

And their high priest, Kar Dathra, commanded them like a god! He waved his staff and a hundred, two hundred at a time emerged from the smoke flames as if they'd stepped off a barge.

They carried the weapons of the ages. Pikes, swords, knives, and bayonets on primitive single-shot rifles, in addition to the modern weaponry they wielded with expertise far beyond what we had expected from the Nistaani farmboys and rabble-rousers whose enthusiasm had hitherto far exceeded their skill and training. Some were weighed down with enough kilos to sink a small boat, but they kept pace with those who were more lightly armed. They all ran with the speed of gazelles, crosscutting between one another with telepathic team-work.

Their movements, which seemed chaotic, totally unplanned to an observer, thwarted the best-aimed shots of all the troops in the hills. Normally our soldiers know how to lead a shot, but the Nistaani warriors—or should I call them ghost warriors?—always seemed a step ahead of the marksmen's aim. At the very least, our men often hit the man behind their preferred target, but the hits were rarely in the heart or head, where they would do the most good.

On the other hand, every hit made a wound that popped like a melon. The manner in which the warriors reacted to the wounds, however, has given rise to much theorizing. Were the Nistaani living men, or resurrected men, or made of clay, like the legendary golems of the ghetto? We shall never know, as no Al'istaani has ever admitted to having been on the battlefield that day. In any case, if wounded in the leg, arm, or shoulder, they paused momentarily, then shook it off and continued.

In this, they were typical. Those who were struck in the head continued for several meters before falling. And those struck in the chest usually fell, but then began to crawl until they exhausted their life-force or were trampled, whichever came first.

Within minutes of their appearance, the warriors were swarming up the hills. I never knew exactly what happened to Marcus' unit that day. I only had bits and pieces of survivors' testimony to puzzle it together.

Some of them say that he had already fallen before Kar Dathra appeared. Some claim that his was one of the units that had misjudged their orders and been too close to ground zero when the furnaces blasted.

Fools. They don't know my husband.

At an earlier battle in northern Al'istaan, March us and a unit of six men held a defensive position for four days before reinforcements came.

Marcus lost three of his men. The Nistaani lost three hundred.

The one thing I do know was that Marcus was down there, somewhere, knee deep in blood and ashes.

Standing like a wall of iron, holding the center of the line. Most likely cursing Central Command at the top of his lungs.

Of course, it was a lot easier for Marcus and his men to score direct hits on the enemy while they were actually being overrun. Within ten minutes the Red Forces who could still stand were doing so on a mountain of Nistaani bodies. How long they could remain standing was the question. I have easily imagined Marcus' master sergeant Anton Slatkin, the man upon whom he most depended, firing one Hailer barrage after another into the faces and hearts of the onrushing hordes and saying something along the lines of "Marcus! At this rate I'm out of ammo in six minutes!"

For in those final few moments of his life, my beloved Marcus must have realized the Nistaani had won. That death was now the only enemy. He told me endlessly that he had no fear of dying in battle. *I know Death's secret!* he would laugh. *Make your weapon his scythe. Kill his quota for him faster than your enemy can. And*

Death will leave you be to do his work. Death always knows who is going to profit him most. But always remember, sometimes Death favors the enemy.

"We haven't got six minutes to live!" Marcus would have said. With a laugh. Then he would have gutted another enemy soldier.

Commander Brusilov on the *Konstantinov* was not oblivious to the plight of the man on the ground. Quite the opposite, according to Urik. Commander Brusilov was most empathetic, and his report to Central Command was very influential.

Perhaps too influential. For Central Command, in all their wisdom, did not order evacuation. Defeat was not an option, I suppose. They ordered a Krawl-drop instead.

If only I could have seen the look on Marcus' face at the moment the Krawl Carriers, all thirty-seven of them, moved overhead. He would have gone mad, he would have said, "Armor?! You're going to drop armor on us, you idiots?!"

And perhaps Anton would not have been so incredulous, as by that time he would have observed he had only three minutes of ammo left. Evacuation or reinforcements—either way, from the point of view of the common soldier, represented a chance.

For the phrase "dropping armor on us" was only an expression. A Krawl was a tank, powered with diesel fuel and protocols. A Krawl Carrier held anywhere from fifty to seventy-five Krawls, and the drop part was literally that. After the Carrier was positioned overhead the designated zone, the Krawls descended in battleshucks, pyramid-shaped shields that floated through the air like dandelion seeds until they turned into great metallic stones and landed with the thud of shot-puts.

Despite the gravity of the situation, Command lied to itself. They believed that sending more of us to die would be the answer.

And why shouldn't they have?

It had always worked before.

There was no reason why my best friend, Alexandra Goncharova, should have known the deep trouble the Red Forces were in. She lacked a sorceress's sensitivity to the ether. She could sense Death was in the air, but the death of tens and the death of hundreds felt exactly the same to her.

And so too the death of thousands. All she knew was, the troops on the ground were trapped and under attack by what rumor had it was a hitherto undetected mass of enemy troops. The rumor was probably bullshit, but it wouldn't have been the first time Alex had gone into battle not knowing what was going on. She didn't have to know. She was a soldier.

That bullshit thing always bothered her, though. She sensed it in their rollout orders:

"This is Drop Control to Krawl Column Eight. Repeat: this is Drop Control to Krawl Column Eight. Rapid Deployment altitude is Optimal. Be advised, visibility reduced to seventy-five percent due to heavy particle debris. Thermals active and shifting, north by northwest. We had one hell of a fire storm out there today."

One hell of a fire storm. That was her first real clue: the sudden tendency toward colloquial rhetoric. Always a bad sign, in her experience.

"Routing calculated. Check HUD's for impact coordinates," continued Drop Control. And continued. And continued. On and on while Alex did the work she had done so many times before that she barely needed to think about it. Which of course could have been Drop's point. So long as Drop Control was sufficiently annoying, then the Krawl Commanders down the line to Krawl noncoms would pay attention to what they were doing simply because they didn't want to justify Drop's aggressive mother-henning.

Her second thought was usually Krawls weren't needed after battlefield immolation, so the enemy must be especially stubborn today.

Stubborn, and heavily numbered.

It didn't matter. Krawl Captain Alexandra Goncharova of the Red Fleet was always spoiling for a good fight, whenever and wherever good socialist men were in danger. The men who were the best knew how to show their appreciation later.

At the moment, however, Alex's mind was completely focused on the noise of the conveyor belts that had her Krawl bucket gripped by two carrier talons. Krawlers who had become astronauts had told her the rumbling and quaking, so hard and loud her teeth rattled, along with every bolt and piece of equipment, was exactly like the sensation one felt as one sat in cockpit of a space shuttle during the first few minutes of takeoff—only when in a Krawl you're going the other way.

And then—silence! And calm!

"That's the last of them!" said Drop. Captains were always the last to be released. "Full column drop complete. The column is on approach to impact zone. This is Drop Control to Captain Goncharova. The column is yours. Impact protocols commencing on your mark."

"Affirmative, Control. All units, this is Captain Goncharova. When we hit terminal velocity, I want those

damn formations kept tight!" She could see the formations were anything but tight, as her immersion-goggles
provided her with a three-dimensional, 360° view of
what all five hundred Krawl buckets were doing and
where they were. Of course, the goggles didn't provide
much of a view of what was happening where they were
going, but she and her troops were trained for every
contingency. She was confident they could handle anything the enemy could throw at them.

"Krawls 23 and 104!" she radioed. "Compensate for
northerly gusts—16.8 degrees. Confirm!"

"Engaging, Commander," sent back #23. "But it's a
helluva headwind!"

"Handle it, Renko! All Krawl Kasters, initiate gyro-
stabilization protocols now. Renko! You pull a corner
impact and it's your ass!"

Alex always did have a way with words. She had
trained with me at the Academy. I probably wouldn't be
mentioning this part of the battle except for one
thing—Alex was the last person I know to see Marcus
alive!

They hadn't exactly been the best of friends, you know.
She amused him, with her tough talk and free-spirited
ways. And I think she merely tolerated him. He was too
much a javelin—straight and tall—for her taste. Sometimes
I believe they only put up with one another because they
both loved me. I do know this: they would have died for
one another. They would have died for one another not
just because they were soldiers, and it was their honor
and duty, but because of their love for me. They would
not wanted to have returned and looked me in the eye,
knowing they hadn't done everything they could have
done.

They would have been surprised to know they shared the same trait.

And they both really could kick ass. And she was thinking maybe she should kick Renko's as the pixel dust in her eyes portrayed Krawl #23 land squarely on the flat of its side.

It was tilting. Was going to fall flat. Falling flat tended to do a lot of damage, to the head and to the machine, but at least Renko appeared to have sufficiently compensated during his tilt to have a good chance of landing right side up.

#124 wasn't doing much better. If anything, he was doing worse. What was the matter with these guys?

"Retro-shock protocols now!" Alex shouted. Her words must have burst the eardrums of the receiving Krawlers, but right now she didn't give a damn. "Brace for impact!"

She watched, virtually, as most of the buckets landed right side up and ready to release. It was happening, the landings came faster than at any time she could remember, as if the invisible hand of Gorkovsky himself was hastening the Krawlers to meet their fate. This heartened Alex; surely Gorkovsky's ghost would have divined the probability of a Red victory, no matter how bad things might look at the moment. She had no idea as her column landed that she had been dropped into what would quickly become a nightmare.

For what she could not see through her 3Ds was how the plumes of ash and dust arose from the bucket impacts. The plumes were fully as large as those a meteor might throw up striking the middle of a small lake.

If she had seen the plumes, she would have figured out immediately that the ground at drop point was not very solid. Rather than kasting protocols, the Krawlers ought to have spent their extra mental ergs asking

Gorkovsky's ghost to put a few good words for them in with the Commissars before they disembarked to that great Red utopia in the sky.

Alex looked at her readouts and realized she had 3.4 seconds to relax. 3.4 seconds to impact.

Thuummpppt!

It was like being smothered by an iron pillow. Alex gasped in horror as she realized her sensors were indicating the bucket was sinking, and sinking fast.

She opened her radio to all units and broadcast the following message:

"Not bad for a bunch of rookies! Whoever lived through that—shake it off and blast those casings!"

She was already a few steps ahead of her own orders; she had tripped her combustible latches and gunned her engine. She could feel her Krawl and bucket lurching to the left and she realized she was sinking, even before she glanced at the sensors. Time was of the essence.

Krawlers called the process of opening the door to a bucket cracking the egg. This time the egg didn't want to crack. Something was thwarting the door, and since the door comprised one full side of the bucket, it had to be something significant.

Screw it! Alex thought, and launched a reserve protocol with the pull of a trigger. She didn't like to waste sorceress might on things one could accomplish just as well with brute physical force—in this case, she could have fired a rocket and blown the door off its hinges—but it would have taken more time to get past the debris, not to mention the risk of filling the entire inside with sand and whatever other crap was clogging up the works.

She extended the Krawl legs, had the Krawl legs the edge of the door, and then retracted the legs, thus pulling the Krawl forward. She lowered the wheels—Krawls had ten on each side—and they settled into the track and started to roll.

Alex was ecstatic when her Krawl hit the sand and was equalized for the first time since she hit her drop point. She gunned it. She knew from bitter experience in training that on certain kinds of ground, particularly after immolation, a crawler was like a shark—it had to keep moving or it would sink.

"Let's move!" she broadcast to the Krawlers under her command. "We've got infantry to dig out! Hey, Renko! Where the hell are you?"

Renko answered back with a distinct whine in her voice. "We undershot by a click, Captain. Goddamn desert wind, it—"

Damn her, Alex thought. The woman could hit a pebble fifty soccer fields away, but she'd complain about a muscle spasm every time she had to pull the trigger. "Shut the Hell up and reprogram your machine. Compensate for the extra distance. If you hit our boys, I'll kill you myself!"

Which Alex and the others knew was probably pure borscht on her part. Krawlers rarely had the chance to kill someone they had to look in the eye, and officers rarely got away with shooting a non-com for incompetence. She hoped Renko got the point, but she couldn't escape her gut feeling that she indeed had something to be anxious about.

So even by the time she'd had her last word, she had pushed off her goggles, opened the hatch, and was about to get her first idea about what the drop zone looked like without the benefit of virtual technology.

What she saw made her heart skip.

Renko wasn't the only Krawler who'd caught the wrong side of a tailwind.

Right next to her, not thirty meters away, another Krawler was trying to pull up its escape ramp while at a 45° angle, only to sink deeper in the sand. All the sand pouring inside through the open door didn't help matters any.

Alex felt sick. She knew this man. Krugolov. If he didn't get out of his machine and climb to the highest point, he'd smother to death for certain. And if both Krawler and hatch sank completely beneath the sand, he'd smother to death anyway. The paramedics and mop-up crews would be digging him out of the earth long after the action was over.

And he wasn't the only one. About one out of four, she estimated, was having trouble. It looked like most were going to make it, were going to wiggle their way out of their self-inflicted sinkhole, but a certain percentage she had no time to think about would not. Either way, they were going to miss the action.

"Goncharova to Drop Control—Column Eight is at 75 percent formation integrity and en route to firing zone."

"75 percent?" exclaimed Command. "What the hell happened?"

"Damned if I know! I haven't seen that much wind turbulence after an immolation since I don't know when!"

The wind was keeping the sand stirred. Visibility, particularly pertaining to the mountains where the Reds were dug in, was poor.

"Remember, children," she broadcast to her Krawlers, "This is a katyusha hunt. Rockets and rockets only! So nobody cry because they don't get to fire off their big main gun!"

Alex and the other Krawlers soon made it onto a patch of land where the sand was not deep, and was supported by a layer of rock, simplifying their equilibrium tasks and facilitating their aim.

Alex peered through her binoculars and saw horde after horde of enemy troops rushing toward the hollow in the mountainside where the Red Forces were dug in. She could not see where the waves of fighters were coming from. It was as if they were stepping whole from the fog.

"Okay, listen close, men," she said. "Nobody fires until I give the order. Your wives might put up with you shootin' off your guns early, but not me! Lev, what's the story?"

Lev, manning Krawler #175, was on the far end of the line. "We'll still have several rounds remaining, sir," he radioed back. "On your mark, Captain. We are ready to fire."

"Very well. Ready!"

The carriages behind the Krawl turrets titled back as one, with the precision of a drill.

"All units: FIRE!"

The first volley consisted of dozens of rockets. The rockets had dirty, inefficient burns, and left behind plumes of dark gray smoke. They didn't have to fly far, but it seemed to Alex the rockets were taking forever. Her heart beat furiously. How many Reds would die during the time it took the rockets to hit their target?

The rockets hit simultaneously, and a wave of destruction swept through the Nistaani. A nanosecond later, the sound struck Alex with a force that reminded her of a face slap.

Yet the Nistaani kept on coming. They hurled themselves through the barrage; they climbed through the relentless windstorm over hills of bodies and body parts. I am sure you have heard, Vanya, their religion claims that to die in Holy War permits you to enter the highest level of Heaven. I suppose that their Heaven is like Dante's, with levels, and where you are positioned is determined by the rewards you have earned in the earthly life. Judging by the piles of faithful corpses caused by Alex's and the other Krawlers' shells, the line to get into the highest levels of Heaven would be long. And yet, Alex could not help but note again, the Nistaani kept on coming. As if Death Himself could not deter them.

It was going to take a few moments for the Krawlers to reload. The process was automatic; the men didn't have to do anything except make sure everything went smoothly. Alex gave her primary focus to checking out the results of the barrage.

She hoped to spot the sorcerer who surely was responsible for the unprecedented power the Nistaani horde was displaying this day.

She adjusted the lenses on her binoculars, for occasionally sorcerers operated just beyond the boundaries of human perception. She reported in to Command: "Scanning impact zone for... There he is! I've got a visual on the Nistaani sorcerer! Prepare to set range!"

She gave the coordinates.

The sorcerer was like a spot of ink against a wall of white hot flame. She could see the silhouette of his staff and the sickle on its point, and she knew enough about magical protocols to realize he was holding a large tome wrapped in chains. But Command had not seen fit to inform her of the sorcerer's two comrades, his guards; surely Alex would have been more quick to recognize the danger she and everyone one else was in if she'd known the sorcerer was part of a troika. And of course, everyone who had a shred of sanity left inside their head would have high-tailed out of there as fast as possible if they'd known the sorcerer was Kar Dathra himself!

"Checking protocol status: he seems to have heavy defenses in place. But wait—"

The sorcerer threw his staff into the ground, and it punctured the rock with the ease of a nail puncturing a potato.

"Repeat, I have confirmed protocol activity. It looks like—the readings are saying it's an attack protocol, but—"

Kar Dathra threw out his arms in a manner that conveyed the ecstasy of power. Alex felt her torso muscles tighten like steel.

The sorcerer was inundated in waves of white and blue light that seemed to originate from deep inside the ground, as if he'd somehow opened a direct channel to the center of the earth. *But that's impossible,* Alex thought.

Then the earth around him rose in slow motion. And he rose with it, always staying just above it. It was as if the law of gravity itself was being repealed for the duration of his protocols.

A line of light began to wind its way toward the enemy horde.

Alex realized she was seeing a prelude to something unimaginable. "Control, do you read? This is Captain Goncharova of the Eighth Column! Enemy protocol magnitude is off the scale. Seismic readings off the scale. What the hell is that?"

One moment, the battlefield had been covered in Nistaani; the next, they had become shadows.

Their battle cries could heard but not seen. From out of the dust and smoke a blade would take another red trooper's life, and then vanish into the air.

It was as if we had angered not only Kar Dathra, but the very soil of Al'istaan itself.

The land and sky buckled and roared at the sorcerer's command.

A power exploded forth from him that threw our forces into panicked chaos.

According to Alexandra, this was when Marcus first made contact with her. It was a general distress call. In the background of his transmission she heard the cries of his men being wounded and dying in the background.

"This is Captain Antares to the Krawl Column. Repeat, this is Captain Antares requesting immediate extraction!"

He might as well have added, *and Central Command be damned*, because normally nobody requested extraction unless a certain implied permission had been granted. It was holdover custom from the days of Uncle Petrel and the Great War, when to quit on the edge of annihilation before the order had been given meant certain annihilation once one got home.

"Marcus? Is that you? Do you see this? My God—the power—it's impossible!"

She averted her eyes. The light had become so powerful that even the few streaks that got past the crook of her elbow were blinding. And the power so great that she felt it shaking the marrow in her bones.

"Alexandra! Listen to me! Get us the hell out of here! It's all over! Alex—"

That was it. He was cut off. Whether through system failure or the sudden need to defend himself, she could not be sure. The other, more obvious possibility did not even occur to her. She had always considered it unthinkable. Still, her concern was immense. She'd heard fear in Marcus's voice before, mostly during attempts to conceal his fear. But there was no shame in being afraid.

Any good soldier was. A healthy amount of fear kept you on edge, increased your chances of staying alive. But this was more than fear. It was panic.

"I'm on my way, Antares. Activate your location marker. I'm on route now!

She got a little distracted, however. As did Marcus. Everyone else got distracted, too.

Even the enemy paused. They savored the moment.

But we Reds were terrified.

For not even in forbidden Transnational cinema had we ever seen a scene during which a skyfurnace was pierced by a beam of yellow gai-powered ectoplasm that ripped its metal asunder from one side to another with meteoric intensity.

Multiply that by three, and you know what Alex and Marcus saw.

That was Kar Dathra's first volley.

The second one was equally potent. The crash of the first one as it struck the side of a mountain made me feel like a knife had materialized in my chest and was trying to stab a hole in the middle of my sternum. The sudden erasure of all this human life—no, strike that, I mean *Red* life filled me with a nausea of Sartresque proportions. I collapsed inside. All the energy drained out of me and the connections between the chamber and myself vanished. My chains of light vanished.

I hit the floor. Though stunned to the core by the blaze of human cries of defiance in that instant before they were snuffed out, my sudden freedom exhilarated me. I crawled up the chamber and looked through the portal just in time the crashing skyfurnace begin its long roll toward the enemy hordes.

The hordes did not appear to care. For the moment at least, they were still intent on overrunning the small contingent of surviving Russian soldiers. They had had their moment when the prospect of victory had been so clear, and now they were getting back to the serious business of killing the heinous heathen.

Why do they hate us so much? I wondered. Even then, I thought that what the URRS was doing was for the good of the enemy as much as it was for us.

Looking back now it seems so painfully clear.

Our nation's propaganda had convinced us that we were the "Defenders of Al'istaan from Transnational Global Ambitions."

The Nistaani didn't think so. Nor did Kar Dathra.

To them, we were alien, an occupying force of strange beings who took pride in our ability to make machines that grant us power over one another.

Against the spiritual might of Kar Dathra, our machines were rendered powerless.

The screaming metal sound of skyfurnace after skyfurnace ripping itself apart, is something I can hear even now.

Each skyfurnace moaned deeply as it fell to earth. A burning, twisted, falling coffin. During the remainder of the battle, if you could call it that, twenty-four furnaces went down. Two thousand crewmembers per furnace. Minimum.

And all thirty-seven Krawl carriers. With a crew of five hundred per carrier, plus one or two men each for the number of Krawlers yet to be deployed.

Then there were the casualties on the ground. I can't say it had been a good day to die the day of this battle, but it was a good day for the statistics of death.

Kar Dathra could have killed us all. Every last one of us. But he wanted to curse some of us to live, to tell this story of our defeat. To bear witness of his power before our people.

Watching part of the horde finally tumble onto the fact that the first pieces of that first crashing skyfurnace were beginning to rain down on them made me realize what I had to do.

I kast a protocol and my uniform flew from my locker and into my hands.

Breaking every fleet mandate I abandoned my post and kast a gate protocol to ground zero.

My husband was still down there. I was determined to bring him back myself, or die trying.

CHAPTER FIVE

I t is an incredible thing to witness the end of an era. To see everything you believed in devoured by flames, to have the hopes of your nation fall to the earth in a twisted wreck.

When that twisted wreck is a skyfurnace full of thousands of your countrymen, it is the discordant agony of their screams, the choking stench of their burning bones, the air so thick with human blood that you can almost taste it, that makes you realize what a fool you were to have ever believed in your nation's leaders.

All the leaders of the world—they are all liars. Petty lords with petty schemes. Our belief in them forms chains we cannot see. Phantom shackles of servitude that make us their willing slaves. Their loyal thrall.

All the while we think we are free.

We are not.

But our leaders must have us believe we are because the perfect slave is the one that believes he is free.

On the battlefield that day in Al'istaan, I witnessed firsthand what happens to such slaves when the schemes of their masters fail.

Their life-forces are extinguished. Snuffed out like candles in the wind. Their bodies do not fare as well.

They are broken, burned, or crushed like discarded playthings. And in the seconds before they die, they are filled with terror. It is no comfort to the living to know that the ending of their lives was quick, that their physical suffering did not endure for long, because their terror is infinite.

And that in the end, their bravery and nobility counted for nothing.

I would have dearly loved to personally visit terror on the Nistaani horde, I wanted them to know what it was like to face death in the fires of Hell.

But that would have been futile. The Nistaani already knew what Hell was like, because Hell is exactly the place where they'd come from, to extract vengeance on the Internationalist oppressor.

Even if I could have retaliated, somehow, no possible vengeance could have inflicted damage greater than what they'd already endured, no possible Hell could be more frightening and obscene than that which they'd already faced.

The battle was lost. The war was lost. What remained of the fleet was evacuating in a panic.

A moment before, I had been on the *Konstantinov*, one of the few ships still airborne. Against all orders and customs, I joined a small team of Warkasters and redeployed with them to the battlefield, via teleportation.

The Warkasters had one duty: rally the ground troops at an evac-zone and save as many of them as possible.

The evacuation rendezvous point was my last hope. If I didn't find Marcus there, he would be abandoned as missing in action.

The Warkasters chose as a rally point a hill overlooking the battlefield.

We got there just in time to see the *Aurora* nosedive

in the center of the battlefield. It nose-dived smack onto a pocket of the Nistaani horde, soldiers who had been so intent on their charge, so focused on their desire to kill a few more Red soldiers, that they'd neglected to look up until it was too late.

Even then, they did not appear to flee from fear so much as necessity. It's difficult to kill Red soldiers when you're between resurrections.

A series of explosions, some magical in nature, ripped through the *Aurora* as it completed its nosedive.

The *Aurora* fell on its side.

On more enemy soldiers who'd been more worried about advancing forward than which way the skyfurnace was going to fall.

The typical skyfurnace is almost three kilometers long, and half a kilometer wide. It weighs almost 300,000 tons and as I've said, has a crew of about 20,000.

The earth shakes for several minutes after one falls.

A few avalanches poured down on Nistaani and trapped Reds alike, but fortunately the ones striking the latter weren't too big.

For a moment, the ruined ship held me in awe. I could not help but loathe the Nistaani high priest, Kar Dathra the Eternal, who even now waved his arms and sent bolts of light from the earth to encircle and crush three Krawl carriers.

Off in the distance, two more carriers lay twisted and burning. The horizon was illuminated by several more fires of a similar nature.

The battlefield was Kar Dathra's stage at the edge of the world. On the jagged teeth of his terrain he composed for us a symphony of catastrophe and devastation.

Then he waved his arms and he was gone. His honor guard was gone.

There was left only the horde.

In the wake of Kar Dathra's judgment was a storm that dragged us with him by the tens of thousands, into oblivion.

In the smoke and the screams I could not help but realize, my nation's path had been changed forever. I swear to you I could feel the future of our people locking into place.

A future of chaos and uncertainty. A future none of us could have imagined.

But perhaps I am, in retrospect, over-intellectualizing what I was able to articulate there, on the ground, in the midst of the chaos.

The Warkasters had conjured the gates immediately upon arrival. I'm afraid I was still too weak to participate; besides, I was saving what little strength I had remaining for the combat I would soon have to engage in if I was to find Marcus.

The gates were a series of blue squares of light, four meters tall and ten long. They could be seen quite clearly through the smoke and the dust. Our troops knew where to go—

—Once they'd thrown the hordes off their backs, that is. Now the horde knew where to concentrate their efforts. The hand-to-hand combat became, if anything, fiercer, more brutal.

A frenzied collection of troopers charged the evac-gates. They came pouring in by the hundreds. Many were wounded or maimed, but at least they were alive.

Blind with fear, they swept over me. I called out Marcus' name, again and again. I called out his unit number. My voice was lost in all the noise.

I was dragged by the mass of fleeing soldiers. The wind was knocked out of my lungs and I staggered, nearly falling. Faces passed me in shadow. None of them seemed familiar; none of them were Marcus'.

The soldiers almost dragged me through the gates, but I managed to break through. While catching my breath, I resisted the temptation to follow them. They might be defeated, frightened, and heartbroken, but they were safe—so long as Kar Dathra did not return to target the *Konstantinov*.

Part of me wanted to step through the blue light and into the safety of the Konstantinov's familiar decks. I'm ashamed to admit it, but I actually wavered.

That was when my friend, Krawl Captain Alexandra Goncharova, found me. "Maya! Maya! It's me!" she said as she grabbed my shoulder from behind me.

Good move, because I might have mistaken her for an enemy, turned around and thrown a rearranging spell on her face.

"Alexandra—" I said. I thought I had already hit bottom, that things couldn't possibility get any worse than the deaths of over a hundred and fifty thousand Red soldiers, but looking into Alex's eyes, her tired, wasted eyes, I knew. I knew instantly she believed Marcus was dead.

"Yes, damn you, don't look at me that way," she said hoarsely. "Of course I saw him. I was on my way to pick him up..." She couldn't finish. A look of anguish like I'd never seen came over her. Belatedly I noticed how tired she was, how beat-up and bruised. I'd never before sensed her aura so diminished. She gestured at the *Aurora* and said, "Look, Maya, that furnace. I could see him, but that furnace tipped over on top of my column before I could reach him. Most of my men are dead, and for a few moments I wished I'd died myself. But then, there was Marcus calling me.

"By the time I'd pulled myself out from beneath what was left of my Krawl, I looked over to where Marcus was—" She shed a tear. Damn, Alex actually shed a tear! "You know I don't lie, Maya, even when it's to make things easier. He's gone! There's no way that he—"

I didn't want to hear any more. "But you didn't see his body. You're not sure, are you?"

"I tried to track his location marker. *I got nothing!* You know what that means! Don't pretend that you don't, just because it isn't what you want to hear!"

"To hell with markers! I would know if he were dead! It's not possible!"

"And so if he's alive somewhere on the field, in the midst of that inferno! So what? Do you think the fleet is going to wait for you to dig your way through that mountain of corpses looking for him? They'll leave you here to die!"

That's when I regretted not kasting that face-rearranging spell. I would have kast it right then and there, had I not been afraid of wasting too much energy from my already exhausted resources. "If you care so much about living, go on then! If you're right, if I've lost him, then I'm going to die with him!"

"Like hell you are—"

Only in retrospect do I realize the narrowing of her eyes indicated a determination not be thwarted. During the Battle of Kar Dathra's Gate, Alexandra Goncharova was the very embodiment of the purposeful heroine. She might have to endure the humiliation of defeat, but she would not be distracted from her main goal. I had just noted the reflection of the burning *Aurora* in her eyes when—

She decked me.

I had been looking into her eyes when I should have been looking at her hands.

I had not known it was possible for a person to literally see stars; previously I had only thought it an expression. But the moment her fist connected with my jaw, a veritable constellation spun around my head.

Then I hit the ground.

"Volunteers!" she called out, as if on the other side of a tunnel. "I need two volunteers over here—NOW!"

An eternity passed. I could see her legs planted near me like ancient redwoods, but her torso and face were in shadow. I was vaguely aware of the black cloud of smoke overhead, but I could not see the light from the flames. I could hear it, though. And I could hear the screams of my countrymen, those who were in the process of dying and those who had already died.

Finally the omnipresent chains of gravity released me, and I felt myself rising from the ground.

Alex's face neared me. It was difficult to tell in the flickering light that now enveloped her, but were those the tracks of tears running down her cheeks? Then her expression hardened and she looked to the two rock faces belonging to the men who had picked me up by the shoulders and feet and said, "Gently with her! She's more valuable than both of you lug-nuts put together!"

"Yes, Captain!" one of the men said.

"I'm sorry, Maya," she said. "But someday you'll thank me." She turned away. Her voice had the volume of a whisper, but I know it was something more than that. It was definitely a near prayer. "Marcus, wherever the hell you are, I know you would have wanted her to live."

The last thing I remember, before passing out completely, was a flash of blue light—the grunts carrying me through the evac-gates.

And that was how I left the field of battle, carried off like a sleeping child, my jaw almost cracked by my best friend. I had meant to rescue my husband and failed. I had gone the abyss to bring him back or be devoured by it. To this day, I wonder how close I might have been to saving him.

If only I could somehow know where he was, where he laid his head down the last time. But of course there is no power in the world that can show me that moment. No goddess so merciful that she would whisper to me his final thoughts....

CHAPTER SIX

Marcus:

Maya, Maya my love...

I am defeated. My army is defeated. My cause is defeated, My country is defeated.

Who will stand for the common man against the interests of the corporate minions now? Who will fight for freedom against the barbaric fanatic horde?

Certainly not me.

And who shall love you in the future?

Certainly not me. Most regretfully, not me.

I lay here, my uniform in shreds, on the twisted wreckage of a piece of skyfurnace that broke off and rolled through my men like a fiery cannonball. My body is punctured in many places. I am undoubtedly suffering internal bleeding. And though the air is hot, and the metal I am using to prop myself up extremely hot, so hot my skin is getting burned, I am so very cold.

Maya, if I could have one last wish, it would be to be with you one more night. You are so loving, so giving of yourself. Making love to you is like experiencing an eternity of passion compressed into a few short hours. You are worth dying for, but more importantly you are worth living for.

Forgive me, I want to believe I will live, but we are no longer children, with our eyes full of miracles.

The battlefield is strewn with the dead.

I am the only one left alive.

At least, I believe so. I do not have the strength to call out, and for all I know, some of the blood that stains me has come from my own throat.

It is so hard to breathe. Is the smoke choking me, or my own blood? I do not believe I shall ever know, nor do I think that it matters overmuch at this stage of the game.

The air stirs from the effects of the heat. Indeed, the air moves as if a gale is moving across the battlefield, making the oxygen that much more difficult to catch.

I am cold. The cold is one thing, but this sudden chill down my spine is quite another.

I shall soon be dead. Maya, if the ghost of Gorkovsky could grant me but one wish, it would be to die in your arms.

Something is coalescing in the chaos. Something gray and black. A vaguely human form wearing a hood and cloak.

It is approaching me.

Is this an ancestral vision? Is my brain attempting to visualize the ineffable in a manner not dissimilar to the way the rest of humanity visualizes the ineffable during their final moments? Or am I merely over-intellectualizing the experience so I can better deal with it emotionally?

Whatever the nature of the thing approaching me, I cannot distinguish its features. I am positive it has a face, an amorphous, hideous face.

The thing looms before me. Becomes larger.

And reaches out with long black fingers. The hand morphs between being whole and being skeletal.

I am beyond panic. Beyond emotion, beyond regret.

The hand touches me, reaches inside me.

It is neither cold nor warm. It is nothing.

In a moment, the world shifts and I am among the dead.

Maya...

Suddenly I am standing. The crash and burning of the skyfurnaces is all around me. The dead of the battlefield are all around me. I sense my body is among them, though I sense equally that I could be mistaken, that it walks with my spirit.

The sky is black with ashes and smoke; the smoke is writhing with spirits. Medieval knights fighting desert warriors. The peasants of the Motherland doing battle with the armies of our historic rivals. Mongrel hordes overrunning the armies of our ancestors. But I see not only ancient wars. I see URRS soldiers fighting Europa Aryans in hand-to-hand combat. I see White and Red Revolutionaries together in the streets, rallying protests against the Provisional Government, and I see the Whites and the Reds doing battle against one another on those same streets.

Is this a glimpse of the world that awaits me, a Dark Valhalla? Or is this the failing vision of a dead man?

Not yet dead, but barely alive, in soul if not in body, I walk beneath these visions, in a storm between two worlds.

The moan of a crashing skyfurnace is merged with the sound of broadswords. The heavy thunder of an ancient cavalry becomes the sound of another furnace exploding in the distance.

I have no fear. I am beyond it. I accept my death.

A dry wind scrapes my armor.

I have seen the herald of Death and now my eyes behold His arrival.

In the sky beyond a scimitar slices through a head. A Mongrel warrior falls and yet his aura staggers on to complete a deathblow that has undoubtedly been duplicated innumerable times before. This is the backdrop to His approach.

From a pool of blood He rises, his cloak forged of blades and chains.

He is a behemoth who glides toward me with effortless ease.

I stand frozen in terror, trapped between worlds, as he looms over me and permits me to look into the infinite darkness of his eyes.

He stops and looks into mine.

Can it be? he says. I feel his words in my ghostly bones as much as I hear them. *After so many generations, can it be a soul whose eyes can see the truth?*

If the life of a Red soldier has taught me anything, it is the disadvantage of being perceived as special. Only in the arms of Maya has the feeling of being special been a privilege. Right now the prospects of being perceived as special fills me with cosmic terror. *Are you real?* I wonder.

What you see, soldier, is no illusion, no hallucination. You behold a truer vision of this battlefield than any soul still alive. Your cage of flesh is the only barrier to an even greater vision. Let it die away. Give your soul to me.

I don't think so. I know something is wrong. My instincts scream in a million voices, warning me against him.

I detach my Hook from my shoulder and hurl it bayonet first at the behemoth. My aim is perfect.

Only problem is, the bayonet does not penetrate him. The Hook doesn't even reach him. With the fleetness of a cat, he raises his hand and my weapon is halted in mid-air.

It hangs there. Impossibly. Not even our most powerful sorceress can do that. Not even Maya.

Do not struggle against me, comrade. We are countrymen. You have nothing to lose but your pain.

A gesture, and the suspended Hook melts and twists and changes and then hardens into a scythe.

Your life fades from you. Only moments now until you are free. Do not fear. In life you served our nation. When your soul is in my possession, you will serve it as never before.

The scythe flies to his hand. My transformed weapon will be the thing that he uses to kill me.

If I am not dead already. I cannot be sure.

He raises the scythe. *I promise you.*

I have fallen. Throwing my Hook exhausted all my strength and I lie like a wounded fox on the bloody ground.

I sense a light overhead, a break in the smoke and the fire. Certainly that is the white light those who had returned from a near-death experience speak of.

Though I will not return.

Maya...

My soul is lost in a storm between worlds. The memory of your voice anchors me. It echoes as the cry of a raven.

I can feel the rush of the scythe cutting through the air. Goodbye, my love.

A noise.

Metal upon metal.

I roll over and see that the white blade of a sword, half-corporeal and half an apparition, has stopped the scythe in mid-arc.

I can now see the light overhead. And a bird—a dove? a raven?—flying through it.

But the strain of looking up is too much and I roll over to see who is wielding the white blade.

Nothing in life or the prospect of death has prepared me for the answer.

A woman in red. She wears a hooded frock with long loose sleeves and a flowing cape, and her arms are muscular and strong. She wields her sword with ease.

She looks at the things trying to take my soul without a trace of fear.

How many souls must you imprison, Troika, before you realize your crimes against our people? Tell your master—

Aha! Death has a name, and a master, it seems.

The days of his iron hold on our nation are over. I am here to end his reign. You will leave this soul to me, or be destroyed.

I am beyond pain. My brain must be surging with endorphins, for my mind is surely beyond reason.

How can it be that two beings fight for the broken soul of this wretched body? Were it not the joy of my love for Maya, I would have long ago given up my life-force to whatever preternatural entity desired it. Though were I to be consigned to an afterworld without love, the abnegation of oblivion would be my preferred destination.

Yet the scrape of metal against metal echoes in my mind as if processed through a phase distortion program. The power of these two entities standing over me, sword to scythe, reverberates like the pulses between two opposing magnets.

Troika, after all these decades you are still blind to the truth, says the woman in red. *So I will say only this, I will not allow this warrior's soul to be your master's slave. Face me, and you will be defeated. I promise you.*

The one called Troika backs off a few steps. The sound of his cloak of chains grates, and the cloak itself leaves a jagged path in the bloody ash and dust.

It is so cold. Despite all the fire and heat, I am cold. My heart is cold. But wait—! This Troika again speaks:

Your perceptions are criminal, Rogue Spirit. In Death, as in life, there is no greater way to serve our nation than by doing the bidding of our glorious and eternal Father.

Who would be whom? My mind is too addled, my emotions too weak for me to grapple with such questions. I had thought facing death would bring, if not peace, then answers to the torment of one's heart. Yet it appears the ineffable shall be forever with me.

The woman in red and the being called Troika circle one another, yet neither yields a centimeter.

Nor do their weapons disengage. The scrape of metal against metal continues to reverberate, the cloak of chains rattles, and yet I notice they leave no footprints. It is as if they exist in a netherworld among netherworlds, in a place where they are neither solid nor transparent.

Your master's ways have never served our people, says the woman in red. *His murderous insanity was the end of our revolution. I will not allow his legacy to end our nation itself.*

My master's ways have made this country strong, says Troika, as he swings his scythe in an arc that will take it through the woman's red hood.

Strong? I cannot begin to imagine the scale of the defeat of which my impending death is but a part. I would be angered if I were not so broken, so tired.

The woman sidesteps the scythe, then strikes it, knocking it from one of Troika's hand.

He is surprised, but manages to maintain his grip with his other hand.

The woman takes advantage of his temporary unsteadiness and steps back. She opens her free hand.

Above her hand floats a crimson diamond shaped like a pentagram.

It glows. Its glow permeates my vision.

With the finesse of a prestidigitator the woman grabs the diamond and hurls it straight up in the air.

Troika averts his eyes, or more precisely, turns his face away so the light will not strike the place where he should have eyes.

He is otherwise unmoved. The meaning of the woman's gesture eludes me, but I do not see how I will survive long enough to learn what it may mean.

I do begin to get the impression that the red diamond has disappeared, as if it is rising into the stratosphere of this netherworld between life and death, but wait—!

The being called Troika is responding to the woman's defiance. He gestures toward the nearest skyfurnace.

Where is it that you hide, spirit? Waiting to strike. Hoping to defeat me, time and time again. After all these decades, you must realize the futility of your actions.

His fingers twitch.

The iron carcass lifts from its pyre like a puppet being picked up by its strings.

The woman in red stands over me. She whispers words I cannot understand.

There is the screaming of metal, deafening, terrifying,

as the skeleton of the skyfurnace breaks into its component parts.

Then there is the sound, equally deafening, that goes skreee! as those component parts, red hot, melting, streak toward the woman.

Toward me. During this eternal nanosecond of my demise, it occurs to me I soon may not possess a soul worth stealing. For surely my soul shall be pulverized along with my body.

The woman in red knees over me. She holds her sword behind her back.

A great white light shines over us.

And deflects the metal parts of the skyfurnace. They careen from the shield of light and scatter like misshapen marbles.

They land in a series of pyres.

The woman in red faces her antagonist. *Look around you, Troika. Can you not see this battlefield for what it is?*

The being in the cloak of chains is curiously relaxed after the futility of his spectacular attack. *Blood shed in war is the fuel of a nation. These are sacred rites more ancient than you or I.*

There is another way, she says. *There has always been. You believed that once.*

I will blame such weakness on the confusions of mortality. I have since seen the truth.

If it is the truth you seek, I will grant you this. It may not be pleasant for you. For the first time I detect a note of fear—no, anxiety, in the woman's voice, as she lifts her eyes to the ashen sky and says, in a lower voice, in a pleading tone, *Please, sister, answer me. I cannot defeat him alone.*

You are a fool, says Troika. *You lie to yourself because you are not yet ready to face the truth.*

She charges him. He seems to have touched a nerve.

They fight. They hack at one another viciously, yet never land a blow. Masters of *cinéma vérité* would have choreographed their fight as a ballet; however it is anything but. While I expect Troika to attack as forthrightly and as brutally, as a bullet train, she is equally brutal, both her defenses and attacks being as barbaric yet strategic as his.

Their fight takes them into one of the small pyres their antagonism has created. They move through fires and hot metal, oblivious to the nature of the debris. The woman in red crashes backwards into a beam; her impact causes the red hot metal to bend, and yet her cloak and indeed her very person appear unharmed. In fact, she shrugs off the collision and pushes forward, attempting to put the being called Troika on the defensive.

But she must be wary. His superior size and the wide strike zone he creates when he swings the scythe enable his attack to be aggressive and I can see why it is difficult for her to mount an effective offense.

Yet nothing prevents her from mounting a psychological attack. *I remember a time when your voice was not a sound of scraping metal—when it rang out loudly against oppression, injustice, tyranny...*

Now *that* touches a nerve. Troika doubles the force of his attack. *I was never such a man!*

They move across an iron grill that was white hot—they kick it apart as if it is the remnants of a campfire.

I remember when your voice could inspire an army of voices to pay any price for freedom, says the women in red.

Silence, witch! Obviously, another touched nerve. This

Troika is very sensitive for a cold-blooded force of nature.

Yes, silence. The man you were has been silenced forever. And in your agony, you have murdered millions whose voice were once as beautiful as yours. I promised I would show you the truth, Troika. She *has been waiting to reveal herself to you for so long.*

If the purpose of the woman in red's taunts is to make this Troika even more dangerous, then she has succeeded beyond her wildest expectations. The being's scythe cuts through the iron and steel as if he was plowing through a field of reeds. Only the woman's sword checks its relentless forward motion. And each time she staggers a little bit more. If he keeps it up, then she shall surely be lost and so will I.

Not that there is anything I can do about it. But I am only a mortal man, on the verge of death. Why do these beings think me important?

I see that the woman in red is worried. Her eyes glance imploringly to the sky, though perhaps the sky is in truth the ineffable. *Sister, I beg of you,* she says. *In the name of all we've fought for, do not forsake me now.*

I do not know if Troika has heard her plea, if the extra ratcheting of violence in his attack has to do with the weakness inherent in her plea or if his rage has simply given him an edge. For whatever reason, he closes in to the point where neither scythe nor sword can connect and he pummels her with his fists.

I said SILENCE!

He puts both fists together and with a wide swing, lands a tremendous blow across her cheekbone.

She goes down. She attempts to scramble up but he kicks her on the belly.

She is too stunned to defend herself, and I fear for her.

I would gladly give up my soul to this monstrous reaper if I could be assured of her salvation.

With his fists on his hips he looks down at her and I almost expect him to laugh. *Where is your righteous judgment now, Witch?*

Both Troika and I are late in noticing the smile on the woman's face as the sky—or the ineffable—answers her.

Thank you, sister. You have not saved me in vain.

I had thought things were happening in slow motion before. Now they truly slow down and become, at least for the moment, almost a tableau.

The woman in red lies still on the ground. She would be a perfect, a helpless target for this creature, but he is totally fixated on the sky.

I sense another presence in the netherworld. The presence is vast, overwhelming, yet as removed from this plane of existence as we are from the land of the living.

It manifests itself as a crimson curtain, an aurora borealis of sorts, moving across the sky.

A pillar of crimson light shines down on Troika. He holds his scythe helplessly, like a little boy caught in the act of stealing.

The hands of a hundred cloaked furies bound by the crimson light grab him. He struggles against them, I sense he is pleading for mercy. But as Troika had been deaf to the horror of his victims—and I surmise there have been millions upon millions—so now there is no mercy left for him.

The crimson furies hold onto Troika and take him into the sky, and he vanishes into the crimson curtain.

I am saved. Not saved from death, for that is inevitable, but I am saved from Troika.

Perhaps that is enough, more than I could have ever asked for.

THE RED STAR

The woman in red stands straight and tall, her cloak swirling in the rushes of air created by the funeral pyres of the Red Fleet, as the presence in the sky recedes into darkness.

It seems she is gliding rather than walking as she goes to her sword and pulls it from the mound of white hot metal into which it had fallen.

Now she is coming for me.

I should be afraid, for surely she is as powerful, as determined, and as mysterious in her own way as the entity she had just vanquished. But try as I might, I cannot believe she means me harm.

She gathers me in her arms. I remember now what it was like to be young, and to be held by my mother.

Marcus Antares, she says.

"Maya... the fleet... the battle," I manage to say.

Rest now, son of Antares. The war is over and you must not be troubled. You see, it was not our people who were defeated here, but our past. And the path to our future begins with you.

That's very nice, I think, but life in the military has taught me the downside to taking on too much responsibility, and this definitely seems like such a case. "Can't I... just die?"

I suspect she has literally read my mind. *Sadly, no.*

And she lifts me. Carries me as easily as she would a child toward a blazing, setting sun.

Above me, the spirit warriors have ceased their eternal battle and they stand in formation, saluting me with their swords. Doves, ravens, and eagles fly about the woman in red and myself as she takes me into another world.

To the next stage of my journey.

CHAPTER SEVEN

This is my station, Vanya," said Maya Antares. "Marcus' grave is... close now."

Vanya smiled to himself. He realized Maya had had no idea they had circled the Citadel National Cemetery.

"I hope you haven't—by listening to my story—missed your stop?" she continued as she pulled the chord signaling the train to let her off.

"No, sweet child," Vanya replied, filled with sadness at the prospect that he would probably never see this woman again. He had not felt such warmth in his soul since the birth of his last grandchild. "As I said, there are so many of my comrades resting in this place, it would be impossible to visit them all. I ride the train, look out over the fields, and let the memories fill my head."

On her way out, Maya kissed the old man on the cheek. "I wish your generation was young again, Vanya. In your day, your comrades feared nothing."

Vanya laughed. Laughed and wished he was fifty years younger, so that he might discover if it was vaguely possible to convince this woman to take another chance on love. "Ahhh, child! That's only because we were farmers. Too stupid to know better."

At the door Maya looked back and said, "It was an honor to have met you, Comrade Vanya. Thank you."

The door closed behind her and the train pulled away. She was alone.

Before her, beginning at the bottom of the series of steps that led to the ground and stretching three kilometers to the nearest forest, were the rows and rows of gravestones. Exact figures of the dead buried or memorialized here were unavailable, but in this section alone, reserved for the casualties of the Battle of Kar Dathra's Gate, there were over three hundred thousand. (There had been more casualties during the battle than that, of course; the families of many of the victims had preferred their sons and daughters be buried in their native villages.)

She had divined Vanya's last thoughts about her. Not just because she was a sorceress, but because men always underestimate the transparency of their thinking. She could not help but be amused, because he never would have stood a chance, not even if he was fifty years younger. The memory of Marcus was always uppermost in her mind, and closest to her heart.

Once she was on the field itself, walking between the tombstones, she did not have to look where she was going. She could find his grave blindfolded. She was just one shadow among many thousands.

She was devoured by the same reminiscence that always overtook her on this leg of her journey. So vivid it was she feared it was more a fantasy than an actual memory, that she augmented it with her dreams and illusions, and with the special filter people always seem to apply whenever they are overcome by feelings of nostalgia.

The day of their first kiss could not have been as bright as she remembered. The touch of his hands as he embraced her could not have sent such warmth through both his gloves and her overcoat. The trembles that shot through the fingers of her gloved hand as she touched his cheek could not have been as strong.

It is not possible for a man to have been that tender and passionate at the same time.

She nearly fell rather than knelt at his grave and laid down her offering of nine blood red roses. His body was not present—strictly speaking this was a memorial—but she believed with all her soul his spirit was. She felt it touching every tear that ran down her cheeks.

Today her grief was even more overwhelming than she'd expected. How tempting it was to shatter the silence of this sacred place and wail like an old woman freshly widowed.

Only the presence of another approaching Marcus's tombstone deterred. She knew of his approach not only because she heard her footsteps in the snow, but because she sensed his more restrained, more resigned grief for Marcus.

It was the grief of her brother-in-law, Urik Antares.

"It's strange, really. Nine years now, we've come here on this day," he said, "to this empty grave."

She knew those nine years had been difficult on Urik. She knew he had been drinking, womanizing, pushing his natural rebellious disposition to the edge of insubordination. He had come close to being court martialed or exiled several times, and yet he had never lost the respect of his men. Or of Maya. She did not need to look to know that his uniform was freshly cleaned, the buttons and shoes freshly shined and his appearance every centimeter that of the model soldier. For the memory of Marcus he would do no less.

"How was your walk, Uri?" she asked.

"Long, Maya. How was the train?" He helped her stand.

"Pleasant, really. I met a solider. A veteran of the Great Patriotic War." She smiled weakly. "It will be a sad day when the last of his kind are gone. I'm afraid I just got here. I spent too much time talking to him."

"I am sorry. If I had known, I would have waited."

"Why?"

"I wanted you to take your time, Maya. It's important that you say everything you need to say to Marcus today. This will be our last visit here, until God knows how long."

"What?" She noticed he had said *God* instead of the customary *Gorkovsky.*

"I don't suppose you've heard then. I wanted you to know—I wanted you to have a chance to say good-bye to my brother." He gave her the newspaper he had brought. "Or possibly to let him know we might be joining him soon."

What she saw chilled her more than a thousand winters.

WAR IN NOKGORKA was the headline. The lead article was posted from Bahamut, Nokgorka. It read:

> FOR CENTURIES, THE MOUNTAINOUS REGION OF NOKGORKA HAS BEEN A PROVINCE UNDER THE LEADERSHIP OF THE LANDS OF THE RED STAR. YESTERDAY, NOKGORKA'S LEADERS DECLARED THEMSELVES A SOVEREIGN NATION, THUS MAKING OFFICIAL THEIR INTENTION TO BREAK AWAY FROM THE MOTHERLAND,

THE RED STAR

THE GOVERNMENT OF THE FORMER UNITED REPUBLICS OF THE RED STAR IMMEDIATELY SIGNALED ITS INTENTION TO RESIST FURTHER EROSION OF TERRITORY THROUGH THE ATTORNEY COMMISSAR, WHO OFFERED NOKGORKA'S REBELLIOUS LEADERS WHAT MANY IN THE DUMA VIEWED AS REASONABLE TERMS OF SURRENDER. EDGAR BURROURGSKI, THE SPEAKER OF DUMA, WARNED THE REBELS THAT "ANY THREAT TO THE TERRITORIAL INTEGRITY OF THE NATION WILL BE SUPPRESSED BY ANY and all MEANS AT OUR DISPOSAL."

THIS STATEMENT OF POSITION WAS IMMEDIATELY FOLLOWED BY A DECLARATION OF WAR. (SEE STORY ON PAGE 3.)

FORCES OF THE RED FLEET HAVE ALREADY BEEN MOBILIZED, WITH ORDERS TO CRUSH THE NOKGORKAN RESISTANCE MILITIA. THE EXACT SIZE OF THE DEPLOYMENT FORCE IS NOT YET KNOWN, BUT SOURCES CONFIRM THAT THIS IS THE LARGEST MILITARY OPERATION SINCE THE CATASTROPHIC WAR OF AL'ISTAAN ALMOST A DECADE AGO.

IT IS A SMALLER FORCE, BUT A NO LESS DETERMINED ONE.

THE NOKGORKA RESISTANCE MILITIA IS MAINLY A SMALL GUERILLA FORCE, HOW LONG IT CAN STAND AGAINST THE MIGHTY RED FLEET IS NOT KNOWN, BUT COMMANDER MURAVIEV HAS SWORN TO HAVE THE REBEL LEADERS IN IRONS BY WINTER'S END.

DESPITE WHAT CONCLUSIONS REASONABLE PEOPLE MIGHT COME TO, THE PEOPLE OF NOKGORKA ARE NONETHELESS UNITED IN THE DELUSION THAT THEY NO LONGER HAVE NEED OF THE GOVERNMENT OF THE FORMER URRS AND ARE FULLY JUSTIFIED IN GOING TO WAR, IF NEED

BE, IN ORDER TO RELIEVE THEMSELVES OF WHAT THEY BELIEVE IS THE TYRANNY OF RED RULE.

WESTERN REACTION HAS BEEN MIXED, WITH LEADERS OF MOST OF THE TRANSNATIONALIST COUNTRIES NOT WANTING ANY PART OF WHAT THEY CONSIDER TO BE A HIGHLY COMPLEX AND EXTREMELY PROBLEMATICAL SITUATION—FOR THE RUSSIANS.

PRESIDENT PERRY OF THE WESTERN TRANSNATIONAL ALLIANCE HAD CAUTIOUS WORDS FOR THE PRESS. "PEACEFUL RESOLUTION OF POLITICAL CONFLICTS ARE ALWAYS PREFERENTIAL. HOWEVER, THE CURRENT WORLD CLIMATE DOES NOT ALWAYS OFFER SUCH ALTERNATIVES. IN LIGHT OF THIS, IT IS OUR POSITION THAT THE CONFLICT IN NOKGORKA IS BEST LEFT TO THE LEADERS OF THE REGION TO DECIDE. WHAT I'M TRYING TO SAY IS, THE TRANSNATIONALS DON'T HAVE A DOG IN THIS HUNT. CATCH MY MEANING NOW, BOYS?"

Maya's eyes glazed over. Of course the Transnationals will not interfere. Why should they, when their ideological foes were busy dividing and destroying themselves, doing the Trans' work for them?

Damn. It is just the Motherland's dumb luck happening during a heated election campaign! she thought, knowing from past observation that the perfect time for getting the worst decision possible out of the incumbent party was to hand them a crisis during election season.

President Moszkowski was stepping down, and the election was wide open, hotly contested between the party of the Reformists and the party of Hard Liners, with all the parties in between jockeying for the best possible terms in the next coalition.

Maya forced herself to focus on the second lead article. It was devoted to the Reformist Party front-runner.

DEPUTY DEFENSE MINISTER VOICES OPINION ON NAKGORKA

"HAD THE PREPARATIONS OF THIS DEPLOYMENT NOT BEEN KEPT SECRET FROM ME, I WOULD HAVE VOICED MY OPPOSITION MUCH SOONER." THESE ARE THE ANGRY WORDS OF THE DEPUTY DEFENSE MINISTER CHIGAYEV UPON HEARING OF THE ANNOUNCEMENT BY CENTRAL COMMAND TO MOBILIZE FORCES AGAINST THE REBEL FACTIONS IN NOKGORKA.

"JUST AS IN AL'ISTAAN, THE MILITARY OPERATION'S LONG TERM AND SHORT TERM STRATEGIC GOALS FOR NOKGORKA HAVE NOT BEEN CLEARLY DEFINED," CHIGAYEV CONTINUED, "I HAVE TO BELIEVE IN ALL LIKELIHOOD THAT PRESIDENT MOSZKOWSKI'S DECISION TO USE FORCE WAS MADE ON THE SPUR OF THE MOMENT WITH LITTLE THOUGHT OF THE OUTCOME. MANY OF THE TROOPS WE ARE SENDING INTO NOKGORKA ARE FAR FROM MORALLY PREPARED TO DEAL WITH FIGHTING SOLDIERS WHO, UNTIL NOW, WOULD HAVE BEEN CON-SIDERED THEIR COUNTRYMEN. HAVE WE LEARNED NOTHING FROM THE BATTLE AT KAR DATHRA'S GATE?"

CHIGAYEV SAID HE DOES NOT SEE ANY WAY OF SOLVING THE NOKGORKA PROBLEM BY FORCE ALONE, AND WOULD MUCH PREFER A CARROT AND STICK APPROACH, AS BEFITS THE REALM OF *REALPOLITIK*.

Another article was devoted to the Hard Liners and their lead candidate.

THE RED STAR

LYULIK CALLS NOKGORKA
REBELS A CRIMINAL REGIME

Minister of State Affairs, Aleksei G. Lyulin
stressed that the Nokgorka issue is a prime
example of the secessionist trend which the
former United Republics of the Red Star must
overcome.

"If necessary the government will use force in
any and all provinces threatening to secede to
preserve territorial integrity," said Lyulin today.
Lyulin went on to say that he considers the calls
to settle the Nokgorka crisis through peaceful
means weak and ultimately hypocritical. "No
peaceful means will ever help us deal with a
criminal regime which is armed to the teeth," said
Lyulin. He argued that comrades of the former
URRS must view their motherland first and
foremost as an indivisible power.

The smaller the nation, the lesser its influence, thought
Maya. The camp counselors of her training days had
stressed that principle. They had also impressed upon
her the eternal truth that the gold standard of the individual is measured by his devotion to and willingness
to sacrifice for the State.

She could not help but wonder how much more she
had to give. She realized she had inadvertently betrayed
her ideals during her conversation with the old man on
the train. She had actually enjoyed the company of a
man for its own sake. More experienced widows than
she had told her—a long, long time ago—that that was
the first step toward putting their grief in its place and
going on to the next stage, and the next love of their

111

life. Maya wasn't sure how she felt about *that,* but now it certainly appeared her love for Marcus was the only one she was ever going to have.

The words on the paper began going in and out of focus. Maya felt unsteady on her feet, and she belatedly realized Urik was helping her stand. There was a photograph on the page, a fuzzy black and white of a city in ruins, its factory smokestacks devoid of fumes, its tallest buildings reduced to naked steel substructure, its streets and sidewalks deserted. A Nokgorkan city, already reeling from the effects of a war just begun. Even the most trained and adept sorceresses were not one hundred percent in control of their abilities during times of stress, and Maya's mind transported itself into the essence of the vision indicated by the photograph.

She saw Nokgorka. A place that soon would be as cold and laden with death as the graveyard in which she now stood.

Trained as a soldier, her mind immediately armed itself with thought duty, country, survival.

Trained as a widow, she saw those weapons as something more than instruments of her own protection. They were more like a cage—a complex system of mental imprisonment that she needed to find a way to believe in once again.

Else she would die in Nokgorka.

She realized her country was too plagued and corrupt to win any war. But to accept that was to become an imperfect soldier—a soldier filled with doubt. And imperfect soldiers made armies that were mere pawns, marching to slaughter.

The soldier in her personality cursed her thoughts, struggled to make her accept herself. The widow was not sure of anything. She pleaded to escape her fate.

On one side of the dark tunnel of her mind, in the future, was the dim winter light of Nokgorka.

On the other side, in the past, Al'istaan burned.

Al'istaan. The place that had claimed her husband.

She had been little more than a child when she entered that war. Only a newly married bride when she was trained to transform herself into a pillar of light that destroyed anything in her nation's path.

No thoughts plagued her then. No questioning of what she was a part of.

She was the heat of her nation's anger, the burning will of the state. She was an inferno, clearing the path of those who resisted.

Between the soldier and the widow, there was only one choice to be made. The widow, her eyes shadowed, hid in the darkness. The soldier stood boldly at attention in the forefront of her mind.

She was Maya Antares, Sorceress-Major of the Red Star Skyfurnace *Konstantinov* of the Red Fleet.

In her nation's service, she wore proudly on her uniform the order of Imbohl—glorious Father of the Revolution in which our nation was born, and the Order of the Red Star, the symbol of our ancient lands.

No weakness would consume her. No fear would lure her into paralysis. If she was to die in Nokgorka, then that was the will of Gorkovsky and the State. With each moment, her fate approached Nokgorka. There were women there, whom she would widow.

Her mind moved deeper into the essence of the photograph. She began to perceive the color of a hazy blue sky, the heightened surrealism of being in a broken city where things had worked not so long ago.

Her mind's eye pulled back from the vision in the photograph and saw the place where the photographer had stood. Saw what the editors of the newspaper had not wanted their readers to see. What the government censors had made clear the citizens should not see.

The rebels, celebrating their victory over the bodies of several dead Russian soldiers. Their minds are possessed by their country's cause. They are fed by a glorious rage. Their flags—particularly the large green one being held by a waif armed with a hammer and sickle hanging from her back—glide on winds scented with victory.

This child Maya perceived as clearly as she did her memories of that first day when she and Marcus declared their love for one another. This child wore a tattered coat, a fishfur cap, and shoes she had stolen from a corpse. This child, a girl of about fourteen, had a wide, innocent face and eyes full of miracles. She believed, as Maya once had, in the destiny of her nation.

Maya was convinced she would one day meet this child with weapon in hand.

And the child's weapon would destroy her.

Marcus... my love. I will be joining you soon.

Either way—life or death—the result would be the same.

CHAPTER EIGHT

<u>Sergeant Razin:</u>
There are many untold stories of the Battle of Kar Dathra's Gate. This is a worker's story. A labor story. A war story.

It's my story.

It begins, as these stories so often do, at a labor camp.

Labor camps are difficult and maddening places.

For instance, the prison regulations of the United Republics of the Red Star are quite clear.

If the temperature is lower than forty below zero, then prisoners cannot be made to work that day.

Of course, there are no regulations that say the labor camps have to have working thermometers.

On some days, even the alarms are frozen solid. And still we must work.

The place where I begin my story was Special Labor Camp SNK5814. Labor camps are denied names so any prisoner who might escape will have no idea where he's starting out from. The code for the camps is top secret too; many a guard has had his mind wiped and then became a prisoner himself because he simply thought about releasing the code to unauthorized folk.

All labor camps are identical, or so they tell me. So

when you're transferred from one fortress to another, it's like you've never left, only the people are different. But that doesn't matter. The guards are always your enemy, and among your fellow prisoners it is a simple matter to make friends as well as enemies.

Each camp is forged of iron and rock, and is of such magnitude that you'd think it'd been forged from a mountain rather than erected whole on the tundra or in the steppe. There are no bars because there are no windows. Ramparts are steep and heavily booby-trapped, in case some fool thinks to scale down one.

The bloodstains are deep.

I am Sergei Razin. I was once the leader of the 104th prisoner squad at labor camp SNK5814. I was convicted of treason because early in the War with Al'istaan I was captured and I escaped without having been tortured. The Nistaani always tortured captives, as quickly as possible, so the fact that I'd gotten around it struck my superiors as highly unusual.

Within a week I'd become just another "zek," scrubbing only slightly radioactive skyfurnace filters, building parts for skyfurnaces, or doing whatever else the State required of its slave skyfurnace labor that day. We work as hard as possible because the prospect of redemption is always held out before us. Meet this quota, and you may be pardoned. Take this risk, and you may be pardoned. Die in the line of duty, and you may be pardoned.

Time means nothing. Every day is the same. Wake, eat gruel, work, work, work, eat more gruel, work some more, then eat and go back to sleep. There are no holidays. The only thing that changes is the weather, which thanks to a bad patch in global warming only goes from tepid to absolute freezing for months at a time.

One morning we awoke to see the skyfurnaces overhead. Their presence meant they were preparing for battle, and needed cheap, disposal labor willing to die for the Motherland. We were naturally willing. Dying a patriotic death is a kind of redemption. Living a patriotic life is better, though.

"Form groups of five!" shouted the guards. "Hurry it up, zeks! Fives, form in groups of five!" We knew what to do, of course, and the guards knew that, but they were trying to look sharp in front of all the brass arriving by land and by air. It was days like this, when something was happening, that a guard was most likely to screw up and find himself suddenly among the zeks. It had happened, more than once. The hazing lasts for only a little while, and soon the former guard is part of the fold. In fact, former military personnel make up a large portion of the prisoners. At least the former guards knew how they'd screwed up. The rest of us couldn't always say the same.

"Look at all those skyfurnaces," said Sharik, who'd walked into the yard next to me. "They're beautiful."

"Anything's that not part of this place is beautiful," I snarled. I was always snarling at the kid because although he was a hard worker, he was having trouble learning the ropes, figuring out how to survive over the long haul. "Now stop gawking and let's get a move on. Stop staring like a goddamned puppy!"

"But look, Razin, aren't you the least bit amazed?"

"The skyfurnaces may all look the same to you, boy, but there is only one of them I'd want to bet my life on. And if that whistle blows and we're not front and center, God knows what piece of junk we'll ship out with."

"Squad 104 assemble in the main yard!" called out a guard standing at the crossroads, directing us like a cop directing traffic. He even had a whistle in his mouth.

"Squad 223 in the main yard! Squad 272 adjacent yard south! Squad 34 you have two minutes! Squad 104! Where is Shukov?"

"He's coming!" said the kid.

I jabbed him with my elbow. "He means it as a rhetorical question!" I hissed. "Shukov will be there or he will be dead. It's as simple as that!" I urged him on. "For such a talented engineer, you can really pull some stupid moves."

Our squad needed every good engineer it could get its collective hands on. And although I was giving the kid hell, I understood what he was thinking. I felt the same way about skyfurnaces when I first arrived at camp. I hated taking them apart and putting them back together, hated the grind, the repetition, but seeing one whole, in the sky—well, that symbolized a way out of here.

Being chosen for the crew meant you actually were getting out, if only for a little while. Sure, they only needed you because there was a battle coming up, and already the bureaucrats were beefing up the prison population pipeline, because a lot of us wouldn't be coming back.

The north field was big, but it was barely large enough to hold one skyfurnace, and the *Konstantinov* was one of the biggest. Looking up at it, one could not only imagine how ants must feel, when a dying whale has washed up on the beach.

"827!"

That was my number, stitched to the scarf prisoners must wear under their hoods, always with the number on your forehead, so guards won't have to try to remember your face.

"827! Where the hell have you been!" demanded the guard, a decent fellow under the circumstances named

Palvo. A lot of the guards looked out for the men whenever they had a chance, and he was one.

"Sorry, Palvo," I said, "the checkpoint guard..."

"I don't give a damn about the checkout guard. Sergeant. Volkov looked like he was going to shoot me right here on the spot for holding up the squad."

He was exaggerating. The sergeant never would have shot him with so much brass in the general vicinity. He'd waited until the brass had left.

Even so, I wasn't worried. Pavlov was just trying to look good in front of the Sorceress-Lieutenant.

And I could not say as I blamed him. Despite her heavy overcoat, you could tell she was strong and slender, and that face was like a vision of purity straight from the literary masters of the past. "Guard, are these the two men?"

"Yes, Lieutenant," Palvo said, turning away from Sharik as if he had been beckoned by an angel. "This is Razin and Sharik of the 104th—as you requested."

"Good. Don't worry about your sergeant. I've spoken to him."

"Thank you, Lieutenant, thank you," said Pavlov, with more gratitude than I'd thought him capable of. "Hey! Where the hell is Shukov?"

"Here, sir!" said Shukov. He was always the last to arrive at any assembly, by the way. It was his fate in life, to always be last.

She had one of those new "invisible" com devices attached to her ears and chin, and she pressed the section on her ear, switching it on. "Konstantinov—come in! Antares here. The 104th is assembled and accounted for. Proceed with loading on engineering decks 18 through 20." She paused, glanced at us, and spoke once more into the tiny microphone, before tuning out.

Then she turned her full attention to us. Suddenly the bitter cold went away, at least in my heart and mind.

"Alright, one-oh-four, form fives and move into the cages. For some of you, this will be the first time aboard a skyfurnace. Where we're going, this will be an excellent chance it will also be your last."

A standard speech, which she delivered with no more or less conviction than the last or the next officer. She was a young bird, well-trained, of that I was certain, but perhaps not as experienced in battle as I was. Even so, she had bothered to show concern for Pavlov's situation; I could only assume she'd felt the same responsibility toward the indentured crew of her own ship, when the time came.

"Brother workers, welcome. This is Red Star Skyship *Marshall Konstantinov*, the most powerful ship in the fleet."

The man speaking to us had the number 854 on his cap. Standing above the heat furnaces, and before the ether containers, on a grid that overlooked the new "recruits" to his ship, he surveyed us with the cool evenhandedness of a blackguard at bootcamp, even though our years of imprisonment had not left us exactly inexperienced in the ways of the skyfurnace.

"Is that him?" the kid asked excitedly, jabbing me. "Is that Torin?"

"The one and only," I said, trying in vain to maintain my typical reserved attitude toward figures of authority. "He was given his freedom years ago, but refused to take it. He loves this ship too much to leave it."

"Why not?" the kid whispered.

"Because he is a military man, a former professor in the Military College, and his crime was delivering constructive criticism about military strategy during a time when the generals didn't want to hear it. What would a man like him do in the civilian world anyway? The worst thing that could happen to him would be to leave the military. For one such as him, it is better to be a prisoner than a free man. Now hush, and let me listen!"

Besides, the rest of the squad was *sshh*ing us by now. Torin stood over us while he bathed in the red furnace light, like an emissary from Gorkovsky himself. His features seemed chiseled from rock or marble, his body was a straight iron plug draped with an air sailor's uniform. "Other skyfurnaces are mighty," he said. "The *Solaris* may boast of speed, and the *Taktarov* can deliver enormous amounts of firepower, but the *Konstantinov* could breach the Gate of Hell itself.

"Of all the prisoners in SNK5814, I have chosen you to fill the ranks of the crew for the battle in which we are to engage. Those who do not love and respect this ship as much as I may leave now. I have arranged positions for you in the frigate fleet delivering rations to the elderly."

He paused, as if seriously waiting for one of us to volunteer for the frigate fleet. That was where the sailors too old and frail to do much good in battle were stationed, and freedom was never, I repeat, never an option of fate for a sailor who'd survived that long in the modern gulag.

The faintest trace of a smile could be seen from below as Torin said, "None of you? Very well, then. This ship sets the marks by which all other ships are judged. I will tolerate nothing but perfection. We, brothers, are the soul of the ship. Without us, she is a beautiful but lifeless sculpture of a goddess. Our lives fuel her wrath. Our sacrifice grants her life. In return, she will defend us as we roam the inferno. And she will bring us all home."

With that, he turned on his heel and left it to his subordinates to introduce us to our duties.

"He is amazing," said the kid.

"That is an understatement," I said. "One time I saw him lift a burning girder off of three men, single handed."

"Burning?"

"Yes, as in white hot. He had come to the camp to supervise the installation of a new container and the girder slipped from its ramp. He just wore a pair of leather gloves that were burnt to a crisp during the seconds it took for him to lift the girder and toss it aside. And yet, I can't even say he was injured. Certainly he continued his work as if nothing had happened."

"That's impossible!"

"I wouldn't believe it myself if hadn't been one of the men who was trapped. I was in a burn ward for weeks, and he didn't even visit. Didn't even get a scratch, near as I could see. He saved my life that day."

The kid was dutifully impressed. "Sounds like it."

"I'd follow him to hell and back," I swore, with the same fervor I'd always used when expressing that sentiment.

"Good," said the kid, "because from what I hear about the upcoming battle, you may get your chance."

Now that was a moment. Usually I was the one who gave Sharik advice. I looked him in the eye. His jaw was set, his expression was grim and determined. Determined to survive. Determined to survive whether he was with me or without me. Soon he wouldn't need me anymore. And that was good.

Besides, the truth was, we workers needed one another. Always had. Always would.

There are no places to meet in secret on a skyfurnace, but if one is careful, two can meet reasonably surreptitiously. I heard it on good authority that immediately after giving us his little talk, Torin walked directly to a part of the furnace area where a man stood discretely behind a bank of steam pipes that rose from the floor to the ceiling.

Torin deliberately refrained from saluting, so as not to give away the presence of the man hiding behind the pipes. "I'm sure I wasn't followed, Sir," said Torin with a wry smile. One of his few smiles. He leaned against a pipe and lit a cigarette. So as to give the illusion, to anyone watching, that he was simply taking a break.

"I'm reasonably certain I wasn't followed either, my friend," said Urik Antares. "We're safe, but I don't have much time. Brusilov has got a hair up his behind about something and he's been putting us all through our paces. But listen, I've arranged for your crewmen to have edible food before the battle. I don't want them eating the garbage that Central Command has provided. Some of that meat was canned thirty years ago, Torin. *Thirty years.* I've got infantry units too sick to stand up from bad food, and I'm supposed to send them into the most important battle of the war."

"What does Command expect them to do? Fart the enemy to death?"

"I can't help them, but I can help you. Just make sure the men don't spread the word about their rations."

"Thank you, Urik. The men greatly need it, and I sincerely appreciate it."

Torin flinched as Urik grabbed him by the arm and squeezed.

"Listen to me," said Urik, between clenched teeth. "Command denies it, like they deny everything, but intelligence and rumor suggest we may face Kar Dathra, the Nistaani High Priest, the Ghost of the Gate himself today. If we can destroy him, we'll break the Nistaani once and for all. Unfortunately, he's officially not supposed to exist, so don't say anything. I haven't even said anything to my brother or his wife, and he's going to front lines and she's going to the isolator tunnels. So don't spread the word. Just be ready for anything. Keep the men fed, Torin. Keep them strong. And if we survive this—" he smiled, like a wolf about to break the neck of a rabbit "—the drinks are on me."

Urik turned and walked away. Watching him, Torin couldn't help making a discrete salute. So long as there were men like Urik Antares in the Officer Corps, the Motherland would endure. She would endure in the face of a hundred Kar Dathras. Of that Torin was certain.

However, Torin would not have been human if, on the day of the Battle of Kar Dathra's Gate, he had not had a few doubts.

Near as we mere members of the indentured proletariat could tell, the battle seemed to be going exactly as planned.

The fleet of skyfurnaces came out of the transfer protocols right on top of the Nistaani air defenses. The Nistaani had weak ships, cobbled together from the ruins of abandoned furnaces they'd scavenged. They'd also built skyships from the antique scrap metal sold to them by unscrupulous western Transnationalists who were supposed to have sold them top-of-the-line material. The Nistaani would have never mounted a defense against the fleet and army of the Motherland had it not been for the covert support and aid provided by the Trans nations, who of course had been delighted when the Motherland had been drawn into a conflict that enabled them to do battle with us by proxy. Perhaps if the Trans capitalists hadn't been so greedy, and the Nistaani ships stronger, we would have been forced to have our final battle a year or two earlier.

In any case, the Nistaani air ships were no match for the repeated blasts of our sorceresses. They dropped like flies, withered by the impact of the ecto-plasmic assaults. Everytime we heard them crash against the ground, we stopped what we were doing for a moment and raised a deafening cheer.

But only for a moment. Torin came alive in warfare. He was seemingly everywhere at once, inspecting this, conjoling us for failing in that regard, praising us for having succeeded in another. Everything about him seemed to become more powerful.

As for the rest of us, we did our duty. We could do no less, and were permitted to do no more. Deafened by the roar of the engines, bathed in the heat of the furnaces, joined in a single purpose: keep this brick from falling.

Then something went wrong.

We had fired off a coordinated ventral immolation that turned the desert into a wasteland.

But the battle did not end.

An entire fleet of furnaces now sat in the air, unable to do anything. The blast tanks had been fired at full power. It would be hours before they could safely fire again.

In the deep tunnels of the *Konstantinov*, there was no way to know what was happening on the battlefield. All we knew was that we suddenly had orders to ready the Krawls for deployment. That seemed strange to us. It had not been part of the plan.

After we dropped the Krawls, things got too damned quiet.

The kid and I and the rest of the squad now couldn't do anything but wait. That's the worst part of a battle, when you know your countrymen are fighting and dying and there's nothing you can do until the times comes when you can do something.

About fifteen minutes passed that way. That's when I got Torin's call.

He was still calling when Sharik and I had joined him on the spike. Each skyfurnace has several so-called spikes that protrude from the body of the vehicle. Basically a spike is like a narrow pyramid-shaped iron frame that acts like a rudder during several fundamental flight maneuvers; they are not very large, proportionately speaking, compared to the ship as a whole—each one is like a spine on a cactus. What drag they add to the sky-furnace is usually offset by the sheer sorceress might used to power these ships in the first place. The *Konstantinov* had six to a side, and we met Torin halfway down port #4.

"Come with me, quickly!" Torin beckoned, motioning us forward. "The ship is in trouble! Something—!"

By forward I mean closer to the edge. Sharik gulped but I urged him on with a look. The *Konstantinov* was in a holding position, and the winds weren't so bad. An experienced airman could maintain his balance with ease, and while Sharik was as of yet inexperienced, there was only one way to change that, and he didn't have the luxury of choosing the time and circumstances.

"We're right behind you, sir!" I said.

"But how does he know?" Sharik asked.

"Shut up and move it, boy! When Torin thinks something is wrong, it usually is."

Torin never looked to see if we had approached the tip of the spike, which was where he was squatting, like an old tribal holy warrior at a campfire. "There, in the distance," he said, pointing.

At first it was difficult to see what he was pointing at. The area blasted by the combined skyfurnace might was still billowing a mushroom cloud of ash and dust. But gradually, with concentration, I began to perceive a faint blue glow through the brown haze.

"Oh my God," said the kid. "It must be as bright as a star, if we can see it through all this muck."

"What is it?" I asked, feeling my gut tighten like a boa constrictor.

"Sorcery, Razin," Torin answered. "Nistaani sorcery. It's our deaths if we don't act quickly. You two get inside and begin to assemble the men in access tunnel 28. Do not alarm then. I need their heads straight. I'll be there in a moment."

"If you don't mind my asking, sir," I said, asking anyway, "what are you going to be doing?"

"I've got to talk to the First Mate. And you two must follow my orders to the letter. Our lives depend on you as much as anyone."

Even the most decisive of men need permission to act when they serve in the military. This is true even in an emergency.

Otherwise, Torin would have acted alone.

Regardless of the personal consequences.

No, he didn't tell me that, exactly, it's simply that was the sort of man he was.

First Mate Urik Antares, he's a more complicated

example, but I think under most circumstances he would have acted alone. Of course, he happened to be on the bridge, which is where a First Mate is supposed to be, when Torin called in. He and the officers were undoubtedly feeling rather proud of themselves, and probably thinking some of those sleepless nights would be a thing of the past.

Officers have their problems, too. Even zeks recognize that. Screw-ups were bad, of course, you get busted bad for screwing up. Busted and/or thrown in the brig for a harvest or two. Abject failure was worse, and could get you standing before a firing squad.

The Battle of Kar Dathra's Gate can be seen, in retrospect, as a whole lot of both. They screwed up because they, not the Nistaani, had chosen to make their stand on the most sacred ground in that quarter of the world, and then they had not fully exploded the sorceress possibilities. The worst case scenario made obvious by the most popular myths didn't make a dent in the bulwark of their collective consciousness. And to make matters worse, they suffered abject failure on top of all their screw-ups.

But at the time Torin got through to Urik via that invisible com. When Urik heard what Torin wanted, he immediately moved to a window facing away from the battleground, and pretended to be doing something important that required his total concentration. "You want to do what—?"

"Reset the firing mechanisms on the central furnaces," said Torin.

Urik thanked the great socialists in the sky that only he could hear what Torin was saying. "This soon after a blast? What is the temperature in the central chamber?"

"I was afraid you would ask. Still at critical—about 2500° Kelvin."

"Well, then, it's impossible to fire the ventral furnaces, Torin."

"No, Urik, it is possible. But whether or not it is a good idea, I urge you in the strongest possible terms to allow me to find out for myself."

"Torin, you sound like an idiot."

"That blue light is Kar Dathra himself!"

"What blue light?" He was looking in the wrong direction.

"You told me to be ready for anything and I'm telling you, this is it! I have never, never seen a phenomenon like that associated with a blast area before. We have to fire the ventrals again!"

"And risk the implosion of the central chamber? What the hell are you saying?"

"In a matter of minutes, we're going to get thrown like tissue paper anyway!"

From the corner of his eye, Urik caught the reflection of a sudden bright light in a window.

Then he heard the sound.

"What the hell was that?" he exclaimed. "Torin, do you see this from where you are?"

"I'm headed inside! I don't need to see it! No time, Uri! No time left! We need the order now!"

"I'll see what I can do! Antares out!"

Below the decks, Torin could only hope Urik was able to get that order from Commander Brusilov. The men would only listen if it came directly from him. At the very least, the most immediate solution to the problem was planted in Urik's head.

But of course, the problem was already there.

Urik, the Commander, and the other Officers stood in

slack-jawed amazement as the first Mayday came in: "Informkaster to all ships! Informkaster to all ships! The *Aurora* has been hit and is spiraling into freefall! Freefall imminent! Repeat freefall imminent!"

"Informkaster to all bridges! The *Yagoda* has been critically hit! Request Warkasters immediately! Request Warkasters immediately!"

Both the *Konstantinov* and the *Yagoda* knew that last part was a fantasy. Warkasters wouldn't have time to get started by the time the *Yagoda* hit the dirt.

"Informkaster to all bridges! The *Beria* has been critically hit! Freefall alert! Freefall alert!"

"The *Vyshinsky* critically hit—"

"The *Kaganovich*—"

"The *Strugatsky*—"

"My God—it's not possible!" said Commander Brusilov. Definitely a case of paralyzed brain.

Luckily someone already had an idea. "Sir, the chief engineer has requested permission to reset the ventral furnaces for another blast—I—!"

"We've got to get out of here!" exclaimed Brusilov. "And since Torin is the only one who seems to have an idea—" He tapped into his com. His words were blasted out loud and clear from the speaker system—loud enough for nearby other skyfurnace crews to hear. "All hands! All hands! Emergency reset of the ventral furnaces immediately! All sorcery corps units transfer to ventral firing chambers! Ignore all temperature data and proceed with blast now!"

"All right, men, you heard him," said Torin, standing on a platform so he could look into our eyes.

Eyes which reflected various degrees of icy fatalism or red-hot terror. We could not see what was happening;

the reactor control rooms did not have windows or portals. But we could hear it, we could imagine it, and it was all something we had never before imagined it was possible to hear, and even now was beyond comprehension.

For no one in the Red Fleet had heard the sound of a skyfurnace exploding before. Every nuance of the sound was like a symphony of dissonance, as if the laws of nature herself were being broken.

And when a skyfurnace hit the ground—! Hearing that was the equivalent of getting kicked in the gut.

We had been so hit several times before Torin gave us a distant glimmer of hope by providing us with a sense of purpose.

"The central chamber is still too hot so we'll have to reset in the secondary zone," Torin continued. "Stay away from the vats or you'll be boiled alive. The instant that you've reset your station, send an all-clear signal. We fire at the first opportunity."

"But Chief Torin," one of the men protested, "what about the blast fuel? The tanks are reading at zero! The reserve blocks are in the central chamber. There's no way that we—"

"The blast fuel is my problem, boy!" Torin shot back; he was clearly in no mood to brook dissent or doubt. "Get to your station and proceed as ordered. *Now!*"

Better to die trying to save yourself and your countrymen, I figured, than to die doing nothing but lamenting your fate. While my comrades and I were manning the gauges and the pumps, our fellow indentured soldiers on other skyfurnaces were panicking and jumping from the decks. They were disobeying orders and some were even shot as they fell by officers seeking to maintain discipline. In the end the extent of their discipline or lack of same mattered not a whit. No action, cowardly or otherwise, could have saved their lives, because they had not been blessed with officers who trusted their men, and they did not serve with men like Torin, who saw what to do and had no qualms about doing it.

At least we were doing something. At least we were able to do something. The officers on the bridge could do nothing but watch. Watch helplessly.

What they saw was spectacular in its own unthinkable way.

A blue wave of enchanted might expanding until it covered the entire landscape and sky, like a cool layer of Hell rising up to usurp the sky.

Brusilov and Urik Antares were among the officers watching. They were trying to pretend to be in command, attempting to communicate, but in the final analysis all they did was watch and wait and hope that their workers were doing what they both believed impossible.

For without the impossible, they stood no chance.

When the blue wave engulfed the *Solaris* and it disappeared in the light, Brusilov dared to hope against the odds. "This is Brusilov to the *Solaris*," he broadcast through his com. "Do you read? Repeat! This is Brusilov! Are you there, damn it!"

Antares, meanwhile, was attempting to keep his commanding officer informed about how their own ship was faring. "Shield reading approaching redline, sir! Power readings on the enemy protocol still showing no signs of decrease in magnitude or range!"

Another roll of cruel thunder swallowed the sky, deafening all on the bridge. Brusilov had ordered thousands of men to their deaths, and he had watched his willing sacrificial lambs slaughter thousands more of the enemy, but this was the first time in his life, I wager, that his heart was breaking. For that roll of thunder meant the *Solaris* was meeting her fate, and every time a skyfurnace met her fate this day, it was another dagger in the heart of the Motherland.

He knew he had no choice but to utter his next words, to radio them to the satellites in the hopes that the blue wave hadn't destroyed them, too. "This is Brusilov to Informkast. Send a distress call to Central Command. The fleet is being torn to shreds by enemy protocol of unprecedented magnitude."

There was another noise, a crash, that had previously been beyond the imaginings of the officers' wildest nightmares—a flurry of dust and debris broke through the blue wave and rose in the sky like a malevolent cloud.

"The *Aurora* has impacted on the surface," said Urik Antares. "All hands must be lost! Who could survive such an impact?"

"Here's hoping we don't find out," said Brusilov, grimly. "How are we doing?"

"Shields at redline, sir. I'd say—not well."

And in the control rooms, the men struggled furiously, turning air valves and manipulating steam release wheels and reconfiguring protocol energies, all in a vain attempt to cool down the blast chambers, which were still too hot from the immolation blast. Even the controls were hot, so hot that our asbestos gloves kept bursting into flames. There was no way the blast blocks, filled as they were with the magical energy of the Motherland's bravest, strongest sorceresses, could be pushed into the chambers. They reacted to heat the way two strong magnets repel one another. Usually it took several hours for the chambers to cool sufficiently; trying to flee the Battle of Kar Dathra's Gate, we were trying to force them to cool within half an hour. The irony did not escape us. We wanted to do nothing less than run like a dog with our tail between our legs. But we couldn't run until the tail was in the right place.

Torin and I were alone, right next to the shields to the blast chambers. Everyone else was at their stations, and would not in their right minds be anywhere close to our location, should the blast blocks begin to move."

"The gauge still reads at critical, Torin," I said. "Hasn't moved."

"There's only one thing to do," he said grimly. "I'm going in."

He stepped toward the chamber shields. Without thinking I got in front of him and put my hand on his chest, stopping him in his tracks. He blinked in surprise and looked down at my hand. I removed it.

"Sorry, chief," I said. "You know I'll never doubt you, but don't you want a shieldsuit at least?"

"Even if there were time to put one on, it would be useless. The heat is beyond the suit's capacity."

"But if you go in there, you'll die!"

"If I don't, we all die!"

"But it doesn't matter! You'll burst from the heat and radiation like a naked astronaut! And then you'll evaporate! There won't be enough of you left to break apart when we crash!"

My voice had risen until I was practically screaming at him. With a shock I realized what I was doing and shut up. Torin would have been fully within his rights to confine me to the brig for the rest of eternity, which the way things stood wasn't going to last very long. I expected, at very least, a severe tongue-lashing.

But Torin said nothing. He simply looked at me for several moments. Then he did something he never did.

He smiled.

He put his hand on my shoulder and looked me in the eye. "Sergei," he said, "I'm going to entrust you with a secret I have confided to no man. By Gorkovsky's beard, I haven't even told my mother, but I am going to tell you."

I nodded. I'm sure my expression was stupid in a comical way, but I was waiting, and overcome with curiosity. "Okay."

"I have talent."

"I know. You're the greatest chief I've ever seen."

"Besides that. I have wild talent."

"Oh." It took a few seconds for the meaning of his words to sink in. "OH! You have talent! Do you say *wild* talent?"

"Yes, Sergei. Instead of majoring in strategy in military college, I should have majored in the sorceress arts. But I had managed to keep my talent hidden throughout my youth so that I would have freedom and options in life. However, my critique of the skyfurnace, which is unfortunately is proving to be all too accurate, irked a few sensitive superiors who were all too ready to prove the dictum that a corrupt man would gladly sell the rope that hangs him to his hangman."

"I see. I guess you have a chance."

"I am no suicide, Razin."

"I know that. But Torin, if we don't make it out of this one, there's still no other chief I would rather have served."

Torin's only response was a curt nod. He wasn't the sort of soldier who endured compliments well. "Open the chamber shields, Razin."

I put my hands over the controls, but could not help but hesitate.

"Do it," he said.

And so I did. I pulled the levers and twisted the knobs and pushed all the right buttons in the proper order and tried not to be too obvious about my crying. My mind was a muddle. I opened the doors properly only because I had been so well trained, so all I remember, really, was that I would have gladly sacrificed myself if it could have meant Chief Torin could stay alive the few more minutes the rest of us had.

The chamber doors opened. A blinding yellow light bathed us. The heat that escaped from the chamber almost set fire to my clothing.

Torin put his head down and walked in like some kind of angel, immune to the fires of hell.

He looked back at me for just a moment. He spoke, but the roar of the heat silenced his words before they reached me.

I watched him for as long as I could, then I had no choice but to turn away.

And close the doors. Sealing him inside.

I thought, how could such a man, such a worker, be a prisoner of any state, and not a hero celebrated before all the world? I said a curse word against the mother of the bastard pig that arrested such a man as Torin. I know it wasn't her fault, exactly, but she should have raised her son better.

Outside, on the bridge, our commanders had no idea what was happening. All they could do was communicate the details of their demise to one another. So as Brusilov clung for dear, finite life to the rail, he listened to Urik Antares count down the final events in the existence of the skyfurnace he had pledged his soul and honor to:

"Contact with radius of enemy protocol in thirty seconds. Shields deteriorating, hull at critical."

The story is, Brusilov grit his teeth and closed his eyes, waiting. After the war I saw him on television and he said the thing he remembered most about that particular set of final moments was the cool detachment in First Mate Antares' voice. Antares might as well have been reading numbers from the black market betting forms.

Indeed, once the *Konstantinov* was engulfed in the blue wave and was beginning to break up, Antares remained just as calm. "Shields negated, hull temperature at thirty past redline and climbing... fifty past redline and climbing." Then he shouted, but only to be heard over the din of the shaking skyship. "Hull temperature at twice critical levels!"

On TV, which was still a State-controlled medium, Brusilov claimed not to have prayed to a higher being of dubious metaphysical distinction.

Antares was more up front about it. He asked out loud what all the officers were thinking: "What in God's name is holding us together?"

For the *Konstantinov* should have broken up the moment the temperature passed twenty-five redline. We should have been riding this giant plug to the ground. But even though we were awash in heinous enemy magic, we were still afloat, and only Antares and myself knew why.

Chief Torin.

During his youth, when he had discovered the exist- ence of his latent sorcerous power, Andre Torin did what was very difficult, and surreptitiously studied and mastered the magical arts on his own. While his fellow soldiers were carousing on the weekends, he was alone in the country, learning how to control the uncertainty principle, bridging the gap between energy and matter with naught but his will. After all, what is a mind, but a form of energy imprisoned in matter? Trained sorcerers and sorceresses, and surely Torin is one, are able to escape their corporeal prisons and transform their bodies into energy and back into matter. But Torin was not only trained, but his talent was great as well, because he did not require mechanic or scientific aid to convert himself. He could do it on his own. Not even the magnificent Maya Antares can do that.

I wish I could describe what happened in the reactor chambers. But even the most eloquent magicians, some of whom are our nation's most revered poets, have never adequately described the unique agony and ecstasy, which transcends all class and earthly affairs, that happens to one when he converts into ethereal form. Many admit their memories are vestigial, more along the lines of a direct encounter with a dream of their ancestors rather than the more mundane pursuit of perceiving reality

I do know this. Chief Torin cooled down the chambers enough so that the energy blocks just slipped in, catching worker and officer alike totally by surprise. I would have liked to have seen the look on Brusilov's face when those ventral furnaces fired. I am certain mine was most comical, and betrayed a sudden sense of awe and wonder.

Hell, it felt like every single one of the furnaces lining the flat underbelly of the *Konstantinov* ignited at maximum blast, which almost never happens, not even at optimal conditions. So great was the force of the blast, indeed, so great was the shock wave of sound and air when the energy struck the ground that the *Konstantinov* was lifted toward the stratosphere like a punctured balloon, lifted so fast I felt my feet begin to rise up from the ground.

They say the Second Mate had to grab Commander

upper skyfurnace decks today, who should have rejoiced with us and shared our new-found freedom.

His back to the sun, Torin stood beside several closed wooden crates at the edge of the deck. He was a man who always stood tall; he never slumped, and his arms were akimbo whenever possible. But today I thought I detected a more relaxed demeanor, as if for the first time in years he felt his full measure of self-esteem. He stepped forward to greet me—when his face came out of the shadows, I saw much to my amazement that he was actually smiling!—and I nearly fainted from shock as he slapped me on the shoulder.

"Razin," he said, "you're a free man now! Take off those numbers for once!"

It took me a few seconds to realize what he was talking about. Meanwhile, Sharik and the others began laughing at me. "I get it!" I said, joining in their laughter. "I understand!" I pulled down my hood with one hand and with the other yanked off my scarf with my penal numbers on it. "Haaa! After so many years I forgot they were even there!"

"Keep steady, Razin!" said Sharik, helping me do so even as he spoke. I had become dizzy and hadn't even realized it.

Torin reached into one of the crates and pulled out a bottle with a familiar yellow sheen. I call it familiar, but in truth it was a long-lost yellow sheen that I had believed I would never see again. Then he filled the cup and raised it in our general direction. "Gentlemen! A crate of Citadel Reserve, the best Steel the Motherland has to offer, compliments of First-Mate Antares. Let's see to it that none of these bottles lives another day, eh? To those who will never make it back from Al'istaan!"

The men cheered. By now we were already opening

the bottles, passing out the cups, and pouring the brew. By the beard of Gorkovsky, the steel tasted delicious! Not for nothing is it called the Nectar of the Motherland!

"To this iron goddess that will bring us home!" said Torin, raising his cup still higher. "TO THE MEN OF THE 104th!"

It had been a week since the battle. We were alive when so many were not. We flew over safe skies, moving slowly toward our homeland, and the sky at that altitude was a beauty to behold. The booze didn't hurt my perception of the scenery either; it merely made both the sweetness and the bitterness that much more poignant.

The bottles we consumed each received a name, and were respected as painful casualties of battle when they poured their last drops and another bottle had to take their place in the ranks.

The zeks—I mean, the boys all talked about what they would do now that they were free.

Big plans, big dreams. The only thing they knew how to do now was repair and fly skyfurnaces. Did they actually believe they could pick up where they'd left off—or been forced to leave off—and return to their drab existences as accountants, teachers, artists, and armchair activists? Especially now that they flew the angry red skies of their own free will! Who did they think they were kidding?

But it was easy to forgive them, after what they'd been through in the camps.

Torin was still Chief Engineer of the *Konstantinov*, but now he was a ranking officer instead of a zek.

Sharik joked that Torin wouldn't work as hard now that he wasn't forced to.

I slapped him upside his stupid rookie head with a bottle.

Such a joke reveals the mind of a slave who cannot see that the most powerful man is one who chooses his own duty.

Ah, he's young. The scar will be good for him. It will remind him of the cost of freedom.

As for Torin, during the celebration, he found a place to be alone. That's his way.

I want to tell the men about what miraculous power Torin has. But I stay silent, as he requested.

He knows I'll keep his secret. That's twice I owe him my life.

How many thousands of days, how many years had we lost forever to the camps?

I knew the number even to the hour.

The old zeks say that lost time is time lost forever.

To have been given the chance to get some of it back?

A happy day, indeed.

CHAPTER NINE

B ahamut. Capital City of Nokgorka. Once a jewel in the crown of the URRS, once the most prosperous of cities, a beacon of intellectual and spiritual light even in the darkest days of the old empire. Her universities and museums were world-renowned, respected even among the Transnationals. Her churches and mosques were historical treasures, her parks bastions of beauty in a jungle of concrete and steel. Great composers and writers had been raised or educated here. On these hills magicians and seers had glimpsed the higher planes of existence. And then there were the captains and stewards of industry who had built the giant factories that had provided an empire with guns and transportation and household goods such as toasters and refrigerators. Of course the air was bad, the water undrinkable, and the children tended to have higher than average levels of lead in their bloodstream, but no crown jewel is flawless.

Nokgorka had been annexed by the Lands of the Red Star after enduring the wrath of the immortal Imbohl. Since then her people had openly called themselves sons of the Motherland, and then loyal citizens of URRS, but when the empire collapsed, they rediscovered their national identity, their traditional culture, their cherished religion, even their nearly-forgotten folk tales. So after a century and a half of servitude, they declared their independence from their former master.

The State was outraged. Not yet wedded to the will of the Red Star, who hated to see their comrades go but sympathized with the Nokgorkan desire to write their own destiny free of Internationalist interference, the State mobilized the Red Fleet "to deny this declaration of freedom upon pain of death."

The war has lasted a month, and at the moment is at a standstill, a standstill the Red Fleet approaching in the sky is poised to break. Makita, a heavily armed child of fourteen, can see the result of her people's resolve and the State's intransigence as she crawls out over the great sword of the ruined statue of the Motherland, a statue that once stood proudly atop a skyscraper, and now lies broken, on top of ruins. The angle of the sword provides Makita with altitude, its width provides her with more than enough purchase, and the statue's weight, plus that of the ruins on top of it, provide her with stability.

Makita stands tall, taking the risk of making herself an easy target for an advance sniper, but she is on a mission and that mission is of paramount importance. She can always worry about her safety later.

Below lies the former crown jewel of the Internationalist empire. It is a city in ruins. No part of the city—not the commercial districts, the residential areas, the churches, the parks, the museums—none of it has been spared. Nearly all the buildings are in ruins, and the parks have been napalmed, to prevent the rebels from using the trees for cover. Bahamut appears as if an angry God has stepped on it. Nothing is as it was, except the air is still bad, the water is still undrinkable, and the children still must deal with lead poisoning. Another kind of lead, to be sure, with more immediate effects, but lead poisoning nonetheless.

Makita squints. She does not see what she is looking for. The pillars of smoke on the horizon are too thick.

Wait—! What is that?

"Okay, Papa!" she says to her communicator. "I've got a visual on your location. In the air, I count two capital ships, furnaces with escorts. They're right on top of you! You and your men should fall back before the ground forces surround you!"

"Negative!" The digital read out of her father's face, bathed in crimson, hovers above her communicator. "There's nowhere to fall back to, Makita. They've scattered deployments all over the city."

Makita bites her lower lip, otherwise tries to keep her expression stoic. Even the crimson and the distortion that are part and parcel of the cast-off technology used by the Nokgorkan freedom fighters cannot conceal the difficulty her father is having in concealing his pain. He has been wounded, she knows it in her gut, and there is nothing she can do about it. She cannot even cry.

"... Unknown numbers of heavy infantry, supported by ground attack fightercraft," her father continues.

Makita squats on the outermost edge of the sword, trying to become a smaller target. She does not believe she possesses the equilibrium to make it back to the ground without falling first.

"It's their largest offensive yet," her father says, choking twice. "We've frustrated them and they're hoping that mass will prevail. And that's not the worst of it. Reports are in that a hydra class Krawl—"

"Hydra class!" Makita exclaims. "Are you sure?" Hydra class Krawls are tanks the size of a small mountain that move slowly but relentlessly. Luckily, they are more vulnerable in urban environments, though that isn't saying much. A squad must be prepared to make sacrifices to stop one. Many sacrifices.

"It rolled in like a nightmare through the northern heavy works plant. Be aware—the border troops said they didn't even hear it until it was right on top of them."

Hydras are slow for many reasons, the most obvious being their size. Their size contributes to their firepower. But they are also laden with mufflers, sound dampers and the quietest engines the Internationalist scientists are capable of designing. Not nearly as compact as Trans engines, but almost as quiet. And to make matters worse:

"The men weren't sure, but they think the Hydra has a stealth protocol the Reds have come up with. A new arrow in their sorcerous quiver. That's all I got before their signal went dead. Two hundred men..."

Makita wonders how many she might have known.

"Now you listen to me and you listen well."

"Yes, sir."

"The mission I'm giving you was intended for me. But I'm not going to make it."

"What do you mean—not going to make it?"

"Don't get sentimental on me now, Makita. Remember what I taught you. You may be a child, but war is not for children. I am *not* going to make it. Is that clear? I said, is that clear?"

Makita feels a lump in her throat. "Clear, sir."

"I know you're on the other side of the city. You must find a way to reach me immediately. How far away are you, exactly?"

"I'm not far from railcar station 82," she says, trying to steel her voice. "If I catch the next train, I can be there in twenty."

"Good. Then get ready to move. Just one more thing: You'll need to remember everything Proto and I have taught you to survive this day, my daughter. Everything! If you don't get here in less than an hour—" he coughed again "—we'll be dead. Do you believe you can make it?"

"Even if I have to run, sir."

"Then run, Makita. *Run.*"

She snaps her com closed even as she whirls, pockets it and slings her machine gun over her shoulder as she dashes recklessly down the length of the sword. She uses the stone face of the personification of the Motherland as a springboard, and hits the ground.

Running.

With 60 minutes to go.

Listen and listen well, her father had said.

She dashes over a pile of rubble.

There's nowhere to fall back to.

Through an alley.

59:18 remaining.

Dashing over more rubble, and down a decimated cobblestone street.

Heavy infantry.

Into a ruined department store, for cover in case a Red patrol spots her.

Fightercraft. A Hydra rolled in like a nightmare.

And out again. 58:15 remaining.

Down blood-splattered steps, over the dead bodies of a freedom fighter and a Red, their hands at one another's throat.

The worst of it is, I'm not going to make it.

Across the street.

You must find a way to reach me.

Already breathing hard, her weapon a heavy weight.

Is that clear?

Into a parking lot filled with mangled automobiles, probably from a bomb blast.

Survive this day.

Finding a working one would take too much time. She must run.

Survive this day...

Failure is not an option.

... my daughter.

57:11 remaining.

She catches a glimpse of the wing of a fightercraft as it passes by the onion dome of a ruined cathedral. She leaps over a stone wall and sticks close to it. She needs the cover, but she can't stop running. Not today.

56:01 remaining.

She frightens a bunch of pigeons, scattering them into the air.

The mission I'm giving you was intended for me.

She climbs up a dumpster and scurries over a fence.

You must reach me.

She jumps and lands with a teeth-shaking thud.

Far away.

She stumbles but continues running.

Remember.

And she runs.

Remember everything I taught you.

And runs.

Do you believe?

She is not...

Run, Makita...

... sure.

...RUN.

It doesn't matter. There is 55:19 remaining. She knows what she must do.

The day is cold. The streets are lined with slush.

Makita's stockings would be keeping her warm were they not torn, but no matter. Her adrenaline and energy are doing that. She cannot think of herself. She is fourteen and in a proper world she would be able to think of herself, but this is not a proper world and she must think of her country first. And her father. For the next hour she must keep her father uppermost in her mind because she knows she will not have another chance to see him alive.

She is distracted for a moment by the sound of a distant explosion. It is followed by waves of gunfire, all equally distant.

She is still running when suddenly she comes to an abrupt stop in the middle of the street.

A fightercraft is flying down the street between the buildings, headed straight toward her.

She sees its nose pull down just a tad, just enough for the pilot to get a sure fix on her.

And since the Reds have long since decided the difference between civilians and freedom fighters is nonexistent, there is no chance the pilot will figure she's just a kid who can't do any harm. No chance whatsoever.

She has just a few more seconds to live, not long enough to make it to cover in any direction.

She has always heard that before the moment of one's demise, one's life passes before one's eyes. Just her luck: she gets one of her father's speeches:

To be born on this soil is to be born a warrior. For as long as our people have wandered the mountains over the Sea of Hyrkahm, we have passed down these lessons to our children. I love you and I want you to survive this war. Therefore you must listen and learn as I did at your age. The first lesson of warfare, my child, is this:

No matter what his rank, the foremost concern of a

warrior is how he will behave at the moment of his death. Concentrate always on the inevitability of your end. Only after having accepted the fact that he is going to die can a warrior truly reach greatness and achieve the highest honor.

The way of the warrior, moment after moment, is the practice of death.

Victory. Defeat. These are imposters, illusions. Every day you must consider being ripped apart by rifle and blade—thrown into the midst of a great fire—being carried away by surging waves—falling from thousand foot heights—being crushed by debris or beneath the treads of a Krawl—fight recklessly toward your own death and this world cannot count you among its horde of slaves.

If you are wounded so badly that there is no hope of recovery, then these are the preparations of a warrior's death:

Speak to your comrades clearly for as long as you remain conscious.

While you can still breathe, offer your final words...

Carry on my will.

If, of course, you do not suffer the fate of dying alone.

Which is what she sees in her mind's eye at this very instant, a few nanoseconds before it actually happens.

The fightercraft spewing rounds of death that catch her in the chest and limbs and send her crashing against the broken sidewalk.

This is her fate. And she would be glad to face it but for the promise she has made, the promise she needs to keep.

But there is nothing she can do about it.

She imagines the pilot smiling to himself as he presses the button to fire.

"Makita! Get down!" calls out a voice behind her.

She turns so quickly she almost gives herself whiplash and sees a tank turning around a corner. In that instant she realizes the fightercraft has been more concerned with the tank than with her.

A freedom fighter has opened the gunnery hatch and is waving at her. He carries a missile launcher on his shoulder. This is the man who has called out to her, who knows her, whose voice is reassuringly familiar.

She hits the dirt. Puts her hands over her fishfur cap and holds her breath.

The freedom fighter fires his missile launcher at the approaching fightercraft.

Makita covers her face.

The roar of the fightercraft and the high-pitched tone of the missile echo throughout the ruins.

Makita can't help noticing that the missile flies directly over her.

There is a direct hit. The fightercraft explodes into flames and rolls over backwards like a drunken bouncer with a glass jaw.

It spins, performing two full rotations, on its way down.

And then it crashes. An inferno, a little pocket of hell brought to the Earth.

Makita releases her breath and uncovers her eyes. There is no way the Red pilot could have survived. He is dead and she is alive!

Still alive! Now she can see her father and perform this mysterious mission. She does not want to think about the implications, not now, not while she is still running.

"Hey, pretty girl," says the man in the tank. "Have you forgotten everything I taught you?"

Makita grins from ear to ear. The man is not a man exactly; he is sixteen, a year and a half older than she, but he is more than a man, more than a friend, more than a savior or a brother. He is—

"Proto!" she exclaims. She has scrambled onto the tank and does not recall having done so. It is like he has summoned her via a protocol.

"C'mere," he says and before they both know it he's planting a wet sloppy kiss on her.

She wants to melt in his arms and stay there forever, but there is the matter of half his body still being inside the tank. "Proto! Papa's in trouble at the front! Can you take me to Station 82?"

Proto grins. He has such a wonderful smile, and those big brown eyes... "Of course! 82's only two clicks away!"

Another hatch opens and someone sticks his head out. Makita barely notices the man's red goggles, his scarf, and the letters D, I, and E written on it. "Hey, hey! That forget! You both! You both! No PDA here! This war zone! Save it for love zone! More duties we have, Proto! Is more enemy ships all over city! We have to go at the speed of light! I mean, yeah, she's cute, but me you want to tell Commander Gurka go we are making at taxi playing? So love scene is about ten seconds left! Okay!"

"All right! All right, Turko!" says Proto, not for a second taking those big beautiful browns off her. "I heard you."

"You did?" Makita asks. "I mean, I heard him, but I didn't understand him."

"Turko's from the hills. I'm the only that can kinda translate his tortured syntax. Anyway—" he sighs "—I'm screwed. I'm sorry."

Makita sighs, shrugs, and without taking her eyes from him, leaps to the ground. She waves. She knows they both understand. This is a big day for the revolution, perhaps the definite day, and they are not entirely masters of their fate.

"Hey!" He blows her a kiss. "I built that ramp for you. And be more careful today, will ya!"

She nods and watches forlornly as both Proto and Turko disappear into the hatches and the tank moves off. Quickly and in relative silence. The freedom fighter protocols aren't doing too badly today, much better than they usually do.

The time is 47:59 remaining as she dashes past the burning wreckage of the fightercraft. If she'd had time she would stay for a few moments, to be close to its warmth. But its sudden crash is bound to draw the attention of Red soldiers or other pilots, and besides, the smell of cooking flesh, even enemy flesh, is none too pleasant.

Besides, the running is enough to keep her warm. And she runs. She has run hard and fast in her time but never this hard, never this fast. She concentrates on keeping her legs moving but maintains visuals on the ground ahead. If her father has been surrounded, that means the heinous Reds are gating down fast, and probably in a complicated, checkerboard pattern. Otherwise her father and his men would have never been pinned down in the first place.

That means, of course, the Reds could show up anywhere, anytime.

Right in front of her, even.

She has a feeling, though, where the Reds will show up. This feeling stems from two sources.

The first is a lesson from her father, quote:

Whenever possible, a warriors chooses the terrain in which to engage the enemy. By doing this, he has given himself the advantage of surprise, and therefore taken the initiative. Even though you may face superior forces, if you have laid a trap for them in this way, you have made their numbers count for nothing.

All that is left to do is attack!

The second source stems from the words of a fortune-teller who cast a protocol on the sticks of the *I Ching* on Makita's behalf the day after her last birthday. Looking at the unusual pattern of the sticks—two stood straight up, perfectly balanced, with no apparent means of support—the fortuneteller squinted, stuffed a fresh pinch of Trans chewing tobacco in her mouth, and took her time mumbling incoherently to herself. After awhile, she said, "The *Ching* says *one cannot choose one's fate but one can choose the place where it happens.* The *Ching* adds one cannot always choose one's level but one can always rise above it."

That caused Makita and Proto a lot of trouble, and they discussed the matter for hours until Makita decided what the *I Ching* meant was that fate had a hidden, hitherto unsuspected reason why there should a ramp concealed behind a particular wall at the ruins of the Sprokivan Necropolis, the graveyard of medieval heroes.

Makita is nearing that very same wall right now.

45:06 remaining.

Behind the wall a blue glow suddenly appears. Makita visualizes the Warkaster protocol in the process of still creating the gate between the skyfurnaces and the ground. The Reds stepping through. Their second lieutenant saying something along of the lines of, "Let's hurry the hell up! I want to move out of here on the double!" Their job will be to secure the ground until the remainder of the platoon arrives.

She does not think. She doubles her speed, staying to

her course, hoping none of them spot her as she goes past the holes on this part of the wall.

She unholsters both her semi-automatic fieldpieces as she makes the turn.

Damn! Another thirty-meter lap to go!

More holes! More chances to get spotted!

She makes it. She feels like her feet haven't touched the ground.

She turns. The next opening is fifteen meters long. She passes it firing both barrels at the surprised Reds.

She's a good shot, which doesn't surprise her. One goes down, shot in the ear. Two more go down, shot in the face and forehead. A third is shot through the leg as he steps through the gate. A fourth bringing up his rifle accidentally shoots one of his own men in the back. The others scatter.

Behind the next fragment of wall, she has just enough time to drop her clips and reload.

They're still scattering when she reaches the second opening. She hits four more, but with one exception they're just wounds.

Now she has reached the ramp. They will be expecting her to come running on the ground when she reaches the next opening, they will be looking at and pointing their weapons to the ground.

But she is running up the ramp.

Two things flash through her mind. The first is the conversation during which she convinced Proto to build the ramp.

"I want it here. Tall. Right to the top." She was sitting on the top.

Proto was standing on the ground. "Here? What for?"

"Because you love me?"

THE RED STAI

CHRISTIAN GOSSETT
CREATOR • PENCILLER • WRITER

BRADLEY KAYL
Co-Writer

THE FOLLOWING PAGES ARE EXCERPTED FROM
THE RED STAR Volume 2: NOKGORKA

HURRY IT UP, THEN, *KOBA!* *THERE*, CHECK OUT THAT *SPG** UP AHEAD!

AW, *BOSS!* THERE'S NEVER *NOTHIN'* IN THOSE DEAD *KRAWLS* BUT PASTED REDS!

SHUT YER *HOLE* AND GET OVER THERE! YER WORSE THAN A *WOMAN!*

* SELF-PROPELLED-GUN.

YOSEF! *ZUGA!* CHECK THE OTHER KRAWLS...

...SEE IF THERE ARE ANY SHELLS LEFT WE CAN SELL THE *GORKAS.*

KOBA, HOW LONG *AGO*, THIS BATTLE?

MMM. LOOKS LIKE IT WAS MORE OF AN AMBUSH. I'D SAY ABOUT A *WEEK.*

GREAT. GODDAMNED GORKAS MUST HAVE *REALLY* PISSED 'EM OFF NOW.

WE'LL BE DODGING VENTRAL BLASTS FOR A *MONTH!*

SHUT UP, KOBA. AND DIDN'T I TELL YOU TO GET THE HELL *OVER THERE* AND *CHECK* THAT SPG?!

...NEVER IN ANYTHING IN THESE CANS, *DAMMIT.*

HEY BOSS, WE SHOULD THINK *BIGGER*, YOU KNOW? THIS SPG? IF YOU TOOK THE CANNON *OFF?*

THIS WOULD MAKE A GREAT *TRACTOR!*

KOBA, IDIOT! YOU WERE A *WORSE FARMER* THAN YOU *ARE* A SCAVENGER! STOP WASTING TIME!

EH--?! *HEY!* I THINK I SAW SOMETHING *MOVE* IN THERE!

HEY, WHO'S *IN* THERE? IF YOU'RE SMART WE'LL SELL YOU BACK TO YOUR *OWN* ARMY! IF *NOT*, WELL... THE *OTHER* SIDE'LL--

--*OOOOHH...* WAIT A MINUTE!

HELLOOOO, MY *DARLING.* DON'T BE TERRIFIED! *UNCLE KOBA* IS HERE--

--I'LL *PROTECT* YOU!

HEY, YOU BASTARDS! IT'S PAYDAY! JUST REMEMBER, SHE'S MINE FIRST!

I DON'T--

SHUT UP, KOBA, LOOK!

OH-OH...

GOOD MORNING, WITCH.

I AM THINKING, HOW FAR THE REDS HAVE FALLEN. THIS AMBUSH JUST A WEEK AGO... AND NOW SENDING OUT A SORCERESS ALONE? NO WONDER THE GORKAS ARE WINNING THIS WAR.

STAY WHERE YOU ARE. YOU'RE OURS NOW.

LISTEN TO ME, YOU FILTHY SONOFABITCH. TAKE YOUR PARASITES AND SCAVENGE SOME-WHERE ELSE.

I'M HERE TO BURY THESE DEAD.

D'YA HEAR THAT, BOYS? SHE'S HERE TO PRAY FOR HER FALLEN COMRADES!

TAKE SOME ADVICE, LITTLE WITCH--

--THEY DON'T HEAR YOU.

I'M ONLY GOING TO SAY THIS ONCE, THIEF. LEAVE. NOW. OR BE BURIED WITH THEM.

HAVE IT YOUR WAY. THE GORKAS PAY *DOUBLE* FOR DEAD WITCHES.

SHIELDS--

RANGE: FIRST
INCREMENT...

...DEPTH:
ONE TRIPLE
ZERO...

...PROTOCOL:
DROP...

...KASTING.

WANDERING
LOOTERS.

PROFITEERS.
THEY SMELL WAR AND INFEST THE
BATTLEFIELDS, HUNTING FOR BLOOD MONEY.

THIS IS AS MUCH A FAVOR TO THE GORKAS
AS IT IS TO THE FLEET.

--NO!

"How many little mouse-holes have I built for you in this city already? I can't count them!"

"I just have this little contingency plan."

"Oh noooo. It's always dangerous when you say that. And if I do, what's next? A house?"

She jumped down and got lost in those baby browns again. "Someday..."

"I don't know. You still haven't told me why."

"I'll give you a hundred kisses."

"Do I get to choose where?"

"Bad boy!"

The second flash consisted of words from her father:

The laughter of our loved ones, in more pleasant moments, is a fragile gift, my child. Happiness is not guaranteed in this world. When you have it, protect it. Let no one take it from you.

For the world will stand against you. Any dream you try and create, there will be those that try to steal it from you.

And when they do, fight them to the death.

She has reloaded. She is near the top of the ramp and is almost visible.

She *is* visible. Her guns are already blazing, both ejecting a stream of spent cartridges. She is mowing them down. They don't dare stick their heads up long enough to return her fire.

And she glimpses, in the distance, the pending arrival of reinforcements. The Reds must have been very daring or foolhardy to risk arriving so close to the train station. Makita decides that since their plan has failed, they were very foolhardy.

The last man she shoots is the medic.

She dives off the end of the ramp and somersaults twice, once before she hits the ground, and once after she hits it. The walls of the Necropolis are always swarming with freedom fighters but she can't pause long enough to cheer them or even to accept a gesture of congratulations for a job well done.

She knows she would not have been able to kill so many Reds if their hearts had been in this war. They were insufficiently dedicated to their cause and because of that they are now dead.

Time remaining is 44:03.

She runs. She believes she is able to make slightly better time now because she's no longer weighed down by two hundred of the five hundred rounds she habitually carries. Before she knows it the time remaining is—

42:52

And she is running up the ramp of wood and chord leading to the entrain platform. The train, suspended from a dangerously wobbly monorail, naturally is the one she needs to catch.

Last call for next train leaving for the front. Repeat: This is the last call for the next train leaving for the front, broadcasts the dispatch telepath. *All units assigned to counterassault have thirty seconds to departure.*

Makita despairs; she isn't going to make it. No way.

Below the ramps, in between the monorail and a reasonably intact example of government housing are three anti-fightercraft guns, each one the size of a small tank, all cannibalized, she thinks, from seafurnaces.

Her keen eyes spot one of the gunners—he's smaller than the other soldiers in the general vicinity, about her size. Meaning he is probably about her age. There is only one gunner she knows of who fits that description.

"Dushka!" she shouts through her com. She does not miss a step. "Dushka! Can you see me on the bridge?" She waves.

"Wait! Yeah! I see you!" He waves back. "You trying to catch the train? Forget it! It'll be back in a hour!"

"I don't have a hour! I have orders to get to the front immediately! You've got to help me! Call the elder in charge of the train and tell it to hold on! Tell him I only need about ten more seconds, that's all!"

"Uh... I don't have my gunner's communicator anymore."

"What? What the hell happened? They're not going to bust you, are they? Not today, of all days."

"They said I was talking too much, so they took it away. Man! I was so embarrassed, Maki. Right in front of all the other gunners. It was just yesterday morning, in the mess hall."

"Dushka! Shut up and ask your superior to try and hold the train!"

"He probably won't. The train is packed like sardines for the front!"

Makita senses his reluctance. She would curse if she wasn't so out of breath.

The train is moving. Clear all doors and step back from the loading platform. The next train for the front will be in one hour. Repeat. Next train for the front from this station in one hour.

41:23 remaining.

'Stop the train!" she shouts. "Stop the train!"

There are quick images she gleans from the corner of her eye: a mother saying good-bye to her son, lines of soldiers waiting for the next transport, men trying to shore up one post that was hit by Red gunfire. She also laments the lack of magical power available to the Nokgorkans; otherwise they too would be able to use Warkaster protocols.

But mainly she concentrates on the train. Pulling away from her.

"Hey! Late trooper!" says one of the men on the train. "There's always one," he says to a friend. "She looks quick! Fifty says she makes it."

"You're on, Robilov! Hey, Simko! Give her a hand!"

She sees the hand; in a manner of speaking, that's all she sees, though she knows she has only a limited amount of running ahead of her—mainly because the platform is going to run out in about twenty meters.

"Damn, she is quick! Sonofabitch!"

She reaches. She runs, reaches, stretches.

The solider reaching for her flicks his fingers. "C'mon, girl! You're almost—!"

He's right! She can almost touch his fingers.

"C'mon! Run!"

"Reach, Simko," says one of the men on the train. Then, disappointedly: "Ohhh, man! That was a good one."

Another says, "Hand it over, Robilov."

Robilov says, "When we get back to the barracks, you cockroach!"

41:06. Makita falls, exhausted, breathing so hard she fears her chest will burst, on the very edge of the platform.

She watches in despair as the train pulls away on the monorail, making a turn, heading toward what used to be the downtown district of Bahamut.

Some of the soldiers wave good-bye to her. They were impressed, she thinks, with her effort.

Then, in the space of a second, her despair changes to utmost shock and revulsion, quickly smothered by an overwhelming numbness.

During that second, she hears a high-pitched tone.

Then there is the explosion. It is as if the train has immolated itself like a monk protesting the conflict.

But of course a section of the monorail is shattered at the same time.

Three of the cars break apart and fly away in pieces; some of those pieces of human.

More cars burn, but they all crash to the ground forty meters below.

It is possible there are survivors, but Makita doubts it. All she knows, at that moment, is that if she had made it to the train, she would be dead now.

She had been running to her doom, and had narrowly missed it.

To think that for a nanosecond, she had actually regretted pausing long enough to ambush those Reds coming through the gate.

Their doom had meant her survival. She could only hope it was for a good reason. For in the words of her father:

In an ambush, it is always the same. The flash of enemy fire. Then the piercing in your ears. Around you will be screams. Panic.

Refuse panic. Always. It is never to be indulged.

Panic leads everyone to think about "what has been attacked?" "Who is hit?" This is secondary.

The warrior thinks: "Where is the enemy?" "Who or what am I up against?" And "How do I kill them first?"

Makita is afraid she knows the answers to all those questions.

The enemy is making a turn, moving past the burning debris of the train.

The enemy is in the Hydra Class tank that fired at the train. Makita gasps. This is the first time she has actually seen such a tank outside of a VR training program, and it is truly awesome: three stories tall, thirty meters wide, with three guns (two immobile, pointed straight ahead, and the third on a turret capable of a 360 degree turn), three tracks, and the heaviest, densest armor the Reds could equip it with. The Hydra was designed and built precisely because the other Red models had failed so miserably during the final battles in Al'istaan. But that did not mean it was invincible. A method to defeat the Hydra had been devised, and it has even been successful upon occasion.

For the moment though, the three anti-fightercraft guns are turned on it, blasting away. The three crews work feverishly.

But one blast from the gun on the turret is a direct hit. Makita sees the crew leap off moments before the anti-fightercraft gun explodes.

She has the sinking sensation this is going to be a dark day for the independence movement.

"Dushka! Come in! It's me!"

"Makita! You're alive!"

She had seen him scurrying for cover, so she knew he would receive her broadcast. "I missed the train!"

"Have you ever seen a Hydra Class before? The elders are mustering an assault team to try and take it out! You'd better get down here! And Makita—"

"I know! Don't be last!"

The support beams for the platforms are each equipped with a heavy rope for the express purpose of quick descent. Makita figures it bodes ill that she is among the last of those who had been on the platform during the ambush to use the rope to climb down into an underground bunker.

Within the bunker, Captain Verdohski, a blonde, bearded man who at twice Makita's age had the air of one who had seen six times the tragedy, is already rallying the troops, who are standing in formation while noncoms hand out the weapons stored in the bunker for just this eventuality. Verdohski is very cool, and does not even flinch when the Hydra guns get the second of the anti-fightercraft guns above them.

"Steady, boys! Steady!" he calls out over the din. "Squad 3! Your job is to take out the rear vents! Squad 4! Left treads! Squad 3! Right treads!"

Makita does not even have the chance to get past Verdohski so she can join the formation. He tosses her the large tubular weapon he has been holding—it is called a sword—and says, "Makita! You're last! Barrel duty!"

The soldiers all look at her and shake their heads sadly.

"Don't look at me like that!" says Makita defiantly. "I'll last longer than any of you would have! And if any of you is too scared to take up the sword when I go down—rot in Hell!"

The soldiers glower; many begin to speak, but are silenced by both the blasting Hydra guns and Verdohski's stern look of disapproval. "You all know the drill! First—immobilize the Hydra! Second—shield Makita! She's carrying the sword! When the sword-bearer falls, the closest trooper takes up the duty."

There is a moment of silence as twin Hydra blasts demolish two nearby buildings. Makita holds her breath as if she has just been submerged in a cold dark sea and looks into the eyes of the men who just moments ago were glad they had not drawn the duty of the sword-bearer. Their eyes are sad, but determined. They will do what they have to do and are ready to sacrifice themselves to save the sword-bearer. Their death sentence, she knows, is no less severe than hers, their possibility of survival no greater.

"Let's do it!" shouts Verdohski.

And like a soccer team coming out at halftime—a heavily armed soccer team—they scramble out of the bunker.

Makita holds back for a few moments—she must give them time to get into position, to fan out, to provide her with the cover of numbers.

Verdohski puts his hand on her shoulder. "Good luck, young maiden! Now, follow me!"

Verdohski scrambles up a nearby ladder and his machine gun is in his hands even before he reaches the top rung.

Makita slings the sword over her shoulder and goes up a different ladder. Already the firefight above is deafening. She has never heard so many weapons going off at once. And the Hydra is still firing. The earth shakes with every impact of the Hydra projectiles.

She remembers the words of her father:

If a Hydra class Krawl ever attacks, do everything you can do avoid barrel duty. However, in case this happens, remember everyone in the assault force is protecting you. You carry the sword.

She reaches the surface and for a moment stands transfixed in horror. She has witnessed death and destruction before, but never on such a grand scale, never so up close and personal.

Every freedom fighter in the vicinity is converging on the Hydra from all directions. The belly of the beast has opened and the Red troops are attempting to fend off the Nokgorkans. Bullets are flying everywhere, people on both sides are falling, and already bodies litter the ground, staining the snow and slush red with blood.

Not ten meters away from her, Verdohski lays flat on

his back, his eyes and mouth wide open, a bullet hole in his forehead.

The moment is over. It has seemed an eternity. She runs, using a cluster of freedom fighters as cover.

They are your shield. They are your diversion. Use them.

The Hydra is moving across the square. Its guns are too big and too close for the Red crew to fire them at the train station platform without having too much debris falling on top of it, potentially slowing it down to a unsafe speed. The Hydra is clearing a path for itself through the buildings, however. Freedom fighters are battling to get close to the treads; most can't break through the lines of Red soldiers but a few are able to toss bombs or Molotov cocktails. The bombs seem to do little damage except to the thrower and nearby Reds, while the flames from the Molotovs have thus far accomplished little or nothing.

Makita concentrates on running; she began near the rear of the Hydra. She must get to the front.

The great tank rolls across an artificial waterway, a deep channel built to control runoff from rain and flood. It is too wide for the freedom fighters to cross without the assistance of sorceresses.

If the tread teams have been wiped out or have simply been thus far ineffectual, then the beast may still be moving, which will make crossing onto its back all the more perilous. If the beast is crossing difficult terrain, then a squad of priestesses will most likely be supplying expanse protocols, but if they get taken out...

Makita moves pass a robed priestess whose protocol has created a flat, narrow red bridge across the channel. There are other bridges, and many freedom fighters crossing all of them. Makita tries to blend in, hunkers down low as she runs across the bridge. It starts to fade.

...Their bridges go with them. So don't waste time watching the light show. Get across that bridge!

And she does, getting one foot on solid ground the instant the bridge goes out from under the other foot. She stumbles, but makes it.

The other freedom fighters still on the bridge aren't so lucky. She can barely hear their screams as they fall—the gunfire is still very loud—but those screams are no less haunting for all that.

But within a second she can no longer hear the screams. Too many bullets are whizzing around her. She has always heard about those people who are blessed in warfare—they seem literally *oblivious* to harm and can pass through a thousand battles without receiving so much as a scratch. Makita has received a lot of scratches and bruises thus far during Nokgorka's bid for independence, but she prays that this once she can be one of those warriors. Just this once, for freedom, for country, for the men and woman who are putting themselves between her and the bullets...

The shield squads will be some of our best. Their sole purpose is to draw fire away from you. Most of them won't make it off the beast, win or lose. Even from the brief moment of you running by on your way to the barrel, some of their faces you'll never forget...

True enough, she learns. A sorceress has created a ramp at an angle leading onto the beast. Indeed, as the Hydra moves, so does the ramp, staying on the right side where it cannot be run over, where the Reds cannot easily stop the "enemy" from lodging on the armor, like ticks on a dog.

"Go, Makita, Go!" cries out one of the men the instant before he's riddled with bullets.

Another freedom fighter has written "NEVER FORGET, NEVER FORGIVE" on his helmet. "Give 'em hell, Makinoshka!"

She intends to. She dashes up the ramp just ahead of a line of bullets chasing her—it's moving too fast, no way she can outrun the moving aim of the Red bastard firing at her—but the line of fire is abruptly cut off seconds before it can reach her. She doesn't have time to wonder what happened to the shooter, heck, she hadn't had the time to wonder where he was standing, in the first place, all she cares about is the fact that she's alive and on the Hydra and then—

She's running up the barrel. Now the Reds should be riddling her with so many bullets her body will be splitting into pieces before she hits the ground, but there's nary a high-pitched whiz to be heard.

As you approach the barrel, remember two things. Mask and dropline.

She pulls up the mask that she's been wearing around her neck like a bad guy wearing a scarf in a Trans western movie. She gags. Only with great difficulty does she prevent herself from projectile vomiting all over the battlefield.

Mask first. It's been soaked with Stimulant D. Smells terrible. But without it the gases in the barrel will knock you out. Still, don't keep it on too long. Stimulant D is a dirty buzz.

Indeed, she can still see long wisps of blue-gray smoke emanating from the barrel. She knows from experience that the Hydra had been firing the big barrel so much that at the moment it is overheated. It can fire again at any second.

And it could be messy if it does.

Dropline. By now, if you have approached the beast and not been hit by autofire—if you have climbed onto its back four stories up and not fallen—it is time for your descent into the mouth of the Hydra.

Trust your dropline magnet. It will hold your weight. Drop it onto the barrel. Hit the release switch on the cable, take the sword into both hands, and jump straight out over the end of the cannon.

She does, in less time than it takes to remember the words.

She is in. She crouches down and peers into an abyss of blackness.

An abyss of blackness that is apt to erupt in a blinding flash of deadly light at any moment!

Assemble the weapon—

It is only three moves.

—And prepare to fire as quickly as possible. If you are not lucky, then the gun crew has already loaded the next shell. In this case the end comes quickly once they fire the cannon.

She is already pressing the trigger—

If you are lucky, then you will see the light at the end of the barrel as the crew opens the breech to reload.

Indeed. She perceives a tiny white crack in the abyss.

This is the moment.

It is unprofessional, but she squints the instant she finishes squeezing the trigger.

Fire.

The missile that had been loaded into the sword is on its way. She has less than a second to make her next move.

Time for your second jump with the dropline. As before, the distance is preset.

She hits a button with her thumb.

Just hit the release and jump.

She jumps. The line provides a little resistance, but not much. She has not even hit the ground when she hears the muffled explosion—a tiny *pop*, really—of the missile going off. There is no ball of flame, no sounds of pieces of metal coming apart, not yet anyway, because thanks to the protocols, the effects of the missile exploding are delayed.

Anyway, as I was saying, the distance is preset for a safe landing.

Then she hits the ground.

Give or take a few meters.

Hard.

"The stars..." she says, speaking directly into some bloody snow. "There are so many of them."

Someone grabs her roughly by the arm and yanks her to a sitting position.

"So many colors... ?" she asks. The earth is spinning, either because of the impact or the buzz. Either way, she isn't sure who she is or what she's doing.

"Makita! Shake it off!" says the soldier holding her up. "You've got through. They sounded the Evac! Let's go!"

She's not sure how he could know. The gunfire is still so deafening, the screams and cries of the wounded and dying so surreal.

Another soldier grabs her by the other arm and the two pull her backwards. Her head starts to clear while she's fixated on the path her feet make while they drag in the snow.

Past the open eyes of a dead freedom fighter.

She realizes only a few seconds have passed. She and the others are waiting, while the bullets are still flying.

If you have survived the unforgiving moments of your duty, and your shot has found its mark, if the dropline has not failed you, leaving you lying broken in the snow...

"C'mon, blow, you bastard!" she whispers.

"Listen! Listen!" says one of the men helping her. "It's starting to go! It's starting to go!"

"So let's not be here when it does!" says the other.

You will hear the thunder of the Hydra's arsenal...

She does.

Ripping out its insides.

The Hydra begins to vibrate. Smoke rises from between the shields, up from the bolts, and above the treads. A man rises up from a hatch and is immediately shot at from every possible angle.

There will be, I can say with certainty...

First: a loud cacophony as the delayed explosion causes a chain reaction that rips through the belly of the beast like a string of nuclear firecrackers.

Second: the rapidity of the gunfire quickly diminishes, tapering off until there is only an occasional rap or pop. The Red troops have all given their lives defending their Hydra. Futilely, as it turns out.

And third:

A great roar of victory.

Everyone who has survived raises their voices in cheer as the Hydra suddenly grinds to a halt, as the welding of its armor breaks, as parts of the guns and engines turn white hot, and walls of flame flicker from every opening. Especially the open hatches.

Makita finds herself coming back down to earth. The dirty buzz is receding. She grins at the two soldiers who assisted her by dragging her to safety. The soldiers pat her on the back, call her a heroine. But she shakes her head and looks at some of the nearby deceased freedom fighters, those who weren't lucky enough to make it through the Hydra ambush.

"I know," says one of the soldiers. "But we are alive, thanks to you. Blessings be upon you."

But Verdohski isn't, she thinks. *Damn...* "Excuse me, fellows, I think I feel nauseous."

She's vaguely aware of the soldiers who had previously helped her being too busy shooting their guns into the air to pay much attention to her now.

Suddenly a pair of hands does steady her. She stands, gratefully, and feels the spin of the earth coming back to normal.

"Makita!" exclaims Dushka, "that was great!"

She grins. At least he made it. Usually she was not a creature to doubt herself, but she was beginning to wonder how many family members and close friends she could stand to lose during this conflict. Probably as many as necessary...

"I brought you some water," continues Dushka, offering her a canteen. "Here. I'm really glad you made it back... I wasn't worried though. I knew if anyone could blow that Krawl, it'd be you! Maybe Emil, too, but he has a broken hand, and he wasn't last like you were. I told you not be last, didn't I?"

"Yeah, I think you mentioned it."

"But maybe it was good you were last because if it weren't for you the Krawl would have maybe rolled over us, and that would've been bad..."

She stares at the top of the canteen for several seconds, then pours water into her mouth.

"Like that time at the river," continues Dushka, "when there were those hovercraft coming across, not like this

one, and you and Proto had to swim with all that gear
on and..."

"Dushka."

"Yeah."

"Sash." She pours what's left of the water onto her
head.

"Okay." He has this dreamy look in his eyes.

She thinks he might have a crush on her. How cute.
She gives him a kiss on the cheek. "Thanks for the water."

"You're welcome."

23:28 minutes remaining.

"I gotta go."

Makita is running. The time remaining is 19:28, and she
is afraid she will be late, she will miss her father and will
inadvertently fail in granting him what she fears is his
dying wish and all she can do is run and try to avoid
the hot spots of battle throughout the city. The only thing
that slows her down is the unshakable feeling that she
is being watched. The feeling causes her to take detours
she knows will cost her precious seconds, it causes her
to hesitate before dashing into the open spaces. But
though she sees no one, though no sniper takes a shot
at her, though the only sensation the landscape evokes
in her is a profound nostalgia for the time when these
streets were filled with happy people going about their
business and the buildings stood whole, the feeling of
being watched refuses to melt away.

By the time there is only 14:09 remaining, she has
done her best to shove the feeling aside and concentrate
on meeting her father.

Little does she know that the plane of existence she is
being watched from is one forbidden to mortal eyes.

One of the entities watching her is the woman in red.

"My dearest Iakos—" her voice always drips with sarcasm whenever she calls him *dearest* "—you must forgive me, but this child? This reckless wolfcub is to bear the message that could save my people from Imbohl's legacy?"

The spirit entity called Iakos, a soulthief by nature and by trade, looks through his red tinted pince-nez glasses and down his nose at her. He is wary at being too arrogant in her presence—she has the Sword of Truth sheathed on her back *and* a magnificent temper—yet her nobler impulses must be constrained if he is to maintain what control he may over the situation. "I told you long ago there were no guarantees, my friend. I still cannot say for certain she will survive to deliver the letter. However, of all the souls in Nokgorka, I feel she is the best chance you have."

"I should not doubt your word. She is obviously of great tenacity. She is courageous, too. And yet too much is at stake. What is it about this child, of all the warriors in Nokgorka?"

Iakos stuffs his cold fingers in the pockets of his black regulation Prince Albert frockcoat. The red insignia on the shoulders are meaningless; the only rank he possesses, at this stage of the game of life, is the rank he has conferred upon himself. "When you approached me to speak to the Nokgorkan ancients on your behalf, their hatred toward the lands of the Red Star was quite clear to me. So many of them were put to death under Imbohl's direct order. Almost a century has passed, yet even in their afterlives the ancients are no more forgiving than when they were mortal.

"Even though I made it clear how the delivery of your message could end this war, and perhaps save their people, it still took brutal negotiation to gain even your passage here, within their realm, let alone surrender the letter to my custody."

"The letter that they had stolen!" exclaims the woman in red.

Iakos shrugs. "Nonetheless, they gave me the letter on one condition: that its next bearer be of Nokgorkan blood. This was their trick, you see. What Nokgorkan could ever want to help the Reds? And if so, then what Nokgorkan could possibly fulfill this delivery, to a red sorceress, and not be killed in the attempt? They presented me with several candidates to bear the letter. All soldiers, of course. I was given time to observe each one and make my decision. It was during this period that I discovered that their deception ran even deeper—

"The Gorkian ancients had underestimated me. They did not know that my abilities had shown me each of the candidates indeed would die, the letter to be destroyed by a fire of an indeterminate origin on this day, before it could possibly be delivered. Of all these, there was one man who showed promise beyond his own mortality. Having traveled the labyrinth of his soul, I realized that upon his death, there was a strong possibility that he would pass the letter on to his daughter: Makita."

And upon the corporeal plane of existence, Makita feels a chill unrelated to the wind and the cold pass through the marrow of her bones. This time, instead of hesitating, she pushes herself to the limit.

"Makita is of mixed blood," says Iakos to the woman in red. "Her father is Nokgorkan, but her mother was a Red. A soldier. The parents met while on duty in Al'istaan, before the Nistaani rebellion. They tried to make a life together here, but the break-up of the URRS and the defeat in the war was preceded by the re-emergence of old ethnic hatreds. The mother was driven out, forced by the husband's clan to leave her child on pain of death. The mother saw no choice but to return to her life as a soldier."

"The mother lives?" asks the woman in red.

"Yes, too ashamed—and bitter, I might add—to attempt any contact with her past. She was very young, barely seventeen, when she gave birth. I think that if the situation occurred today, the clan would think twice before coming between her and her cub."

Makita cannot see them, but as she runs through a park square, with snow-covered statues of Nokgorkan heroes of yore, she passes between the soulthief and the woman in red.

The entities' gaze follows her.

"The father raised Makita here in Bahamut," says Iakos. "I took mortal form to meet him, to give him the letter. He's dying, as we speak, but I assure you..."

"He will pass this letter to her!"

Iakos grins. "If we're lucky, my friend. If we're lucky."

"If we're lucky? Then how can you confidently assure me of anything?"

"Have faith in this little wolf. I have not felt a spirit such as hers since...since I first met you!"

The woman in red makes a face that is almost a snarl, then disappears from the plane that permits her a direct view upon the mortals.

Iakos shakes his head. He'd thought he was beyond such petty traits as admiration, even devotion, but the woman in red can still manipulate his karma like a bunch of harp strings.

Meanwhile, Makita freezes. Both literally and in her marrow.

She is certain she is being watched. Her eyes dart this way and that. She grabs her gun and whirls.

And sees no one.

The only tracks in the snow are her own.

She doesn't have time to worry about it. There is only 10:57 remaining.

Now there is only 8:48. A sister freedom fighter hands her a canteen and says, "You made it."

"Thanks a lot," says Makita, panting severely. Her heart is pounding and her temples are throbbing, as if she is on the verge of having an aneurysm. She must hold it together; she cannot have gotten this far only to permit her own body to betray her.

"Drink," says the sister. "And for God's sake, keep your head down."

As if to punctuate her words, bullets whiz overhead and a fightercraft buzzes a street on the next block. There is the sound of an especially large handheld missile launcher firing, followed quickly by an explosion. Makita and the others instinctively turn their heads away as a bright ball of smoke and flame illuminates the decimated cityscape where the freedom fighters have been making their stand. Makita notes with sadness that the puppet theatre, where she had spent many a happy hour as a young child, has been reduced to rubble.

But she has no time for sentimentality. "Thanks a lot," she says, returning the canteen to her sister fighter. "Is my papa still...?"

A young man—well, not that much older than she, salutes her and says, "I'll take you in. It's hot in here. Full of Reds coming in through gate protocols. So catch your breath and keep your head down."

"I heard the first time. Let's go."

6:14 remaining, and Makita greets her father in a makeshift hospital where the Nokgorkan have dragged their wounded. The roof has been blown off, and lies in pieces on the ground. Many of the dead lay in heaps outside the building, but those were most likely the ones who had expired in the hospital, as she had seen many dead comrades in arms laying in the streets, presumably where they had fallen. Several soldiers are at the windows, firing at any enemy soldier who dares to raise his head. Sometimes they fire mere pot shots, other times they shoot sustained barrages. This place is not likely to be a hospital for long.

And looking at her pale father, his greatcoat stained with the blood that has hemorrhaged through his bandages, she knows that what happens to this place in the near future will not make any difference to her father. Although he is the same bear-size man he has always been, it seems the air has been let out of him somehow. She tries not to choke, she holds back her tears, and his words on the eve of this conflict come back to haunt her:

The first lesson of warfare... the foremost concern of a warrior is how he will behave at the moment of his death... the way of the warrior... the inevitability of your end. I love you. I want you to survive this war.

And she wants to shake him and proclaim that she wants him to survive, that she would give everything she would ever have in this world and the next if he would just live, somehow, while the bullets are flying all around them both, but of course there is nothing she could do except buckle up and try to put on a brave face because that's what he wants her to do, to be a brave soldier and his little girl at the same time, no matter how many bullets fly.

"My child," he says, beckoning her to come close with a weak gesture. "You've made it. Come. Time is short. I am lucky...not to die alone. I have one final mission for you, before I'm gone. I was entrusted with a message, a sacred mission, but as you can see, I will be unable to complete it."

"It's all right," Makita says, trying not to allow her lower lip to tremble, trying in vain. "I'm sure the person will get the message, somehow."

He smiles and shakes his head. "Promise me, Makita, that you will complete this duty for me."

She nods.

"The message you will bear may save our people, our nation's future. Do you understand?"

She shakes her head. "No."

He laughs, coughs a trickle of blood that runs down his chin. He reaches into his greatcoat and withdraws a bloodstained envelope. He gives her the letter and his daughter only barely stops herself from bawling. The blood on the letter is his, of course. He has protected this letter with his body. "The name is here," he says, pointing to the writing on the envelope. "She is here, in Bahamut. We fought together at Al'istaan... before the break-up of the republic. It is your duty to find her, my child. When you do, give her the letter."

"I will," says Makita, her head bowed, her voice breaking.

"My brave little cub. You are everything a patriot and a soldier would want his child to be. I want you to have my weapons. Take them."

Makita's eyes widen. These are not regulation weapons, these are personal implements of battle, tools her father had forged for himself when he was Makita's age and which he had spent a lifetime mastering. Makita had practiced with them some, but... "Father, I am not worthy."

He laughs again, chokes again. "If not you, then who?"

She takes them. They are cold, and stained with his blood. One is a square hammer, forged of the hardest steel, and the other is a large sickle, razor-sharp. Both feel heavier than usual in her tiny hands.

"Promise me," he says, "promise me that no matter what the future brings, you will deliver this message at any cost."

"I will, I promise."

"Your spirit is steel, my soldier, pure shining steel. I know in my heart that you will not fail me."

"I don't understand. Why is this letter so important?"

"I do not know. I have never read it, and neither shall you. You know how impolite it is, to read another's mail."

Makita blushes and shrugs.

"Do not even take a peek," says her father sternly. "Promise me that, too."

"I promise."

"There is something more I must tell you, my child. I should have told you a long time ago. I thought there would be time, and now there is no time."

"Oh my father..."

"It is about your mother. What you think you know about her is not the truth at all. It is only what my family and my clan wanted you to believe, and that was wrong. It was my weakness that permitted it to happen..."

"What? Papa?"

She has buried her head in his shoulder and is holding onto him with all her strength. Perhaps if she is strong enough, she can hold his spirit onto this earth.

"Wait," says her father. "The shooting. It's stopped."

Makita gasps. She had not noticed. She was used to

the sound of gunfire, nearby or in the distance, either way... Now the silence is eerie.

"Furnace overhead!" someone calls. "Descending into blast position!"

A shadow grows around them. They look up to see a massive skyfurnace looming in the sky, its great coils staring down like the indifferent visage of a multi-eyed god. The sound of a switch turning on echoes through the ruined city, and the coils begin to turn yellow like those on a stove.

"That's impossible!" says a nearby medic, a sister with a wounded leg. "They've still got troops on the ground!"

"Most of a battalion," says Makita's father.

"The Reds are monsters," says the medic. "But even they wouldn't immolate their own men."

"Yes, they would," says Makita, whose hatred of the Reds was such that none of their myriad atrocities could astound her. "Papa..."

Her father took her, gently, by the arms. "My time is done, my beauty. Yours begins. Run. Run as fast you can, do you hear me? Run!"

The other patients encourage the medics to run as well, and they do so, joining the soldiers who had been defending this position in a mad dash for survival.

More shots ring out; some of the Reds cannot resist the temptation to shoot at the easy targets. Clearly the ramifications of what is happening have yet to sink in.

"You must run too," Makita's father says to the medic with the wounded leg.

"Alas, I cannot," she says. "I can barely limp, let alone run. I will stay with you."

Makita's father turns back to her. "Do not look back, little one. Not one glance. Not one!"

Makita signals she will obey with a nod, but the tears stream from her eyes.

"Go!" says her father, pushing her away. "The firing has again stopped!"

"The Reds have realized they are being betrayed by their own command!" says another wounded freedom fighter, laughing with a profound sense of satisfaction, indeed, vindication. Indeed, most of the wounded—those who are conscious anyway—know they are doomed, but find the situation of the Red soldiers hilarious.

"I'll be watching you from the heavens," continues Makita's father. "Always. And Makita... Carry out my will."

There is 2:51 remaining on the original hour her father had given her. Not enough time by any stretch of the imagination, but it would have to do.

Meanwhile, elsewhere on the ground, a grizzled Red soldier, scratched, nicked, bruised, dirty, and dead-dog tired, communicates with his high command. "This is Aralov to *Konstantinov*! Skyfurnace *Taktarov* is descending into ventral blast position and is not responding to my signal! Request *Taktarov* abort blast! They're right on top of us!"

On the bridge of the *Konstantinov*, Sky Marshall Urik Antares hears the words with a combination of anger and disbelief. What Taras Volkov, the commander of the *Taktarov*, is obviously contemplating is unthinkable. Not only has Urik's entire training focused on the practical and moral necessity of not permitting one's own army to be immolated in a blast, he regards it as downright sloppy as well, the best way he can think of to damage the Red Army's morale in the future. And while he can not say the battle has been going well today, from the Red Star point of view, he certainly doesn't think things are so hopeless that the sacrifice of the very men who have entrusted their lives to him is warranted.

"It is confirmed," says Olga Shibolet. "The *Taktarov* is preparing to immolate the entire battlezone!"

Urik slams his fist on a console. "Gate our men out! Immediately!"

"Too dangerous, sir," she says, in that cold, impersonal—no, make that *inhuman* voice Urik has grown to loathe whenever they've been in the midst of a crisis situation. "We'll get blowback right through the gates!"

For a moment, Urik is tempted. The odds are great against the *Konstantinov* coming through gate blowback without sinking like a meteor, but they are not impossible. Still, they are very close to suicide. Urik has never been impressed with the example of kamikaze pilots in the past. What good is it to be courageous, if you know you are never coming back alive? Bravery comes by taking a chance with one's life, not with assuring its end. And Urik considers the fact that if he is dead, then who is going to imprint his fingerprints on Volkov's neck in the future?

Urik opens communications with the finesse of a jackhammer. He practically breaks the controls and negates the protocols with his violence.

When Volkov's bald dome, bathed in the crimson light of the *Taktarov* bridge, appears on the light screen before him, Urik would gladly trade his soul for a sorceress amoral enough to kast a reality/bender protocol. Then all Urik would have to do would be to stick his hands into the light and Volkov's neck would literally be within his grasp.

"Volkov! What the hell do you think you're doing? Burn your own troops all you like, you sonofabitch, but I've got most of a battalion down there!"

Volkov rubs his goatee as if he's picking whores in a red light district. Indeed, he reminds Urik of the devil himself, deciding the fate of men while lounging in his throne room in Hell. "Please, Urik," he intones just as inhumanly as had Olga, "we may have failed in our primary objectives today, but we must at least show the 'Gorkas the price of their resistance."

"What the hell you talking about? This is a siege! What difference does it make if it takes a week, a month, a year to defeat them?"

"Too long. Central Command has decided the Motherland cannot afford to be seen as weak in the eyes of the world. Your troops will be heroes. Their sacrifice will be remembered."

"You're going to kill them because of public relations? I'm only going to say this one more time! Abort that blast—now!"

Volkov grins, as much as he is capable. His skin appears about to crack. "You've never had much of a bluff, Antares. Volkov out. Lieutenant? End communication!"

Meanwhile, on his own bridge, Urik feels that the pomp and power associated with his command are entirely meaningless. His fist slams helplessly on the console as he hears Captain Aralov radio in:

"Gate us out! Gate us out—now!"

The fear in his captain's voice fills Urik with shame.

The sound of the coil ratcheting up another level can be heard through the skies above the entire battlefield. Urik knows all too well that as of this moment, the coils are red hot and the vats of magical fuel are ready to explode.

"Volkov, you bastard," he mutters. "I swear, I'm going

to drink your goddamned blood for this. Then I'm going to piss it on your grave."

Makita runs. She knows that being under a skyfurnace blast isn't quite as bad as being caught in the blast range of a small nuclear detonation—there's no atomic radiation, for one thing—but the survival ratios are identical, ranging from zero to zero.

She too hears the sound of the coil ratcheting up. It inspires her to redouble her efforts, but the effort is dangerous—she nearly stumbles and falls flat on her face.

There are others running around her—friend and foe alike—their faces betray their fear, they are just as afraid as she is. Now the Reds know how their vanquished foes have felt in the past; dying in an immolation is not the same as dying in battle, dying like a soldier. It is more like being executed by a coward.

Good! she thinks. *If only I don't have to die along with them to prove my point!*

The other soldiers fleeing on the street completely bypass an intersection. Makita makes the turn. She doesn't want to be caught dead feeling sorry for Reds, especially when freedom fighters are dying with them.

The vats open. The sound is a scream across the sky.

A torrential downpour of protocol-invigorated fuel emanates from the vats, as if a faucet of doom has been activated and within moments begins filling the streets with the heat of the Motherland's anger.

It is a considerable heat indeed. The soldiers on both sides who refused to run, or could not run are the first to be immolated. Whether they prayed to God or the ghost of Gorkovsky, they were now dead, dissolved into atoms. Their souls, their pasts, perhaps even their legacies perishing all in the same instant.

But not her father's legacy. Not if she can help it. *Of course,* she thinks, *you better find a place to hide fast, munchkin, unless you want to disappoint your papa.*

She decides she doesn't like the sound of that angry hiss. It's becoming louder. She has no choice; she must slow down long enough to glance behind her.

And sees a wave of red-hot lava coming at her with the speed and intensity of a tidal wave. Not even the ruins can stand against it.

Her turn to pray—she prays Papa hasn't made it to Heaven yet. She doesn't want him to be looking down and see her dissolved before she even has time to get swept away. She does not want to disappoint him. Not even in death.

But she must admit, she's not sure what to do next. Her father may have given her sage advice on how to die with dignity, but nothing he said left her a clue as to how she might survive being inundated in a six hundred degree wave of magical ectoplasmic goo.

She turns down another intersection and it's all she can do not to stop dead in her tracks. No pun intended. Death is behind her in the form of the fuel wave, it's already melting the opposite side of the buildings to her left, and yet death is just as surely ahead of her in the form of Reds and freedom fighters shooting it out over a bunch of immobilized tanks.

Makita knows they're immobilized because the treads have been sabotaged and are lying all over the street. She knows the two factions are fighting because not only are there dead bodies lying all around the treads, but several soldiers are still firing at the other camp, trying to use the tanks for cover. The tanks are valuable because they have parts that can be cannibalized. Not that it's going to make a difference in the next few moments...

Unless one is inside a tank.

It is too late to try to arrange a truce, and it is doubtful the Reds would permit it in the first place, since only the attack by the freedom fighters got them out of their tanks in the first place. The hammer and sickle strapped onto her back, her father's weapons, are not much good at this medium range. Thank goodness! she exalts—she still has her trusty firearms. Without missing a step she fires at the nearest soldier in a Red uniform, a soldier who just happens to be taking a bead at a freedom fighter.

She dispatches him with a single shot. He hits the street as if he'd been thrown there. If he isn't already dead, he soon will be, because he isn't going anywhere.

At the same time the freedom fighter she was trying to save also falls, shot in the back by one of his foes.

There are four other soldiers still standing and she knows they are all Reds, not only because of their uniforms, but because all four have now turned on her and have started to aim their weapons. They are fast, but not as fast as she, who takes advantage of surprise and shoots a second Red in the mid-section.

She doesn't notice if he falls down or staggers down—either way, he's probably out of the picture—because she's too busy ducking behind the bench at a bus stop. The bench is sprayed with bullets and she comes out from behind it with both guns blazing and at the very least wounds two more before she does a roll behind a line of metal garbage cans. The Red bullets go right through the garbage cans; she might as well have hidden behind a sheet on a clothesline.

Now she is close enough to a tank to use it for cover. Two things are most important: all the dead bodies in this part of the scene are freedom fighters, and off in the distance the wave of Motherland anger is surging between the buildings even as the buildings fall.

A Red looks out from behind a tank, the prelude to firing at her, but she gets him between the eyes before he has the chance to so much as take a bead on her.

Another Red panics and comes around the tank with his automatic rifle already blazing. But his aim is wild, while hers is not. In less than a second he lies sprawled on the ground.

Makita reaches the tank closest to her, climbs up the rear, and shoots the first Red she sees right at the base of the neck. She gets the other two surviving Reds just as easily and is about to jump into the open hatch as if it were a pond in the park when yet another Red pokes his head through. He just has time to widen his eyes before she shoots him in the left one. He falls onto the tank, his body half out of the hatch, and Makita manages to pull him the rest of the way the moment the wave of red hot fuel touches the tank and begins to lift it.

She gets the hatch closed in the nick of time. That is, in the instant before the fuel rushed over the hatch and the instant before the hatch became too hot to touch. Not ten seconds inside the tank and she is already sweating like a fishmonger. The tank is being buffeted along with the wave and she wants to hold onto something but she can't because everything is too hot. She bangs her head on one wall, is thrown over the commander's seat, and bangs her head on the opposite wall.

Time ceases to have meaning, but motion does not. She is on the verge of becoming sick—she wonders what she could possibly have in her stomach left to vomit—when suddenly she feels the tank beginning to slow. Gradually it comes to a stop. Soon after that the world ceases to spin.

Makita has no choice but to wait several moments until the hatch cools down enough for her to deal with it. Her gloves provide only minimal protection because she'd torn off the fingers long ago, the better to shoot with. After dithering with the locks and controls, she kicks it open.

She falls out—the wave had turned the tank on its side—and hits the ground, only to spring up again as the earth is still very hot. Fortunately her boots are not particularly worn and the soles are able to shield her from the hot soil.

The heat is already dissipating—magical fire tends not to linger—but a thick cloud of ashes flitters about the air like so much confetti. The sky is red, and the sounds of battle continue to rage in the distance. Makita is still alive, but at the moment she fears she has lost everything she is fighting for.

To be born on this soil is to be born a warrior.

He'd neglected to tell her that when one is warrior, one pays.

I will be watching you from the Heavens. Always.

She remembers the letter, the reason why she was not permitted to die with her papa. She takes it from the pocket stitched inside her coat.

The letter is addressed to *Antares.*

Whoever she is.

CHAPTER TEN

Field Report to Central Command
From Skymarshall Urik Antares,
Commanding officer:
R.S.S. Konstantinov.

After sustained aerial and artillery bombardment, air superiority has been attained by the skyfurnace detachments over the city's recognized northern and southern hostile districts.

As ordered, the fleet has successfully surrounded the separatist forces of the Nokgorka resistance militia within the city of Bahamut.

I have received your orders to launch a ground assault into the city via armor drop and to conduct the immediate capture and/or elimination of any and all forces loyal to the illegally formed local government.

Special forces recon teams have been dispatched to street level. Those units that have survived have met with furious enemy resistance.

It is the opinion of this officer that such an offensive has little to no chance of achieving desired objectives at this time.

Further, from the recon reports, as well as from my vantage on board the Konstantinov, the city of Bahamut is a burned-out ruin. Its streets offer enemy units a labyrinthine fortress impenetrable to armored assault.

The enemy forces have survived a bombardment of 4,000 heavy detonations per hour, 24 hours a day, for the past 40 days.

After this bombardment of almost four million denotations, after an estimated one hundred thousand enemy casualties, we offered terms of surrender.

Their only response was as follows: TO DIE OR LIVE IN FREEDOM IS OUR FATE.

Another concern is in regards to the troop versus troop profile.

1. Armament versus defense:

Although no standards exist, most frontline Nokgorka troops are armed with the RKG-41, an antique slug-thrower with low rate of fire. Any well-trained Red trooper engaging his hook's defensive rotation shield should be immune to this caliber of weapon.

Unfortunately the level of training has fallen to such a miserable degree that the RGK-4 must now be considered a threat.

2. Morale:

I believe I've clearly established the extreme level of sacrifice our enemy is capable of.

May I remind the Council that for three
hundred years we have attempted to force the
people of Nokgorka under pain of death, to
fully submit to our rule once and for all.
Their reaction, now as ever...
Fury.
As for our troops, where to begin? They are
unprepared, unwilling, and overwhelmed. They
are not soldiers, gentlemen.
For them, Nokgorka is simply a nightmare,
and they have no idea when or how it will end.
With all due respect, this is not the same
Red Fleet that once held half the world in fear.
I can assure you of that.
To speak plainly, Nokgorka is a wasteland.
A frozen ruin populated not by trained armies,
but by packs of desperate wolves devouring
each other. As Commander-in-Chief of the
Nokgorka attack fleet, I request a delay of any
ground assault into the city of Bahamut. To
proceed with such operations at this time
insures catastrophe.

Sincerely,
Skymarshall Urik Antares.

It is the morning after. Her father has not been dead for twenty-four hours and the new scar on the city of Bahamut is not yet twenty-four hours old. She does not think she will be seeing the sorceress to whom the letter is addressed any time soon, but in the meantime she will be satisfied with the hunt for Reds.

Ever since the immolation, the Reds and the freedom fighters have been roaming the decimated urban jungle and have been picking one another off like feuding families of stalkers. The Nokgorkans have to stay out of sight of the Reds in the skyfurnaces and other aerial ships, they must avoid being pinpointed by radar. But the Nokgorkans have the advantage of knowing every tunnel, every corridor, every staircase, every delivery ramp, every basement level store and apartment. The Reds know such places exist, but they have no idea where they are until they stumble across them or are ambushed by a freedom fighter holed up in one of those spots. It is a deadly game that only the Nokgorkans seem to enjoy, and on this morning no one is enjoying it more than Makita.

She treads lightly in the fresh snow in the park, sticking close to the wooden fence. She listens intently and hears nothing, but her senses are in a state of high alert, and she has learned to trust her instincts. At the moment the scene of devastation before her is so complete and thorough, she can easily imagine herself the last surviving person on the planet, and she cannot shake the feeling that someone is going to reduce the world population by a factor of one sometime soon.

Very soon.

Cautiously she makes a turn at the end of the fence.

And comes face-to-face with a startled Red soldier. He is at least two meters tall and has shoulders as broad as an elk's—the better to carry his armor and padding with. His weapon is as long as he is tall and is fitted with a bayonet the size of a battle-axe.

In contrast, Makita carries a heavy, chunky firearm half her size and a quarter of her weight. It was given to her this morning by a freedom fighter who had no more use for it because he was dead.

In that first instant of their encounter, they look one another in the eye. Each takes the measure of the other.

He is afraid. She is not.

On some hidden level he believes it is wrong to kill a child for whatever reason; he has ingrained social constraints against committing violence on those he has been brought up to think of as innocent.

She labors under no such hindrance.

He does not want to be in this war.

Now that she is in it, she has no problem with it.

He is bigger, stronger, theoretically more trained in the art of combat than she. She has no problem with that either.

She fires.

The Red activates his defensive rotation shield—it is half mechanical, half-protocol controlled and its purpose is to deflect any bullets or other projectiles coming his way. Of course, the shield's main problem is its tendency to cause ricochets resulting in death by friendly fire. Since there are no other Reds around, the soldier can use it without compunction.

Unfortunately, he cannot use it well.

Makita grins. If this man had been well trained, he could have killed her with one of her own bullets.

A bullet rips through his side and he falls. He glances at his wound in absolute terror, he cannot bear to look at it.

Makita smiles and without thought to personal injury picks up a handful of shattered glass lying next to a pile to rubbish left over from the inefficient days of the peace and hurls it into the Red's face.

Now he is totally consumed by his fear and he begins to stand. But not before the smaller, shorter freedom fighter, the wisp of a girl, has grabbed him from behind, her tiny arm over his eyes and bloody face, and is holding onto his shoulder with her sickle at his neck.

He has no idea what has hit him.

Rather, he has no idea what has cut his throat.

He struggles, tries to fall or roll away, anything to get this girl off his back. He can feel his warm blood running down his body and he can feel the earth spinning and his life slipping away and there is nothing he can do about it. Nothing. He can't even breathe.

He goes limp and Makita lets him fall. He lands in the bloody snow with a thud.

And she feels very satisfied, as if she has just performed a dance she has practiced to perfect a long while. Papa's death has been avenged, however slightly. She wonders how many more will be enough.

She takes the dead soldier's rations and disappears into the urban desolation before the aerial spies have more of an opportunity to see her.

Viewed at night, from high above, the ruins of Bahamut possessed an eerie beauty, like a luxurious maze in the middle of Hell, or an oasis of the dead nestled between the verdant farms of the steppes. Crimson and golden ash from the immolation still flickered throughout the air space above the city. Skymarshall Urik Antares could see practically the entire expanse of the desolation through the large windows of the war room of the *Konstantinov*. He tried to tell himself that he wasn't responsible, that the immolation would eventually serve its purpose to break the will of the freedom fighters, that there would come a day when his heart and soul wouldn't feel so heavy, when remorse would be a thing of the past, but somehow he couldn't bring himself to believe it.

"That report I sent yesterday," he said aloud. "It almost cost me my command. Central didn't listen. We've been ordered to proceed with the ground assault." He paused, and wondered why it was a man could be standing hundreds of meters above the surface of the world and at the same time feel lower than a worm. "It looks like the bastards are going to fight this children's crusade until all of Nokgorka is bled white."

"What the hell is 'children's crusade' supposed to mean?" demanded Alexandra Goncharova. There were only two people on the planet Urik trusted implicitly, and though he was sometimes loathe to admit it, Alex was one of them. She stood on the opposite side of the protocol map of Bahamut, a ghostly 3D projection of what the city had looked like before the bombing, the fighting, and the immolation.

"The 'Gorkas have children in their ranks, fourteen, fifteen year olds, some younger."

Alex narrowed her green eyes. "Well, I've never met a soldier that wasn't somebody's child!"

"That was cold, Alex, even for you. What the hell are you saying?"

"If the 'Gorkas want their independence, then they know their goddamned price. If all they've got is children to pay the reaper, then to hell with them. It's not on us."

"You're taking this rather personally!"

She shrugged, and her lips began to form a sneer which she evidently thought better of, because she stopped it.

Urik suspected he knew what was really on Alex's mind, the real reason why she viewed the enemy in this conflict with uncharacteristic contempt. After all, her remark had affirmed and denounced Nokgorkan humanity at the same time. "You're wrong. The responsibility is on us! What's left of our nation is hanging by a thread. Any wrong move could mean complete civil war. Our choices could be the difference betw—"

"Our choices?" Alex laughed. "We choose? Since when, exactly? At what moment does a soldier take control? You've got no choice but to send in the assault tomorrow. And I've got no choice but to go!"

"Conduct, I'm talking about conduct. Sure, we're warriors, we're trained to kill and to make no bones about it. We don't have any of those sissy counseling sessions for so-called post traumatic stress syndrome that the intellectually corrupt Transnational soldiers have. We don't worry about our penchant for violence. We make use of it and that's it. But we're not butchers. We do not execute children!"

"Urik, sir, look down on that city. It's a slaughterhouse. And as hard as it may be to believe, some of those children are right now slaughtering our own loyal countrymen!"

Urik blinked. "Now *that* I would find difficult to believe."

"And if not, our men and women are killing children right now."

Urik shook his head. "They wouldn't. Only if there was no other way. They would just incapacitate them somehow."

"How?"

"I don't know. Somehow."

"Are you telling me that no children were killed when you passed on the order to burn it to the ground?"

"I did not—!" But he stopped himself cold. He had not passed on the order, he had tried to stop it. If his own friends thought he'd committed a crime against humanity, what would other people think? What chance did he have to convince others he was innocent in that? "Look, I have no problem killing the enemy fairly, in combat. Even if I have to shoot him in the back—"

"That's enough! Damn the both of you! Are we going to plan this assault or is it also the Red Fleet who is employing children?"

Those words were spoken by Sorceress-Major Maya Antares. If looks could turn people into green lizards, Urik and Alex would have been scurrying for cover beneath the protocol image in an instant.

"Very well, then," said Urik, indicating his desire to concentrate on business. He was worried about Maya. He was afraid she had a deathwish, that she saw this conflict as her big opportunity to join his brother Marcus in an afterlife he didn't believe in. He took a deep breath and stared for a moment at the quarter moon in the bright starry sky. The only clouds there were those caused by the horrors of war. He wished with all his heart he could wipe those clouds away and step into a world where warriors were superfluous, where a man could satiate his need for adventure only with extreme sports or mountain climbing. Even hunters would be banned in this world.

He turned toward his friends, who had been staring silently at him, waiting for him to become their commander again. "First the bad news," he said. "The map is of Bahamut before the bombings began. We haven't been supplied with any revised map protocols, so the effects of the bombing can't be taken into account.

"Alex, you'll lead the 131st armored column in from the north toward the river. Set up a bridgehead near the train station and hold until we can reinforce the position. The approach is narrow. You'll have to run in single column formation, but last recon shows no fortified enemy positions *en route*.

"Maya, you'll be coordinating the attack from up here."

"I wanted to talk to you about that," Maya said, interrupting. "I think it is a mistake not to send me down there with a command on street level."

"Discussion is over!" said Urik, perhaps a little too emphatically. "You're a major now, Maya. The frontlines are for hardasses like your friend here."

"Didn't know you cared, sir," said Alex easily.

Urik almost said *"I don't"* but he checked himself because he knew it wasn't true. On his loneliest nights he often wondered how things might have developed between him and Alex, if only certain other developments had worked out differently.

"And the good news is..." continued Alex.

"There isn't any. In all seriousness, as much as I'd prefer Central Command not to send us in tomorrow, the 'Gorka's have been battered to hell. They've got to be ready to break. If the recon holds up, this whole mess should be over by 15:00 hours."

At 15:30 hours:

Alexandra Goncharova hunkered down at the front of her Krawl and put her arms around her head as bullets whizzed by on either side of her once-proud machine. Her helmet lay a few meters away from the Krawl—she'd forgotten to strap it and it had fallen off her head as she'd rolled down the front of the tank to minimize the time she would be in the enemy's sights. Now there was no way to retrieve it, not if she wanted to live to make the com kast she'd been trying to make for the last thirty minutes.

Thirty minutes which she'd spent completely pinned

down. The Krawl column she'd commanded, what was left of it, was stranded, trapped in the street between two rows of manufacturing plants. The buildings were only partly intact, and the upper portions of their facades were pretty much non-existent. Yet the buildings were strong enough, and the facades complete enough, to have enabled the Nokgorkan Resistance to place several hidden artillery batteries. Krawls at the front of the column and Krawls at the back were decimated, blown to so many pieces they blocked the way, and now the enemy was picking them off, one by one—seemingly at their leisure, but always in such a manner that they never revealed their position. The Krawls usually only had the chance to shoot a few rounds before they were hit—and it seemed that no matter where they aimed, it was at a place where the enemy batteries and snipers *used to be*.

Alex was still alive for one reason and one reason only—ever since the Great War, it had been the custom that Krawl commanders never be positioned at the head or the rear of a column, that they be embedded in the middle somewhere. Otherwise she was certain she would have been dead by now. She figured it was a distinct possibility she would soon be dead anyway.

She spoke into her com unit, doing her best not to sound desperate, hopeless, or panic-stricken. "Goncharova to *Konstantinov*! Goncharova to *Konstantinov*!" She was so startled she nearly jumped into the line of fire when she finally got an answer.

"It's Maya. We've got you, Alex, where the hell have you been? Four hours since our last contact!"

"The 'Gorkas are running powerful protocol resistance shields. They're blocking our communication and our navigation systems! We've been ambushed near the train station. That recon from Central Command was useless!

Where are the other units? I need reinforcement immediately! It's a complete disaster down here!"

Alex could hear the catch in Maya's voice as she said, "We've lost contact with most of them! The 81st and 124th have been all bit wiped out. We ordered the 19th and the 76th to break through toward your last known location, so they're on their way!"

Alex waited until a nearby Krawl attempted another shot at the artillery. Its trajectory was pathetic and the rocket missed, landing somewhere at least three blocks away. Alex hoped it got somebody.

Then she waited another moment as the enemy artillery scored a direct hit on the offending Krawl. It burst into flames. Men and women scurried out like rats on a sinking ship. Most of them were on fire. They were all picked off in a matter of seconds.

"Alex—?" Maya asked.

"Uh, negative on the 19th. They got the hell out of here under heavy fire! The ones who didn't make it managed to block one of our possible escape routes too. Nice of them! No sign of the 76th, as of yet." She paused. It was a terrible thing, knowing you were going to die while you still had regrets. "Pass a message on to Urik, will you? Last night, at the briefing, I know I gave him hell, but tell him he was right about one thing: there wasn't any good news."

Alex smiled grimly. She figured Urik would find the irony in that, if nothing else. Then she happened to spot a flash, the reflection of a large piece of metal in the sun, as it was being moved from behind one end of a facade to another. She hastily gave some coordinates and said, "This is Goncharova to the column! Whoever's left—fire at will!"

A couple of guns went off, but they all missed. And

now the enemy didn't even grant them the courtesy of immediately wiping them out.

"We haven't got much left, Maya," she said into her com. "Goddamned recruits wet their pants when the lead Krawl got hit. All Hell broke loose after that. "Gorkas' anti-Krawl guns are positioned perfectly. Up high in the buildings, angle too steep for our rockets, too steep for our main cannon. And they just keep pouring it on!"

At that point Alex had no idea her communications were being monitored, though perhaps if she hadn't been so rattled, she would have suspected as much. Of course, she had no way of knowing that the enemy was in danger of running out of ammunition, and from her com kast knew the moment had come for the next move: suppression and cover fire, giving the ground fighters cover. The enemy planned to scavenge as much as the Krawls as they could, to use against the Reds on the very next day, if necessary.

Indeed, Alex noted that the bursts of gunfire were accelerating an instant before her Krawl was rained on with bullets, bullets that ricochet off the other tanks as well off the buildings. She would have hunkered down except the rain of bullets was accompanied by a distant blood-curdling battlecry.

The battlecry was accompanied by more gunfire.

Alex's loader, Renko, a tough broad from the tundra, shouted, "Infantry! Infantry charging position!"

But the three Reds who were just hit knew that already.

"Maya, we got—" said Alex.

"I heard her!" Maya said. "I don't understand why the gate protocols haven't been kast yet!"

Alex would have loved to say something pithy in reply. But she was too busy stepping into the line of fire and delivering several heavy bursts at the streams of the enemy coming from the buildings. "They make that same damned battlecry as the Nistaani. No good screaming sons of bi–"

"Alex–"

"I'm just a little busy, Maya!" She whirled back to her former position behind her Krawl. She examined herself quickly. No blood emanating from a fresh hole in her body. That was good.

"It's the gate, Alex!" Maya shouted, forgetting the coms could pick her up perfectly. "They're not working!"

"The protocol resistance!"

"Affirmative. The shields are tougher than we thought. Reports are in from the transfer decks. We can't kast anything in or out of your area. We'll have to send a new squad outside their defensive radius. It won't be easy for them to get to you from where they'll land."

Alex felt her soul drop into a swamp. "Maya, damn you, just say it. How long as we talking?" No answer. More gunfire. "Maya!"

Her friend's reply was heavy with regret. "Three hours, Alex. At best."

"Don't send them."

Back on the *Konstantinov*, Maya felt her grief explode into a wave of anger. "Don't play that martyr BS with me! I'll transfer down with the rescue team myself. You just keep–"

Alex began laughing.

"What?" Maya demanded to know.

"That's as close as I've ever heard you cuss before. You got to understand, by the time you get here, we'll be food for the dogs. That is, if the enemy doesn't eat us themselves. I'll be sure to tell Marcus–"

"Alex! Damn you!" shouted Maya, slamming her fist on the control console. "You listen to me!"

"—how much you've missed him. Goncharova out."

"Don't you dare shut down this comline on me! Alexander!" But Maya sensed the line was indeed shut off. She did not dare grieve, not yet, but she could not help thinking of the old man she had talked to at Citadel. Vanya. Surely he must have gone through times like this during the Great War,

Of course, no patriotic future historian worth his salt would ever call this a Great War.

Meanwhile, Alex and Renko stood between two Krawls; Alex fired at the enemy coming in from one direction, and Renko the other. There weren't as many attacking as Alex had first feared, though the number was high enough, more than high enough to get the job done.

"Looks like this is it, Renko," she said.

"Yeah, I heard," said Renko.

There was a lull in attackers, though there was still shooting and fighting elsewhere in the stranded column.

"Goddamned Nokgorkia," said Alex. "Of all places. I never should have come back to this rathole."

"Well, so much for my trip to the West," said Renko.

"Ahh, you're not missing anything from what I've heard," said Alex as she picked off a guy trying to run past the two Krawls. "They say it's damn hot all year round."

"Cold all year is better?" Renko replied,

Alex took a bead at an enemy soldier trying to sneak past a pile of brick rubble several meters away. "Not to mention that the no-good sons of bitches never stop smiling. I've always hated Westerners for that." She took her shot. A direct hit. "Know what I mean?"

No answer.

"Renko?" She looked at her friend.

Who sat on the ground, slumped against a tread. Her armor was extremely bloody.

Alex sighed. "Oh, Renko," she whispered. "You clown." Suddenly Alex's limbs felt extremely heavy, as if the earth beneath her feet had turned into a neutron star. She knew she had to get moving, she had to stay frosty, even if she wasn't exactly sure what difference it would make...

Then she heard the distinct sound of someone running on top of her Krawl. The person was trying to be silent, but lacked as much as skill as he thought he had. Alex guessed from the intonation of the sound that the person wasn't very heavy.

The person also made an involuntary gasp as he—no, it was a *she*, leapt from the Krawl. Obviously she was going to attempt a silent kill.

We'll see... thought Alex.

Makita can barely contain the urge to utter an exuberant battlecry as she leaps from the Krawl toward the back of the unsuspecting Red soldier below her. Makita holds her sickle in one hand and with the other gets ready to rake her fingernails across the Red woman's eyes. The silly soldier doesn't even have her helmet on. *This is going to be easy*, she thinks.

Makita doesn't have time to remember what her father told her about the unexpected because in less time than it takes to tell, the Red woman looks upward, reaches out, grabs Makita by the belt, and then redirects her energy into a meteoric plunge onto the snow. Makita lands on her back and her breath makes a jump out of her body into the stratosphere. She starts to get up, but gets as far as her hands and knees when she freezes and realizes she should already be dead.

The Red has her automatic rifle pointed squarely at Makita's heart.

They look one another in the eye. Each takes the measure of the other.

Alex sees that her victim-to-be is afraid, that this child is not used to controlling her fear.

Makita sees that the Red's eyes are green, just like hers, but it's what Makita doesn't see that's important: the killer instinct.

The Red is hesitating, and Makita has no idea why. For a moment time is stretching into eternity, almost as if Fate had ordained it. Makita wonders, *Can this be the sorceress? She doesn't look like a sorceress.*

She cannot know, can never know what the Red is thinking. Some of the Red's own words are coming back to haunt her:

> *I've never met a soldier that wasn't someone's child.* And:
> *They know the goddamned price. To hell with them.* Plus:
> *When do we decide to stop being controlled?* But who was it who said something about:
> A slaughterhouse.

"You're a stupid little girl to be out here!" the Red snaps.

Makita tries not to move, tries not to think. No Red who wasn't insane would have hesitated this long.

"Who the hell would send a goddamn child into a... into a slaughterhouse?" the Red says. She has suddenly grown more thoughtful.

And Makita, much to her confusion and dismay, has suddenly grown fearful for her.

"No more. No more. Go on, damn you," the woman says. "Go on and live."

The woman stands there and looks at Makita, at an enemy girl too amazed to move. Indeed, the woman stares at Makita as if she were something out of a dream, the fulfillment of a desire she had never known she had.

Someone appears between the tanks. "Makita! Stay down!" says the freedom fighter.

"Proto..." says Makita. "No! She—!"

"Brave little girl," the woman whispers. She closes her eyes.

Does she do it because she's relieved to have made the decision to show mercy? Because she believes herself fulfilled? Because she wants to commit suicide by enemy fire? Makita needs to know.

But once Proto fires, she knows she never will.

The sound of his gunfire seems like it is the only noise in the entire world.

He scores a direct hit through the back.

Death is instantaneous.

After Urik had left the war room on the *Konstantinov*, Maya and Alex had taken a few moments to stare at the quarter moon together.

Alex pointed out that the moon had seen all the wars of all time. "For as long as we've been killing each other, it's watched us."

"'For a thousand years the castle burned'," said Maya. "'Hopes and dreams in its ashes. Kingdoms born and razed. Generations sacrificed on the pure. And yet, shining untouched, the knight's moon watched, and in its silence, wept.'"

"Well, if you want to get all mystical about it—say, that's from old book you love so much, isn't it. The illegal one?"

Maya laughed. "Yes, you witch. *Castle Justice*, and it's not illegal anymore."

"That's right. I forgot how much has changed."

"And how little. Like how fast morning rears its ugly head before a battle. There. That was mystical. 'Morning is ugly.' Get it?"

"Well, funny girl, if you're feeling mystical, I can loan you my copy of it."

Alex shook her head. "I don't know. Romantic fantasies. I like real stories."

"This is a real story." Maya had forgotten how much she'd always wanted Alex to read this book. "It's a bloody, brutal, real story. The fantasy is just a disguise."

"With a happy ending, I'm sure," said Alex with a smile. She had no intention of ever reading the book. "With a happy ending, I'm sure. Well, I'd better get back then. Morning is getting uglier by the minute. Goodnight, Maya."

"Goodnight, Alexandria."

CHAPTER ELEVEN

I had too much to dream last night. When I woke up I wrote it down so I could remember it, though I haven't looked at my notes since. I remember it so vividly, at least the parts that I *can* remember, I recall vividly. Parts I remember with clarity. Perfect, frightening clarity. No, they are not what you would call "good parts." It isn't that kind of dream. Sorry if I disappoint you.

I was lost in a wasteland. It was a ruin. A graveyard. A battlefield. Colossal monuments made of steel lay all around me on a snowy terrain. They lay as if they been hurled from the sky by a cruel god blinded with jealous envy. They lay in heaps, or end on end. Layers of ice coated their surfaces. I walked through their shadows and felt a chill in my soul that made my body feel warm in comparison. Were these monuments, these twisted relics from another time, all that was left of the civilization that birthed me? What of the dreams of man? What of the love in my heart? Were they destined to be less than ghosts? The totality of the devastation was nothing compared to feeling of the existential dread that was to come, of that I was certain.

Then—an angel appeared before me. An angel bearing mercy.

She smiled down at me as if she had known me for a thousand years. And I had to admit, she seemed familiar somehow, but I could not quite focus on her face or her uniform. A name I could not read was sewn on a patch above her right breast.

She spoke and my heart flew into heaven, but the meaning of her words flew into darkness like shooting stars. I've tried to remember them, but their sound keeps eluding me. I think it's something like *Pray for the living. Pray for the living.* Which is interesting because that's something I already do.

She looked down at me, leaned forward as if to kiss me on the cheek. But she never quite touched me.

I gave her a flower. It was then I realized how small and innocent I was. In my dream I wasn't the person I am today. I wasn't the adept sorceress who has seen and meted out so much death. I was a small girl, with a cloak and a hood, carrying a bunch of flowers like I was in a fairy tale.

She told me she had to go, she could no longer watch over me. I implored her to stay, of that I am certain. I didn't want to be alone in this place that only showed me the futility and desolation of the dreams of man.

Then she told me it was too dangerous for me to stay in this place. I could not help but agree. I then realized that one of the structures that had been frozen here was the cracked face of a giant statue of Gorkovsky. The God of Communism was part of this desolation, perhaps even the cause of it.

The angel told me it was dangerous to stay because it was the past, and I could no longer live in the past. She wasn't mean about it, but her words were harsh. Those

I remember. They went something like, "If you keep it up, you sentimentalist witch, I swear I'll haunt you off a damn cliff."

I had to look. The ground beneath my feet was solid. Frozen and covered with snow, but solid. No footprints though, as if I no longer had anything I could leave behind.

There came a storm. A strangely calming, distant storm that opened a great hole in the sky that beckoned the angel home. She took a flower I had offered her—it had glided in the air from my hand to hers—and began to fade away. She spoke to me for the last time, and during that time her words merged with the storm, they became the storm. She said, "I've searched for him, Maya, I've searched for him. And you know something? He isn't here. *He isn't here!*"

Sorceress-Major Maya Antares stood in the war room of the *Konstantinov* and looked down on the cold vista of the battered Bahamut. It had been a week since the immolation, a week since the death of Alexandra, a week since the blizzards had allowed any military action of any significance to be taken on either side. Now the only lights in the city were those created by the fires started by citizens and/or freedom fighters trying to stay warm in the freezing weather. There was no power, of course, but there was a blockade that wouldn't be lifted until the Nokgorkans gave up their bid for independence. Maya felt ambivalent about their aspirations, but she surely loathed all the killing that had been done in the name of freedom.

"That was how the dream ended, Urik," she said. "It seems ridiculous, now that I've said it. Dreaming of an angel like some child. Not in this world...

"Look at the smoke rising from those bombed-out buildings," she added, changing the subject abruptly.

Urik acknowledged her statement with a grunt. He put his feet on his desk, poured a shot of vodka, then leaned over and put the half-full bottle—or was it half-empty?—next to his pack of cigarettes. He was taking a big chance, drinking even though he wasn't on duty. But at the moment he didn't care. Alex's death had inspired a lot of unexpected fatalism and indifference in him, and he really did not care what his superiors thought of his off-duty activities.

"This could be anywhere, Urik," Maya said. "Anywhere. Today it's Nokgorka. Some small nation no one knows the name of. Tomorrow? Who knows?"

"Hey, that's really touching," said Urik, punctuating his sincerity with a protracted belch. "Hey, I got a story too. Theze two ol' boys've gotten drunk, an'—and, oh, no! The bottle runs dry! And one of 'em says, 'Not to worry! I have some booze I made myself! The Trans' call it hooch! Best damn high you'll ever get! There's only one thing—it's mostly engine coolant! We'll probably go blind!

"And his friend says, 'Well, haven't we seen enough of this world?!'" Urik belched, laughed, and hiccuped practically at the same time. He slapped his knee. "Get it? Don't you feel the same way? Haven't you seen enough of this world?"

Maya raised an eyebrow. "Charming. If you want to drown yourself, go on then. I'm going to find Alexandra's body."

"What?" He made a face. "Gross."

"It's undoubtedly perfectly preserved, thanks to the cold. She saved my life once. The least I can do is bury her. I never got the chance to put my husband to rest, He was left to rot in Al'istaani."

The face Urik now made was one of anger.

"Oh, I'm sorry, Skymarshall Antares," said Maya, her voice oozing with a lethal combination of sarcasm and honey. "I must sound so cruel. You're my husband's brother, aren't you? I'd forgotten that, Uri. That must mean you're my brother-in-law or something like that."

"I *was.*"

She harrumphed, opened the door with a snap-of-the-finger protocol, and strode out of the war room like a tigress. She did not look back. Urik was tempted to stop her; going to the surface would be a direct violation of orders from Central Command, who had promised another strategy for a direct assault that Urik knew they were still haggling over.

He had another drink. Then yet another. He knew her well enough to know he couldn't stop her, and he didn't see the point of setting a bunch of soldiers against her, to try to keep her on the skyfurnace against her will. They probably could, but what would be the point? It would just be a big hassle. For her, and for him especially.

He felt sick to the stomach. Usually he didn't get dizzy when he was drunk—or so he told himself—but pretty soon he would be spinning like a top.

The door opened again. Kyuzo entered and saluted smartly. He was armed and ready for bear, but then he always was, probably even when he went to the head.

"Sir," he said, "Maya's leaving for groundside. As her guardsman, I request permission to follow."

Urik felt himself sink into a swamp. He was under the mistaken impression it was a swamp of anger, but for a terrible moment he actually believed he could live quite well in a world without Maya. "Damn. The smart ones really know how to hitcha, huh? Damn witch! Go on, then, Maya, GO!"

"Sir! I am requesting a follow order–"

"She wants to go die, to Hell with her! Think I can bring them back? What the hell does she want me to do? Bring them back? Bring them back?"

Kyuzo took his reply to be a yes.

The logo on Urik's *Citadel* brand bottle of vodka was a futuristic picture of the Ministry of Defense. The drawing was red and green against a pale yellow background and had a big red star above the tip of the building. Through his tears he could almost imagine it looking exactly like the real building, indeed, as the real building had looked that night in St. Petersberg when he and his brother Marcus had slipped away from their mother standing in the bread line and ran to the train station where they'd been told a new inspiration poster had been put up. The night was cold and the snow thick in the air. The adults entering and leaving the train station seemed remarkably indifferent to this exciting event, but Urik could hardly wait to see it.

"C'mon, Marcus!" he shouted. "Hurry up! It's over there! C'mon!"

Marcus dashed over to him and Urik took his hand and he practically dragged his little brother to the place where they'd been told the new poster would be.

And there it was, illuminated by fluorescences on all four sides and from the rear as well, so that none of it would ever be in shadow. Urik felt his heart stop the moment he got his first full view of it. He had no idea what Marcus thought because for a few moments he'd forgotten he even had a little brother.

213

THE RED STAR

The poster itself was of a chiseled-jawed man, clean-shaven and sharp-eyed, standing against a background of various shades of red, all in patterns originating from the Red Star logo that was the symbol of the Motherland. The poster read: YOUR FATHER FOUGHT. HONOR HIM. And at the bottom: JOIN THE RED FLEET. The man on the poster wore a uniform of armor and chain-mail and a crimson cape, a form of dress perhaps more appropriate for a Roman centurion than a modern Internationalist soldier, but there was no doubt his kind belonged to the future.

A future Urik wanted to be a part of. "Isn't it great?"

"Uri–"

"I can't wait! Only one more year until the Academy!"

"Uri–!"

"But then forever until I graduate to a skyfurnace. Six years! Aw, man, how can I wait that long?"

"Uri–!"

"You have to wait even longer, Marco! Let's see–you're seven, so that's eleven years! We'll probably have already conquered the west by then! Don't worry though. You can read all about it in my memoirs. I'll–"

"URIK!"

"What!?" He could not believe his brother was interrupting him again. Always interrupting!

"Tell me the story of the Red Star again."

"Oh, come on! Again! Every day in school you hear it!"

"You tell it better. C'mon, Uri. Please. Please!"

"Okay, okay! Don't cry." The truth was, he was flattered his brother preferred to hear the story from his lips rather than from those of others. *There was once a knight at a crossroads. Before him, our nation lay in ruins. Above him, Heaven was dark. The light of Truth, the Red Star, had long ago fall from the sky. This burning gem was held prisoner, locked deep in a fortress of lies. Its guards were the souls of ancient slaves, made to serve their masters after death.*

"With fear in his heart, the knight tried to ride away. But a voice called to him, sad and beautiful, begging to be free. 'I am Pravda, Goddess of Truth,' she said. 'My sister, Krivda, Mistress of Lies, has stolen the star from my crown.

"'And all the people in the world wait in darkness for its return. The champion that retrieves my star from its imprisonment shall free us from deception and restore the light of truth to all the world.' The Red Fleet is the Army of Pravda. Her star is the symbol of our duty: To fight in the name of Truth, until the world is free of evil.

"Someday, Marcus, somewhere, we'll fight that final battle, and we'll win. We'll be the ones, Marcus. I know it."

And now Marcus was dead, and in fact had been dead for nearly a decade. The pain, the sense of loss Urik felt was no less than what it had been during the first days since he'd gotten the news, Making matters seem even more futile was the overwhelming realization that in the final analysis, there was no Truth to be found, anywhere in the world. Once this battle in Bahamut was won—and Urik had no doubt whatsoever that it would be won—he would return home a hero of the State. Few would know, and fewer still would even care, that the Red Fleet had massacred thousands of its own to achieve victory.

Taking stock of his situation, Urik was certain only of four things: One: he had not prevented the immolation of loyal Red Forces. Two: Marcus was dead. Three: Alex was dead. And as for number four: well, chances were, pretty soon Maya would be dead too. She had misinterpreted her own dream. Marcus was nowhere to be found in the afterlife because the only thing one can find in the afterlife is oblivion. Complete and utter oblivion. An oblivion Marcus found in no small part because he looked up to and admired his older brother.

What a dickhead I am. Forgive me, Father, forgive me.

He decided he was glad his brother was dead. Glad his brother wasn't alive to see what had become of him: the alcoholic Commander of a battered skyfurnace of a faded empire. Who would want to see that?

It was time for another drink.

Forgive me...

Makita is oblivious to the skyfurnace quietly passing high overhead—usually she is highly cognizant of the possibility of being spotted—but at the moment she is too busy carving the word "MERCY" on the piece of wood she has nailed and strapped to the marker she has improvised for the grave of the woman she has just buried. The nametag of the Red woman—"Goncharova"—is nailed to a second piece of wood.

This is only the second grave Makita has ever dug in her life. She never had a chance to dig one for her father and on some level which she barely understands, she believes this grave makes up for it somehow. Her only regret is that it has taken her this long to come back and do what she felt obligated to do. Whether it was from respect, some sudden love for mankind, or simply as a matter of honor, she was not. She only knew she had to do it, and now she has.

Her eyes well up with tears. Never before has it occurred to her that a Red might be as human as the next person, just as worthy of survival. No one had ever told her that a Red might have a reasonably coherent personal morality that would supercede the laws of war, in other words, that a Red might draw the line at shooting a child. Sure, it was the first such Red in Makita's experience, but she should have been told. She should have been warned. When speaking of Reds, no one in her clan had ever given her a clue such things might be. It seems unfair, somehow.

There is grief to work through, to be sure, but there is also the matter of survival. And although her heart is so heavy it seems it might never be uplifted again, her stomach is growling. Obviously the first order of business is to find some food.

There is probably some food among the rations in these Red Krawlers, she thinks, but she has lingered here long enough. The Reds haven't dared to wander the streets to retrieve their wounded or dead, but they have lobbed a few protocol explosions and more than a few plain old bombs at such sites, to discourage scavenging.

Besides, there are plenty of incapacitated Krawls in the city that have yet to be fleeced.

Plenty.

She comes upon a promising specimen a little more than two kilometers away.

It is promising because there's still a dead Red lying in the open hatch. Whistling a Trans pop song that had been popular before the fighting started, she pulls herself up the Krawl with casual proficiency. She stands over the dead Red. He has begun decaying a little bit because there've been a few warmer afternoons, relatively speaking, in the week or so that's passed since he was killed. But he doesn't stink. Much. Not yet.

With surprising ease she pulls the dead Red from the hatch and shoves him off the Krawl. He lands with a thud that echoes like a muted drumbeat from the ruins. His back and neck crack audibly.

She lowers herself in. Judging from the general wreckage, it appears a small bomb had gone off inside, probably sent by a Nokgorkan transfer protocol. Some of those elder witches and warlocks could do delicate work when the situation called for it. There are two more dead bodies, but as they haven't been directly exposed to the sun and have maintained a temperature closer to freezing level, they haven't degraded as much as the one outside.

One of the men had been groping toward the medical kit when he expired, though how he expected to do much about the intestines falling out of his gut with an anesthetic and a couple of bandages, she has no idea. He has done her a favor, though. The shelf with the med kit is often the one with the rations, and there's a full compliment, though some of the packages are quite bloody, thanks to the other man inside, who was very close to the bomb when it went off. Very close.

She finds a bar of chocolate-covered multi-vitamin fortified essence of trail mix, unwraps it, and climbs halfway out of the hatch so she can have a relatively bloodless view while she eats. Though she's trying to force herself to put the events of the past few days behind her, as she has seen many seasoned yet tragic professionals do in the past, she is discovering it is not as easy as it looks. She tries to hum the pop song while she chews the ration. It is very dry and she'll have to eat some snow to wash it down. But it should keep her going for hours—

What's that?

Someone is talking. The someone is not yet visible, he is behind a stone wall, but he is clearly coming in this direction. What's that he saying?

"Anything left the damn 'Gorkas haven't taken?"

"Only one way to find out," someone says.

"I don't think the Reds have been back yet," says a third. "Hard to tell..."

Makita drops back inside and through a tiny portal in the rear of the Krawl sees a force of about twenty-five men walk hurriedly but without discipline toward her. She catches her breath. These men are neither Reds nor freedom fighters.

"Hurry it up then, Koba!" says the one who is apparently the leader. He doesn't realize he is pointing directly at Makita. "Check out that Krawl up ahead."

The one called Koba replies, "Aw, Boss! There's nothing in those dead Krawls but pasted Reds!"

"Shut yer hole and get over there! Yer worse than a woman!"

Koba strides toward the Krawl she is hiding in. She can almost see a black cloud over his head, due no doubt to the probability that he doesn't like to expend too much energy unless it's absolutely necessary.

The leader—Boss—says, "Yosef! Zuga! Check the other Krawls down that street! See if there are any shells left we can sell the Gorkas."

There's a good deal more than that, thinks Makita. These men are clearly scavengers, looters, rogues who go from battlefield to battlefield in search of quick money on the black market. Men such as these are not famous for their scruples, and women have been known to commit suicide rather than fall into their hands. It's too bad there are so many of them, otherwise she'd try to take out as many of them as possible before running for it. Now the best thing to do is wait. To huddle in the darkness and be small.

Yet not take her eyes off the scavengers.

"Koba, how long ago, this battle?" asks Boss. He is a brutish man whose callous demeanor is reinforced by the scar tissue that covers one side of his face from the forehead to the neck. He looks like someone threw him into a hot oven.

Koba, who has a beard, rotten teeth, and a lot less scars than his leader, looks around and lights a cigarette. "Mmm. Looks like it was more of an ambush. I'd say about a week. Great. Goddamned Gorkas must have really pissed 'em off now. We'll be dodging ventral blasts for a month."

"Shut up, Koba," says the big Boss man, "and didn't I tell you to get the hell over there and check that Krawl?"

Koba strolls up, Makita hunkers down, and he raps his gloved knuckles on the exterior armor. "There's never anything in these cans. Damnit. Hey, Boss, we should think bigger, you know? This Krawl? If you took the cannon off? This would make a great tractor!"

"Koba! Idiot!" says Boss. "You were a worse farmer than you are a scavenger! Stop wasting time!"

Makita narrows her eyes. Koba'd seemed proud of his idea, and now he seems seriously deflated. She wonders if it's possible to will herself to the size of an atom.

She pushes against the wall to her back as Koba begins checking the portals, one by one.

"Hey!" he exclaims. "I thought I saw something move in there!" He peers into the darkness. "Hey, who's in there? If you're smart, we'll sell you back to your own army. If not... well... the other side'll... Oooohhh—wait a minute!" He grins and shows his blackened teeth. His breath is so bad, it fills the chamber with a foul odor. Like vodka mixed with rotten vegetables. "Hello, my darling. Don't be terrified. Uncle Koba is here. I'll protect you." He blows smoke into the chamber.

Makita coughs. It's suicide to make a noise now but she can't help it. *Forget it*, she thinks as she muffles another cough. She's already caught. The only question is: *Now what?*

"Hey, you bastards!" Koba shouts to his comrade scavengers. "It's payday. Just remember, she's mine first! I don't—"

"Shut up, Koba!" shouts the Boss, in tones that strongly hint he is completely unconcerned with anyone Koba may or may not have discovered inside the Krawl. "Look!"

Makita watches as Koba's jaw drops so far his cigarette falls out of his mouth. He goes pale. "Oh-oh," he whispers.

Makita scoots over to the portal the moment Koba steps away. The scavengers' backs are all turned toward her; they face a newcomer, a stranger, a Red sorceress in a gray greatcoat who faces them with an otherworldly confidence. Makita can't be sure—the angle of her view isn't so great—but she gets the distinct impression the sorceress' feet do not touch the ground.

"Good morning, witch," says the Boss. "I am thinking how far the Reds have fallen. This ambush just a week ago, and now sending out a sorceress alone? No wonder the Gorkas are winning this war. Stay where you are. You're ours now."

If the Red sorceress feels any fear, she certainly does not show it. Her only movement is opening and unclosing her fist, once. "Listen to me, you filthy sonofabitch," she says in cool tones that imply the emotion of hatred is too good for this crew. "Take your parasites and scavenge somewhere else. I'm here to bury these dead."

"D'ya hear that, boys? She's here to pray for her fallen

comrades! Take some advice, little witch: they don't hear you!"

The sorceress does not react for several seconds. The men wait. The wind blows strands of her blonde hair across her face. Makita notices she has a long braid that is partially concealed beneath her wide collar. She also notices the sorceress is very beautiful. She did not think it possible that a Red could be so beautiful.

Finally the sorceress makes a move: she smiles.

The scavengers laugh nervously.

"I'm only going to say this once, thief," she says. "Leave now. Or be buried with them."

"Have it your way," says the Boss. "The Gorkas pay double for dead witches." He signals and he and his men fire. Makita guesses that between them, they get off a hundred rounds in a few seconds.

Their aim is true but their bullets don't even get close. The sorceress raises a shield protocol. The bullets ricochet in all directions and the scavengers duck. One bullet hits the Krawl just above the portal through which Makita is looking, but she doesn't even flinch. She is too mesmerized by the sorceress, who is confident to the point of perfect composure behind the squares of crimson energy.

Makita is glad there aren't too many Russians like this one. She will be gladder still in a few minutes.

The sorceress speaks. "Range, first increment..." Her eyes go pure white. "Depth, one triple zero." She is bathed in crimson light. "Protocol drop..."

The scavengers stop firing. Belatedly, they realize something is up.

"*Kasting!*" says the sorceress.

Then comes the silence. A plangent silence, as it were, so great that it reverberates in Makita's mind like grisly news. It only lasts a couple of seconds.

During those seconds the snow on the ground melts, extending a radius of at least thirty meters around the sorceress.

A red maze appears on the ground. The straight lines form a hodgepodge of classic geometrical shapes. The overall effect reminds Makita of a fractured fractal.

Then the ground begins to drop away.

Or disappear, she's not really sure which.

In either case, it vanishes beneath the feet of the scavengers one shape at a time in rapid succession, much too rapidly for the men to move from the area affected by the protocol.

They fall. They grab onto the edges of the land remaining, but that part of the ground is always in another square or rectangle and it's always among the next sections to go. Judging from the diminishing echoes of their screams, their falls are long ones.

The sorceress stands on a small straight pillar of land that remains in the center of the deadly circle she has created.

The circle that keeps expanding exponentially.

Toward the Krawl Makita is hiding in.

She feels herself hanging in the air. The Krawl is dropping all around her!

She hangs only for a fraction of moment. Then she realizes, somewhat belatedly, that if the Krawl is dropping, then she must be dropping too!

She reaches the hatch just as the Krawl is turning sideways. She pulls herself out and stands beside the main artillery gun and within an instant knows what to do.

She reaches for the sickle strapped to her back and leaps.

The Krawl falls away from her.

She stretches, strains to reach a piece of sewer pipe sticking from the solid ground, thus far unaffected by the sorceress' protocol. She feels very heavy, and she curses herself for stealing those heavy boots.

To make matters worse, there is so much dust and debris created in the havoc of the protocol that she can barely see the pipe, much less what might be happening to the scavengers or the sorceress. She prayed they were all falling.

She hooks the sickle around the pipe. The metal blade cuts a full centimeter into the steel pipe, just enough to provide her with the stability to make her next move, whatever that will be. For the moment she hangs on, literally, for life.

Below her the Krawl lands with the sound of a thousand bombs and raises a thick cloud of dust.

She manages to grab both hands around the pipe. Thankfully she'd cut the fingers off her gloves long ago, otherwise she surely would not have been able to maintain her grip.

She happens to glance downward, as if she needed additional motivation to avoid this drop, and sees the letter her father had given her sticking out of her coat pocket.

Not just sticking out, but protruding precariously, at an ever-steepening angle.

It falls.

"No!" she shouts, as if the sound alone could change things.

In less time than it takes to tell—and certainly in less time than it takes to think about it, otherwise she wouldn't have even attempted this action—she releases one hand from the pipe, grabs her sickle, and brings it

down with the finesse of a butcher decapitating a chick-
en.

The point of the blade penetrates the letter. She
rejoices. She has caught it! She will not fail her father!

Now all she has to do is live through this protocol.

She throws the sickle and letter onto the ground. She
hates to be separated from either of them, but this is a
necessity. The pipe is starting to tilt and she knows she
doesn't have much time. Less, even, than before.

She pulls herself up and, moving hand-over-hand,
reaches the edge of the pit.

She digs the fingers of one hand into the frozen
ground, finds a foothold in the wall, and pulls herself
onto the surface. Only then does she dare contemplate
the possibility that she has once again avoided her
demise.

She grabs the sickle and the letter and runs away from
there as fast as possible. She does not look back until
she feels she is a safe distance away, about a hundred
meters.

"Damn witches!" she exclaims, panting. She kisses the
letter. "Close one, Papa," she whispers. "Close one."

Makita sees the witch is walking away, disappearing
into the smoke and the rubble. She puts the letter in her
pocket—her upper pocket, inside her coat, this time—and
slips away in the opposite direction. She does not want
to admit it—it is very contrary to her character—but right
now she wants to get as far away from that sorceress as
possible.

Maya watched the ground slip away and the scavengers
fall with a heavy heart. Her power was fueled by anger
and a thirst for vengeance, though not against them in
particular. They happened to be convenient targets. As

wandering looters, men devoid of idealism or ideology, patriotism or nationalism, their disposal was as much a favor to the Nokgorkans as it was to the Fleet.

Damn you, Urik, for protecting me, she thought. *I should have been here with Alexandria's column a week ago. Not exterminating parasites after we lost the battle.*

She waited until most of the noise at the bottom of the abyss she had created had ceased. The protocol had left a narrow land bridge but it wasn't very sturdy and would remain standing for only a little while longer. So she could not tarry long, unless she wanted to waste ectoplasmic energy on an anti-gravity spell. She did pause halfway across the bridge though, to peer down into the darkness which she had created.

Where are you, Alexandra? I would have died in Al'istaan if not for you. This time I'm not leaving. And you're not here to save me. Either I find you, or the 'Gorkas get me first. Either way.

I've seen enough of this world.

Minutes passed, and for time the scene of Maya's protocol seemed as uneventful as a tableau of a deserted battle-field. Dust settled, a few more rocks fell, that was all.

Then a large gloved hand grasped the edge of the abyss and the scavenger Koba pulled himself up. "Bastard—red witches—didn't—get—me! Not Koba! Not me!"

Koba was exhausted. The long climb up the abyss had been the most physically strenuous undertaking of his life. He had no idea what his next move would be; it would probably be twofold: ingratiate himself with another gang of scavengers, and stay as far away from that witch as possible. But for the moment, he had to pause and catch his breath before pulling himself all the way onto the surface. He drank in great gulps of cold air. They were marvelous. It was too bad all his buddies were dead. Too bad. But he was alive! Alive!

Suddenly he heard the crunch of gravel beneath a heavy booted foot. He knew that sound because he had made it himself, many times, and so had his comrades, the ones who were now dead. Belatedly, he realized he should have been paying more attention to his surroundings.

A man stood not two meters before him. A big man with a bald head and narrow steel eyes. Judging from his uniform, and all the redundant connections between his body and the heavy automatic rifle strapped to his arm, he was a Hailer. A man whose sole purpose in life was to guard and protect Red witches.

"Oh no," said Koba. He was not above begging. It had worked before. "Please. Please. I didn't shoot at her. I mean—I mean—"

The Hailer stepped forward and raised his weapon.

Koba got a good view of the barrel. It had the largest diameter of any such heavy automatic he'd ever seen.

"Mercy!" Koba said. "Mercy!" He would have cried if he'd known how. "Mercy!"

Kyuzo tightened his fist around the trigger.

One shot, that was all it took.

The scavenger's brains splattered in such an arc that gray matter made it all the way to the other side of the abyss.

Kyuzo waited until he heard the impact of the falling body against the bottom of the abyss. It wasn't a long wait, as these things go, but it was satisfying.

He turned toward the tiny figure of Maya Antares, far in the distance. It was second nature for him to visualize her determined stride down this corridor. She would find what she was looking for, and she would dare any man or woman to stop her.

He opened up a telepathic channel. "Guardsman Kyuzo to Sorcery Corps. This is Kyuzo. Come in, Corps. I'm groundside with the Major. No, nothing she can't handle yet. But she's headed into a Gorka zone. Just ready a strike team. Hailers, and track my position. Have them standing by to drop in. Tell them to be ready—for anything."

He continued to follow, a respectful distance away. If she wanted to be alone, he would allow her to think that she was alone. But there was no way he would permit harm to come to her. No harm would ever come to her. Not so long as he had ammunition to fire, and a drop of blood in his heart.

CHAPTER TWELVE

In the week since the Krawl column ambush, the Nokgorkan Resistance Army has been pushed back to several, less strategically significant sectors of Bahamut. The Reds occupy the airport, train stations, the few remaining food storages, the ruins of the buildings of government authority, and the museums, which they were busy looting. But the Reds in no way control the city. Makita had had no trouble reaching the latest anti-Krawl artillery position. It was only a few kilometers away from the gravesite.

She found Dushka leaning against the carriage, his elbow resting on the elevating wheel, and his helmet tilted back on his head. His eyes were watching something in the smoky sky, no doubt something found only in his imagination. Next to the great gun, he looked like a mouse resting against a giraffe.

He was alone. Her sudden appearance surprised him; he nearly jumped out of his skin and choked on whatever it was he was chewing. A trickle of brown liquid ran down his chin, and his complexion was rather green. When he regained his composure he leaned on the other side of the gun and spat out the Trans chewing tobacco.

Makita smiled. She'd heard some Trans contraband

had come into town before all the fighting started. The others had found some black market stash and Fushka was trying to keep up with the men in the outfit.

It was good to see him. It had been a week...

"Makita. I heard about the Red counterattack after the ambush!" he said. "I heard you were wounded."

"You heard wrong! There's a Red witch in our zone! A mean one! Where's the rest of the gun crew?"

"They're on patrol. We've been short-handed lately."

"Yeah, I heard. What if—?"

"Oh, me and Olga can fire her. It just takes longer."

"Where is Olga?"

Dushka shrugs. "I think she's seeing somebody." He points to some ruins across where there used to be a street. "She said she'd be right back, but I don't think she's going to be." He winks. "Got a target in mind?"

"No, by the time we've got the angle, we'll have no shot. Give me your field glasses."

"Where's Proto?"

Makita freezes.

"Makita?"

"Give me your field glasses, I said."

He nods and hands them over. "It's just that a lot of people haven't been heard from since the ambush, but everyday someone you think is—is—you know, somebody pops up."

Makita guides him to the steps of a nearby ruin. From their vantage point, they have an excellent view of the corridor below, and the solitary figure walking in the middle of the street is wide open and clearly daring someone to make a move.

"You see?" Makita asks, focusing on the Red sorceress. "She's a strange one. But powerful. I saw her take out some black market boys who were scavenging near the ambush zone."

Dushka takes a rifle sight from his coat pocket and gets her in his crosshairs. He regrets not having the rifle to go along with it, but then again, he isn't noted for his accuracy with projectiles. "Is she lost?" he asks.

Makita shakes her head.

"Maybe she's gone bye-bye. Snapped. One too many protocols or something."

Makita adjusts some controls and the blue picture of the sorceress pushes in. The woman lacks definite survival skills, in the wolf cub's opinion. She looks straight ahead, but never around. As if she's a pre-cog who could predict the trajectory of a bullet.

Only problem with that concept is, pre-cogs are very rare. After all, pre-cogs are only human, and humans make mistakes. When a pre-cog makes a mistake, it tends to be definitive.

"No, you haven't seen her up close," says Makita. "That one has the fire of the Devil in her. She's looking for someone. Best to take her out while we have the chance. Dushka, give me your comline. I'm going to call Yarka."

"Okay, but don't misuse the privilege. I just got it back!"

Makita has just about dialed in Yarka's code when suddenly it occurs to her: "Is this a secure line? How long since you checked it?"

Dushka slaps his forehead. "Oh Makita! It's fine! You always make everything so complicated!"

"Fine. Idiot. Don't cry to me when the Reds attack your position and blast you to paste!"

Dushka reached for his comline. "You don't have to use it. But you'd better make up your mind before the Red's out of range!"

Makita considers her options. She pointedly dials Yarka's code. "Yarka! Come in! It's Makita! Witch in our zone! You should see her now."

Yarka is a sniper; his current position is in the top floor of a ruined skyscraper, a former KBG building. He had really been on the lookout for Krawls—he is a precise but unimaginative thinker who tends to follow orders so closely to the letter that he cannot see the words—but Makita prods him into focusing on the tiny figure walking down the center of the deserted streets. Ya. There she is. What is she, crazy? What the Hell is she doing down here?"

"Don't know," Makita answers. "Don't care. But I know she has auto-shields—do you have any protocol piercing rounds on you?"

"Not that I'm willing to waste on one sorceress! Got to save them for Krawl-busting."

"I didn't ask your opinion! Get a shot and take it!"

Dushka buries his face in his hands. You don't talk to a sniper that way, especially one who is (in)famous for being very particular about his targets.

"Hey, hey, my little Makinoshka. I took orders from your papa, God rest his soul, not from his little girl. Besides, what's in it for me—especially since you are just a little girl?"

"I won't be little forever," Makita replies.

"Hmmm, fascinating, but bitter experience has taught me some investments don't pay off."

"To Hell with you!" Makita shouts. "You're a lousy shot anyway. I'll call Belomor! I'm sure he wouldn't mind having a witch on his kill-list! Why would I think you'd want to finally do something in this war anyway?"

"Why you little—!"

"Curse me on your own time! Take that shot!"

Yarka feels himself capitulating. What kind of man is he, he wonders, to be so susceptible to the manipulations of a little girl. Well, perhaps she is right, perhaps she'll live long enough to be a big girl and he will be able to take her advantage, as the Asians say. "Alright, already! Anything to shut you up!"

Immediately he regrets being so undiplomatic. Well, he knows how to make it up to her.

He gets the sorceress in his sights. She has a pretty little head. Too bad she is about to lose it.

"I'll show that scrawny little cockroach some shooting," he whispers to himself. Yarka is a careful shot. Some call him too careful, but he rarely misses. "Breathe... slowly..." he says; he is always working on his technique.

The protocol-piercing bullet slips into its chamber. Yarka waits. He likes to have a perfect shot. "Come now, pretty sorceress," he says. "Stand still—for a moment—Yes!"

So intent is he on his target that he neglects to pay attention to his survival training.

In other words, he forgets to watch his back. He fails to notice the big Hailer creeping behind him.

Even if he does notice the Hailer, it will do him no good. He will be dead the second he turns his head around, meaning he will be dead a second later, that is all...

On the ground Makita and Dushka wait. They wait for several minutes. They know that sometimes Yarka can be too meticulous for the good of the cause, but this is ridiculous. Makita watches in frustration as the sorceress slowly but surely moves out of the sniper's range. "Now! Now! What the hell is he doing?" she asks aloud. "Why the hell didn't he shoot?"

A rhetorical question, Dushka figures, so he says nothing.

Makita opens the comlink. "Yarka! What the hell happened?"

No answer. Not even static.

"Yarka! Come in! Come in, damn you! Yarka! Damnit!"

What she doesn't know, but gradually begins to suspect, is that Yarka is somewhat hung up at the moment.

And as her suspicion turns to certainty, Makita scowls. "Who are you, witch? What in Hell is watching over you?"

She strides off.

"Makita? Where are you going?" asks Dushka.

"I'm finished trying to rely on anyone. I'll kill her myself!"

"Makita! Wait! Don't go! *Makita!*"

But he cannot stop her, he cannot leave his position. Indeed, if the gun is needed before Olga gets back from her tryst, they could both be court-martialed. Meaning that they would be summarily found guilty and executed.

On her way out of the Nokgorkia zone, Makita sees Yarka, hanging from a rope ladder near his position high up the building. *Whoever did that to him is obviously making a statement,* she thinks, *but I am not listening!*

Unaware she was being followed by friend and foe, and in fact, still unconcerned if she was being followed or not, Maya Antares thought of a book she had read and reread during her days at the Academy.

The princess, alone, stood shivering in the city of the dead. Whispering to herself so as not hear the moaning of the damned. Lifeless faces stared back at her.

She wondered how the idealistic youth had evolved into the hopelessly romantic yet emotionally barren woman she was today. It could not have been merely the loss of life, the tragic waste, the shattered ideals, the cynical government betrayals, the physical pain she had endured, witnessing the degradation others put themselves through to escape reality—others had lived through all that and more and come out the other side nobler and wiser creatures. The old man Vanya, for instance. No, there had to be something more. There had to be a reason why she would not, could not let go of her passion for Marcus. She did not dare think it was her destiny to love him and no other, that was presumptuous, and she certainly did not believe he would have stayed as true to her if their circumstances had been reversed (though part of her hoped so). But Marcus had been too vital, too much alive every second of the day, to close himself off from the opposite sex simply because it was within his power to grieve afresh every day for a decade. He would have grieved and then he would have gotten on with the business of living.

Of course, Maya did not think living should be a business. That was a Transnational way of looking at existence, a way that had infected the purity of the quest for utopia.

Then again, there was the example of Alexandra. She too had endured a profound disappointment that was in its own way far more tragic than what Maya had endured. And yet Alex had not believed for a minute that she should put the rest of her life on hold because things hadn't worked out like she'd planned. It had been difficult, extremely difficult, but she had done it.

More thoughts, similar thoughts worried Maya when she reached the immolation area and came upon the couple that had burned and died together in an embrace. There was no way of telling if they had been freedom fighters or merely civilians who happened to be in the wrong place at the wrong time. Their clothes and skin had been burned off and all that remained, really, was simply charred meat. Now they were frozen and would remain so until the thawing of the spring.

Maya saw no reason why they should wait for the final desolution to come. She closed her eyes, waved, and said softly, "Rest now. Rest."

Their legs and torso began to crumble. They sank into ash and dust of their own making. Throughout their embrace remained, their heads continued to touch.

"It's the least I can do," said Maya. She dropped her hand and tried to control the overwhelming sorrow welling inside her. It grew even as the two dead lovers dissolved.

"So many ghosts, Alexandra. How will I put you to rest?"

There was nothing else for her to do but to continue, to continue onward.

Unbeknownst to the Red sorceress, the wold cub named Makita watches. She does not understand—what does this witch want? What is she searching for?

Yet, as she stares at the pool of white light that emanates, then fades, in the place where the burned lovers had been locked in their unending embrace, she whispers aloud, "Hmmm. Not a bad way to go to the next life."

Better than any she has ever witnessed.

None of this dampens her resolve. She has a mission, and that mission is more important than any other consideration.

Utilizing her stealth training to the utmost, she shadows the sorceress.

Unbeknownst to Makita, the Hailer named Kyuzo watched her. He had no idea what the wolf cub was thinking; he did not care what thoughts might have occurred to her as she watched Maya scatter the lovers' ashes.

When the cub was out of hearing distance, but not yet out of sight, he opened up his telepathic comlink and said aloud, to spare his head from aching, "Kyuzo to Sorcery Corps. Reporting on the Major's status. We're closing in on the exact location of the ambush that claimed Captain Goncharova's column. But the Major has picked up a scout. Order stands as called: have my strike team ready to drop in immediately—if and when I give word. The scout won't be any problem. When she makes her move, I'll drop her."

CHAPTER THIRTEEN

The rays of the setting sun hit stretches of ground that had been inaccessible to it before the rebellion, when Bahamut had been a rich and thriving city. The buildings possessed only remnants of their former facades, and the steel of their substructures exposed and twisted like massive pieces of stale candy.

The air still reeked of ash and smoke, the lingering evidence of the protocols used to power and augment the battle equipment. The odor always hung in the air that way, impervious to the sweeping of the wind currents, for weeks after the conclusion of battle.

Broken Krawls, burnt-out husks, ironic reminders of the former might of the URRS, littered the streets like the forgotten toys of an indifferent giant.

There were the bodies, of course. Red and Nokgorkan Resistance alike. Left behind to freeze in the winter, to thaw and decay in the coming spring, until the fighting was over and the cleanup could begin.

At last I'm ready, Maya thought as she walked on the battlefield. *Ready to leave forever. I've got nothing here, nothing left. Not for ten years now. The sun sets one last time for me. I've come to put us both to rest, old friend.*

Then Maya Antares realized she was too late.

There were two makeshift graves on the battlefield. Each had two pieces of wood nailed and tied to the markers. One grave read PROTO, and then LOVE, carved with a knife.

The other read GONCHAROVA—it was her nametag—and MERCY. Also carved with a knife.

Alex had already been buried. But by whom? And for what reason?

As for this Proto... well, Proto was a Gorkian nickname. Maya had served with a couple of Protos, before the province had tried to break away. Who in the center of this conflict—this bitter conflict—would single out a Red and Nokgorkan for burial?

Love? And mercy? Maya thought. *I've stepped into the surreal. A dreamworld. This can't be.*

Breath, damn it. That's it. Be calm. I've planned well. I have the perfect protocol for this mystery...

Meanwhile, waiting over her as usual, Kyuzo hunkered down on the fifth or sixth story—it was difficult to tell which—of a decimated skyscraper. From here he had a good view of the entire battlefield. He too was curious about the graves (though he could not read the markers) and he wondered why the Major had paused for such a long period.

He received a communication.

"Go ahead, Konstantinov. I'm here."

"We can't locate the enemy scout. If she is reporting to the Gorka command, she must also be using a transpathic signal protocol."

"Hm. So we both lost her."

"Do you think you were spotted?"

"No, she just knows how to keep her head down. She's good. No matter. She's not far. Kyuzo out. Standby."

He did not know that the scout he was moderately

worried about—he had no doubt that when the time came, he could snuff out her life like a candle in a rainstorm—was on the opposite side of the battlefield, hunkered down on the first floor of another ruin.

Makita wonders why the sorceress has paused at the graves.

A telepathic signal comes in—rummaging inside her head like a buzzing fly of monstrous proportions. *"Makita! Report status of the Red Warkaster!"*

Makita wasn't ready; she is still trying to formulate her thinking on the matter. "She looks like she's... praying."

"Praying? Why the Hell would a godless Red be—"

"You heard me. So listen. Until the Elders finally decide to send me some heavy attack support, stay out of my brain. Damn transpathic signal protocols give me a headache! Hmm.... Can it be? It's almost as if... as if..."

"As if what?"

"Nothing. Just thinking. Go away. Makita out."

Makita watches, and thinks. Her need to kill this woman, this *dangerous* woman remains undiminished by all other considerations, especially those of her personal safety, yet she once again must suppress the disconcerting feeling that a Red can be human.

Maya walked between the graves and surveyed the battlefield. *Love and mercy,* she thought. *Strange words to see here. Dead Nokgorkans, dead Reds. We were countrymen, not long ago. Often reluctantly, yes, but is this better? The living, the dead, all of us hardening in the cold?*

She opened her comlink. She spoke in her normal tone of voice, confidently, assuredly. "Major Antares to Central Informnet. Notification of use of advanced protocol being registered at Mark 81668-33-Bahamut, former Republic of Nokgorkia."

She had to wait a few minutes. Confirmation would not be verbal, but she would feel it in her energy level, in the ectoplasmic increase.

The wind moaned as it wound through the stranded Krawls. Maya looked at the bodies buried under a minute layer of snow and shook her head. A man laid nearby with the back of his skull torn complete off. A woman was slumped against a Krawl and a Red soldier lay in three pieces on the top of a Krawl that had suffered a direct hit by a projectile blast.

Maya had no illusions that what she was about to do would have any effect on the future, but she hoped it would give the future meaning, somehow. That she would know all this death wasn't simply useless warmongering.

She received the confirmation.

Very well, then. This will be a painful Kast. But I simply have to know.

She unhitched her backpack, opened it, and took out what was called in the vernacular a Merlin Cocktail, but was officially designated a Temporal Dislocation Trigger Flash. Basically it was a pewter vial with an iridescent fuse that was ignited by breaking off its shell cap. She broke it and tossed the vial high in the air, augmenting her strength with a silent anti-gravity protocol providing her toss with that extra push needed to take the vial above the forty meter mark; anything less and she would have wasted a valuable Cocktail.

"Kasting: Reenact protocol!" *Remember to close my eyes. The first flash is always the worst.*

As usual, Kyuzo had no idea what the Major was up to until she actually began doing it. He felt his gut tighten the moment she threw the Cocktail higher in the air than she could have done utilizing merely her own strength. At that point it was possible for the resulting light to have been any number of colors, depending on what type of spell she was kasting.

The initial glow was crimson; that should have been Kyuzo's first hint to to close his eyes.

As it was he was a second late, long enough for the brilliant white flare to seer his optic nerves with agonizing sensory overloads. Even after his eyes were close, the flare hurt. Even with his head turned away and his arm over his eyes, the flare inflicted torture.

"Damn R.E. protocol!" he exclaimed. "Damn sorceress engineers! Why do they have to make all the powerful protocols so painful?"

On the opposite side of the battlefield, having been caught in the flare without warning, Makita expresses Kyuzo's sentiments in far less lofty terms.

"Tracking time of death of Captain Goncharova, 131st Armored Brigade. Tracking to Time of Death to five minutes."

Maya felt her teeth grinding so hard she was afraid she'd have to prevail upon the State Dentist to provide her with several rows of fresh caps. *R.E.P.—always the same*, she thinks. *Light so blinding even with eyes closed. Body always refuses to expose the eyes to it.*

But the protocol required for the kaster to open her eyes before the light would diminish enough for her to perceive the events reenacted, indeed, before the events would even begin. Right now the images from the past were caught somewhere between the two points in the dimension of time.

Always have to force them... force them open... force them to see...

Suddenly she was there, wrapped in an illusion of the past. The illumination decreased just enough so she (and other onlookers) could see without suffering undue agony. Colors were washed out, but faces, uniforms, and actions were all clear, with the illusion of spontaneity complete. Maya knew something of the chaos of combat so before she even tried to get her bearings she said, "Protocol, slow it down. Run scenario at two-thirds."

Slowing to two-thirds speed, said the protocol.

Maya saw combatants on both sides fighting and dying. A Krawl was in the midst of being consumed by flame, fueled by gasoline thrown in a homemade bomb. Maya heard the sounds of weapons. The sounds of people yelling in frustration, and screaming in pain. The deep bass tone of a Krawl exploding somewhere, perhaps outside the radius of the protocol. But any sound which had reached the ears of the people represented by these images would also be recreated. Even the shadows of blood splattering from freshly opened wounds was recreated.

It was all there, just as it had been on the day Alex had died. At two-thirds speed, the combat seemed like a tragic dance of violent patterns, a horrifying ritual sacrifice. The words of the Fleet Manual came to mind: *The R.E.P. is the sorceress's ultimate forensic resource for unlocking the events of the past.* Maya regarded those words as Lies. With a capital L.

The past is a prison, she thought. *Its bars and chains forged by the Lord himself. No one has ever escaped. These illusions walk lines of fate that can never be broken. As they fell that day, so do they fall before me.*

As if to prove the veracity of her observation, a free-dom fighter shot a bullet that passed completely through her, striking a Red soldier behind her. Well, it was the illusion of a bullet, and it struck the illusion of a Red.

"Protocol, locate... locate Captain Goncharova."

Locating, said the protocol. It guided Maya to the other side of a tank, where Alex and Renko were caught between factions of freedom fighters.

"Freeze scenario!" Maya ordered.

Holding.

Alex was bringing her weapon around to fire at a Nokgorkan trying to run past the two stranded Krawls. She and Renko were watching one another's back. They were both brave fighters, and they refused to give in to defeat, perhaps because unlike Maya, they were always sure about what they were fighting for. Maya found it bittersweet seeing the image of Alex doing what she did best for the last time in her life. She wanted to touch her, but knew it was impossible. What she saw was only an artificial recreation of her friend. Light and sound, nothing more.

The soul had long since fled.

"Resume scenario," said Maya, her own soul feeling quite weighed down at the moment. "Change speed to eight-tenths."

The replay had reached the point where Maya and Alex were communicating via comlinks. Maya's stomach turned to acid as she heard anew the controlled under-current of desperation in her friend's voice.

She cared for hearing her own, shrill and helpless, even less. She was one of those people who couldn't stand to hear recordings of her voice under the best of circumstances; this one was just painful, so she had the protocol erase the audio track containing her voice.

She got close to Alex as her friend leaned against the Krawl. Maya could see clearly what she had been afraid to imagine before: Alex's face as she struggled to accept the fact that this situation was at last the one she would not get out of alive.

Damn you, Urik, she thought. *If I had been here, I could have saved her. I could have saved all of them.*

Actually, she could not a hundred percent certain of that. But the enemy in both Al'istaan and Nokgorkia tended to be a lot more cautious whenever a sorceress was assigned to a combat unit.

"Maya, stop it," said Alex a week ago. "By the time you get here, we'll be food for the dogs."

"I'm sorry, Alex," cried Maya.

"I'll be sure to tell Marcus—"

"I'm sorry I wasn't here!"

"—how much you missed him."

"I failed Marcus at Al'istaan. I failed you here."

"Goncharova out."

"Why, Alex? Why am I the one who lives—while everyone I loved died around me?" She fell to her knees and her real tears began to fall in the illusion of snow. "I came to say, I came here hoping, hoping that your ghost might be waiting for me."

"Looks like this it, Renko," said Alex.

"Yeah, I heard," said Renko.

"Because I can't be alone anymore," Maya cried.

Wide-eyed and filled with her own measure of grief, Makita comes to the conclusion that the sorceress *did* know the woman of mercy. She has no idea what this means, or what difference it might make in the near future, because her ambition to kill the sorceress remains undiminished.

But it *is* interesting.

Makita watches as Goncharova's fighting companion

goes down. She knows what is going to happen next, but it no less disturbing for all that.

She has never watched herself in the past before. She has not suspected such things were even possible.

And for a moment she admires herself, she is proud of the way she leaps from the tank with her sickle held out, and she thinks it only right and proper that she tried to kill the enemy.

Then she is ashamed at the expression on her face, which she can perceive even from a distance. It has never before occurred to her that she could be just like those on the other side: an inhuman killing machine, fighting not for one's country or ideals but simply to can fight and kill.

Makita watches in horror as the Goncharova woman catches her in mid-flight and hurls her to the ground. Makita had never suspected the move was accomplished so easily for this woman, who surely must have been a master warrior. For the first time Makita recognizes the full extent of Goncharova's mercy. This woman could have snuffed her out at any moment.

This woman may have been the only human being on the battlefield. Everyone else was simply an animal.

This woman. No one else.

It cannot have been this way. "Damn witches," mumbles Makita, her hand over her mouth. The witch must be manipulating reality, somehow. She must be.

"Freeze Reenact!" shouts the witch.

Holding.

"Protocol. Will Captain Goncharova pull the trigger on this child?"

Makita angrily bites her lower lip, stifling the urge to speak up. Who's a child?

Negative. Nokgorka trooper does not terminate within temporal radius of protocol.

That's better. The spell calls her a trooper, at least. Respect from the ether is better than none at all.

Spatial radius, however, indicates...

"Is the weapon that will kill Captain Goncharova within protocol radius?" interrupts the sorceress, who evidently doesn't respect the ether nearly as much as the ether respects her.

Plotting shot trajectory... Affirmative...

The sorceress turns her head and her jaw drops.

Makita gasps. Not having been privy to the purpose of the spell, it had not occurred to her that the events to be portrayed would include the death of the merciful Red woman—and what came after.

"My God, Urik was right," the sorceress whispers, just loud enough for Makita to make out her words. "They're all so young!"

Command inaudible. Repeat. Obviously, the protocol is easily confused.

"Nothing to command. Can you I.D. the Gorka?"

Scanning...

But Makita knows. She huddles against a stone, and when she looks one way she can see the shooter, and when she looks the other she can see the sorceress and the image of the merciful woman.

She knows what is going to happen. And she does not think she can bear to watch it again.

"Proto," she cries, softly. "My Proto. Not again."

Proto has a bead directly on the Red woman's back. And she has a bead directly on the image of Makita. This is the moment when Goncharova hesitated, the moment Makita knows she will never fully comprehend.

Scan failed. Unable to identify Gorka trooper.

"No matter," says the sorceress. "Resume. Resume Reenact."

"Who the hell would send a goddamned child—" says Goncharova.

And Makita has tears streaming down her face as she looks at the image of Proto, the grief she has denied herself all this time finally overpowers her with the force of a tidal wave, she experiences rage, denial, loss, and futility simultaneously, each emotion more powerful than she believed herself or anyone capable of. Together the emotions are greater than their component parts.

"Please, God, please, God," says the image of Proto. "Don't... don't take her away from me. Can't miss... can't miss... will NOT miss. Just hit it, Proto, just hit the target, boy. Makita! Stay down!"

And he fires.

The end, of course, is preordained, not by fate, but by history.

"No more, no more. Go on, damn you. Go on and live."

Those were the last words spoken by Alexandra Goncharova, and they were also the words spoken, like a prayer, by Makita as the tears streamed down her face, as she wondered why human bodies did not break under the weight of such sorrow.

At that moment the protocol informed Maya Antares that Alex had less than two seconds to live.

But she is a survivor, thought Maya. *They say she can dodge a bullet before it is even fired. She would never let down her guard. Why?*

With a wave of the hand Maya kast a telepathic protocol. Peering into the mind of a reenactment illusion was painful, never easy, and could cause brain damage in the not quite adept. Maya was extremely adept and what's more, she knew that only in this moment did she have a chance to discover what was going on in Alex's inner space. Only there could the real mystery of her demise be solved.

And what Maya saw—no, what she experienced was profound depression, a mammoth attack of existential futility and despair that seemed more insightful and more noble than any Maya had assigned to herself.

So Alex's skill and instinct had not failed her after all. She simply had an uncharacteristic moment of weakness, brought upon by the sudden and inexplicable feeling of love she had for the wolf cub who had tried to kill her.

And there was no fear, no despair, no regret indicated on Alex's face, only complete, consummate love, as she looked upon the wolf cub and said, "Brave little girl..."

Those were her last words. The shot rang out and she fell. And the only thing she felt as she died was love, love for the girl, love for the boy who had killed her, love for Maya, love for Marcus, and love for the men she had loved, even love for Urik, whom she had thought she had not loved. But she had. Maya could read that quite well. In fact, she was on the verge of loving him more than she had ever loved anyone. If only she had survived this bloody, useless war.

Maya covered her eyes. She did not think she could endure this image any longer.

Then the boy—Proto—shouted, "Makita, are you all right?" He had jumped up, the love and concern were plainly apparent in his voice, but what was missing was the studied detachment of the genuine warrior. He had exposed himself.

YOU buried them, didn't you, little girl? thought Maya, forcing herself to watch as a Red soldier spotted Proto and shot him in the back of the head.

"Proto! Behind you!" shouted the image of the girl.

The projectile exited his forehead. Most of his skull was blown to bits.

"Get down!" said the image, too late.

"Get down!" said the girl herself, rushing out of hiding. Running toward the image of the boy who'd thought he was saving her life.

Maya gasped. She recognized that the wolf cub was quite a soldier, but essentially just a child. And although Maya was surprised to see that the girl in question had been eavesdropping on the protocol, she was not surprised at the girl's reaction. The child had simply forgotten that it was all an illusion of things that had been. Maya found it painful to see the realization overtake the child, to see her remember, that she had already lived through this and could never go back.

The real girl tried to join her illusion and embrace the illusion of the dead boy, the poor dead boy who she had been able to hold in her arms for the last time one week before. But of course she could not embrace the illusion. She could only watch in frustration as the girl of a week ago was comforted and saved by the older, wiser freedom fighters, who reminded her that Proto was gone and they were still in the middle of a fire fight.

To see an R.E.P. for the first time often had such effects.

The girl's reaction was typical. She was filled with white-hot rage. She believed the person who kast the protocol was the person responsible for her pain.

She took her hammer and her sickle off her back, screamed, and charged.

Maya had an instant to assess the situation. She understood that the boy was the girl's "Love" and that Alexandra was the stranger bearing "Mercy." Both of them had been ripped from her in one bloody moment. Maya and the girl were much alike: they were two survivors who had not wanted to survive their loved ones. They were two scavengers crawling through a ruin. And they were two enemies sworn to destroy one another.

Maya made her decision. She turned toward the rooftops of the ruined buildings and shouted at the top of her voice, "Kyuzo! Hold your fire!"

And from those rooftops, there was only silence.

Maya smiled. She could easily imagine Kyuzo scowling, fighting his every instinct to do away with this nuisance once and for all.

Then the girl jumped Maya and tried to bury the sickle in her heart and bang the hammer on her head. Maya grabbed the girl's wrists and tried to control her. The girl was fast. Strong. For a moment Maya wondered if she'd made a mistake. Hand-to-hand combat was never her forte.

The girl managed to punch Maya on the jaw.

This only made Maya angry, and her anger fed her strength. "Damnit, if I wanted to kill you, you'd be dead. You know that!"

"Go to hell!" said the girl. She spit on Maya's face.

Maya put her hand on the girl's face and pushed her away. "You want me to kill you! Fine, then! I'll do it!"

But of course she did not. Like her friend Alex, she didn't have the heart for it. They struggled, and Maya talked, saying the first things that popped into her head, hoping to penetrate the girl's rage until some common sense kicked in. "I've seen what you lost! How long now since Prorto's been gone? A week? That's a terrible time. A lot of hatred, guilt, tears. Tears when you're alone. When I lost my love to war, I knew there would never be another like him—another who loved me the way he did. Please, I know what it is that's been taken from you—how brave he was—how scared he was to lose you. I saw him save you. Please, don't let it be for nothing."

Makita did not know how it happened, but suddenly she had stopped fighting and she only had the strength to cry.

"That's it," whispered Maya. "Let it go. Let it all out. Soldiers can cry, too. Don't let the boys fool you. Thank you, by the way, for putting Goncharova to rest. From what I've seen of you, little ferocious one, you and Alex would have gotten along perfectly. Tell me, is Makita your real name, or your soldier's name?" Maya felt the girl relax and so she released her just enough so they could look one another in the eye. "I'm Maya. Maya Antares."

The girl dropped her sickle. She pushed back and grabbed the lapels of Maya's coat and for the first time could see the nametag on her uniform. "It can't be!" she exclaimed. "It can't be you!" *Papa, why didn't you tell me?* "Let me go! Let me go!"

"What's wrong?" Maya was not quite ready to release the girl, but the girl struggled so fiercely she felt she had no choice but to let her go.

Makita fell on her rear and scooted back. She did not try to get up. "I know of you!"

Maya raised an eyebrow. The expression on the girl's face was almost worshipful, and although Maya recognized that she possessed many sterling personal qualities, she had not thought herself capable of eliciting that sort of response. "How? Why do you know of me?"

Makita got on her knees. "I made a promise. A promise to my father. He told me... He told me you would know."

Maya tensed as the girl reached into her oversized coat with her left hand. Her every combat instinct told her the girl was reaching for a weapon, that she was being treacherous, but she had learned long ago that most combat instincts were in truth the conditioning brought about by combat training, and did not necessarily apply to every situation, even in a war zone.

Makita withdrew the letter and held it for Maya. The letter was in even worse condition than it had been when her father had given it to her. It was crumpled, had gotten wet, and there was the hole Makita's sickle had made in it when she almost dropped it down the pit Maya had made.

But the condition was the last thing on Maya's mind. The handwriting on the folded page—spelling out the word *Antares*—was in a disturbingly familiar style.

Disturbing because she had not seen a fresh sample of it for nearly ten years.

The writing is in his hand! she thought, accepting the unbelievable.

She tried to read the words, but her hands shook too much and her eyes welled with tears. Breathing was more difficult than seeing. But at the bottom of the page was the single most important thing: the signature.

It read simply *Marcus* and it was genuine!

In the city of the dead, my love returns to life, she thought, and the world is new once more! Marcus. I've found you! I've found you!

Not really, of course. She had been able to grasp enough of the meaning of the letter to know that this modest communication had been achieved against great odds, that it was merely the first step of their journey toward reunitement.

Maya put the letter next to her heart and fell on her knees before the child and looked down into her eyes. "You beautiful child."

"Me?"

"You beautiful beautiful beautiful child. Thank you, thank you." *Alexandra, if you had pulled the trigger, I never would have known.* "You say your father knew me?"

Makita nodded.

"Well, we Russians and Nokgorkans weren't always enemies, at least not to this extent. What was your father's name?"

She told her.

Maya gasped. She would have thought the news that Marcus was still alive would have made her immune against more shocks derived from this terrible war, but obviously that was not the case. "Of course, I knew your father. We fought together during the war in Al'istaan, but I knew him better before the war."

"Did you know my mother?"

Maya nodded. "I met her...once. You have her eyes." *Oh Alexandra, if you had pulled the trigger, you would have killed your own daughter.*

From the spirit plane, the woman in red looked down on what had transpired with a mixture of trepidation and gratitude.

Well done, my little wolf. Well done. You deserve this moment of comfort, both of you. Enjoy it, while you can. You have found the path. The path to Marcus. The path to our people's hope. But the road is long, comrades. Long... And an army of the damned stands before you.

CHAPTER FOURTEEN

The clear sky in the moments before the dawn is an indication that the thaw of spring is coming, however precipitously, but as far as Makita is concerned, the temperature remains as cold as polar bear spit. And it is no wonder, as this is the first time Makita has experienced the extra bone-chill of standing on a skyfurnace deck a thousand meters above the ground.

It is obvious that she is airsick and having difficulty maintaining her balance. Three or four times already the huge hand—and she means *huge*—of the Hailer Kyuzo has clamped down on her shoulder and prevented her from going over the railing. She does not appreciate his touch, she endured quite enough of it when the Sorceress Maya Antares "suggested" she return to the *Konstantinov* with them. When Makita suggests what Maya Antares could do with her suggestion, Kyuzo simply grunted, picked her up like a flask of vodka, and carried her through the transfer gate.

"I'll kill you!" she said.

And as he stepped onto the other side, Kyuzo merely smiled. "The Chihuahua has a loud bark," was all he said.

So far she has a low opinion of the Reds gathered alone on the uppermost deck of the skyfurnace. They have demonstrated some trust of her for reasons she cannot understand. Why have they not disarmed her? Why is she here with them, theoretically participating in this exclusive, secretive meeting? There is Kyuzo, of course; he shadows the sorceress with the grace and ease of a thought. Every time Makita sees him, she cannot resist glaring. She tells herself she has killed bigger fish than this one, but she suspects she has at last met her match.

As for the Sorceress, she is staggeringly oblivious to Makita's sarcasm, resentment, suspicion, warriorlike bloodlust, and loathing of all things Red. Makita is not certain who Maya sees when she looks at her, but that person is a nurturing, loving individual, someone Makita believes died when Proto died. Makita has done her part; she has given the sorceress the letter, now why won't the sorceress leave her alone?

Then there is this Chief Engineer, Andre Torin, who leans sullenly against a rail and smokes a cigarette. Makita has seen many men such as he in her time, men who pretend to be less than what they are; but those men usually pretended to spare themselves the dangers of sacrifice and service. She feels Torin is simply a man who has found it prudent to hold his abilities in check so that they might be stronger when he absolutely needs them. He watches others closely, that is, he watches all the others but Makita. Evidently he doesn't think her much of a threat either.

Most perplexing of all is this Commander Urik Antares, the sorceress' brother-in-law. Once they had transferred to the skyfurnace, Maya had Makita and Kyuzo follow her as she marched into Urik's war room. This Urik was having a deep and personal conversation with half a bottle of vodka, which he was drinking straight. He was unshaven, disheveled, and on the verge of passing out. But when Maya said, "Marcus is alive," he opened his eyes as if he'd just been stung by a bee. He stood up, straightened his uniform, and took his bottle with him to the head. When he reemerged, he had shaved and the bottle was empty; he threw it overboard.

Only then did he ask who the Nokgorkan child was. When Maya told him, he too lost all antagonism and suspicion and looked at Makita as if he was seeing someone else instead. It made no sense. It makes no sense.

And now Makita is surrounded by strangers who are apparently insisting that she give up her fight and join theirs.

She wonders if there is a parachute handy.

Urik read the letter aloud: "Dearest brother. Beloved wife. If this letter has found you across the years and the miles, then perhaps there is still hope for our land, and our people. I did not fall at Al'istaan. Yet on this day of our nation's defeat at Kar Dartha's Gate, I entered Hell. Urik, Papa always that if we were not careful, the State would separate us from each other. Damn his blessed soul if he wasn't right."

His brother's words inspired in Urik the memory of the dawn of the battle, when the ground forces were about to deployed. When Marcus embraced him and said good-bye. Urik told him to watch himself. Marcus replied that this was the day they had always dreamed of, the day they would win the war. *Just be careful, all right?* Urik asked. Not exactly flowery language, of the sort that always moved Maya so, but the sentiments were genuine.

"By the time you read this," the letter continued, "I'll

be in a world impossible to describe. I may never return, so this letter that may never find you is my farewell. It was important to me to somehow try and let you know that I survived the battle. By a miracle, through the arms of mercy, was my life spared. Still, for the sake of our people and our Motherland, I cannot return to you."

Kyuzo scowled. he too recalled Marcus' final words to him. *Kyuzo, I can only tell this to you. I don't want to threaten Maya's chances of surviving isolation duty by worrying her. Urik knows that Central's plan is a catastrophe waiting to happen. It will be a miracle if I come back. You've always been like a brother to her. If I don't live, protect her. Beyond duty. And protect her from your love for her as well. Please. Otherwise it will blind you.* Kyuzo had no choice but to agree. Some men can fall in love but they are constitutionally unable to grasp the implications and responsibilities of love. He feared he was one, and had spent the last decade finding love in ways he knew Maya, if she knew, would never comment upon, but also would not approve of.

"Maya, my love," said the letter, "forgive me. It is your memory that will sustain me on this journey I must take. There is some small chance that we might find each other again. Yes, the road between us is long, my beauty. It is a path of sacrifice and struggle—and if by some blessing you find these words and yet do not wish to follow me, please know that I love. That I will always love you. This fragile paper is the only messenger I can send. It may turn to ashes before it ever finds you. But if it survives, please grant me one wish:

"Speak the knight's vows."

Maya shook her head as if someone had thrown cold water on her. She had been recalling their last kiss, which they had taken while standing on this very spot.

"Maya, do you know what this means?" Urik asked.

"Yes, I do," she said, dreamily. "It's a passage by a poet we loved, from a book: *Castle Justice*. The night we were married he spoke the words to me."

No one noticed Makita covering her face with one hand. All this sentimentality and good will were torturing her, and she did not know how much more she could endure.

"Speak the words," said Urik.

Torin and Maya both tensed up immediately, the latter more noticeably than the former. Kyuzo grunted and nodded. While Makita wondered if she could survive a thousand-meter jump, because she didn't think she was going to make it through this conversation.

"He just signs it, *For Eternity, Marcus*," said Urik. "Say the words. I want to hear them."

Maya nodded. "*It is impossible*," she quoted, "*yet here you are before me once again...*"

Urik gasped. The letter was shaking, yet his hands were steady. "Maya, it's—"

Shards of crimson light rose up from the letter. Urik released it, yet it did not fall.

"It's got to be some kind of protocol."

"Say the words, Maya!" demanded Urik. "Say the words!"

"*How many lifetimes now, my sentinel? How many, all too brief, have we shared and lost? Only to cheat the vast darkness of infinity and be bore into each other's love anew? As the ages pass away, and the scheme of man dissolve, I have loved you—I will love you—for eternity!*"

As Maya spoke, the shards of crimson light appeared with greater frequency and began spinning. The light bleached out the words and then with a sudden burst blinded them.

The letter disappeared, was disintegrated in the cool red light.

And in the letter's place hung a red-robed woman, hooded, with white hair and glowing white eyes. She was young and beautiful, or rather, she would have been young and beautiful if she was human, for it was immediately obvious this creature existed on a plane beyond the normal realms of the human experience and imagination.

On her back was strapped an extremely long and narrow broadsword, fashioned from a crimson metal of indeterminate origin. Her expression was serene, her overall demeanor one of wisdom and compassion, her inherent power both reassuring and frightening.

All those who witnessed her arrival via the letter protocol had difficulty keeping their bowels in check, like a green footsoldier coming under fire for the first time. Nothing in their experience, not even in Maya's experience, had prepared them for such an encounter. In addition, Kyuzo wondered how well this lady could use her sword. Makita wondered if this woman was the goddess of the Reds and if she would lose her power if someone stole her sword. Torin speculated on what her power source might be, and Urik decided that the letter had been permitted to escape the vague plane of Marcus' imprisonment solely to provide this creature an opportunity to make this really terrific entrance. While Maya's thoughts were on the future; surely this woman in red was going to request something of them. Something arduous, that would require sacrifice. Maya wondered if any of them were ready.

Comrades, said the woman in red, her voice as steady

as a rock, yet musical. *Your eyes are shocked, as are all mortal eyes that look upon the Spirit Realm, even though it is always just beyond the vision of the living.*

Heed closely all that I say, for the time I have is brief. To make myself seen across the ravaging currents and vast temporal chasms between the realms of the living and of the dead, is to risk oblivion.

My arms carried Marcus from the battlefield that day. My words alone can lead you to him. Your brother's fate and your own are linked to that of our nation's future, and yet your quest began decades ago, in the pivotal moment of our nation's past. The Great Revolution...

I lived then. A Sorceress-Commander in the Red Army. For three hundred years we had suffered underneath the monarchs of the ancient dynasties. They had unimaginable wealth. All of it given to them by generations of our bloody labor. After centuries of deceit, we refused to live as their slaves any longer. A belief took hold among us and spread like fire.

INTERNALIONISM

The idea that out lives, and the lives of all common people, all over the world, were worth more. That it was time we stopped being grateful for the scraps and crumbs that fell from the table of those we had made rich. Everything they had we had given them. We gave them the gold of our ideas. We gave them the precious heart-beats of our brief lives. From these, our gifts, they prospered and gave us nothing in return. All of their comforts and riches were rightfully ours.

Defiant thoughts became whispers. Whispers shared grew in volume, until from every corner of the land a cry rang out.

REVOLUTION

We would suffer these injustices no more. Even now I

can recall the joy in our hearts as we dreamed of the great utopia that we hoped to build.

How could we have known?

How could we have known that the very man who led us to victory would betray us all? Imbohl was a colossus, a man of iron—a mighty sorcerer. Mountains moved at the sound of his voice. A gesture of his hand, and thousands upon thousands of us performed his will.

Our enemies, decadent after years of luxury, were no match for the combined might of Imbohl's cunning and our desperate resolve. Relentlessly he drove us to victory, and then enslaved us all.

Our dreams were shadows he used to gain our loyalty. Imbohl had desired power, and we had given it to him. We never imagined the monster he would become. What he had kept secret from us was his greatest strength: the ability to see into the Spirit Realm. No one could ever plan against someone whose spies counted among the darkest souls of all damnation.

We were powerless to stop him. To speak a single word against him meant exile in the frozen wastes of the eastern tundra. By the millions, brave soldiers of the Revolution were sent to their deaths.

Yet not even in death could we escape him. To die was truly to become his slave. Wielding his power of sight and sorcery, he built across the vast plains of our country a network of prisons in which our souls were damned. As long as they are allowed to keep our brothers and sisters from the sleep of their final rest, Imbohl's unholy immortality will be sustained as well.

Only their destruction can free us of his legacy. I do not have time to speak at length of my own unjust murder or the horrors of my time in the camps. Suffice it to say

that the blessed spirit of our Motherland, our goddess
Pravda, took pity upon me.

I was chosen.

My eyes beheld the light of truth, and I was transformed from wretched spirit to our lady's champion.

My sacred duty is to fight for our liberation. To battle
the forces of Imbohl, seeking those with the strength and
courage enough to defeat him. After years of wandering,
after failing to save generation after generation, my tears
were answered.

At last, a savior.

At the battle of Kar Dathra's Gate, your brother,
wounded and near death, looked into the Spirit Realm.

And the agents of Imbohl looked back.

Harvesting souls on the battlefield for their dread lord,
they witnessed a mortal perceiving them. Only Imbohl
himself had ever done so before.

Whether or not they sought to destroy him, or somehow
deliver him for their master's judgement and dark pur-
poses is a mystery I cared not to explore.

I had to save him from them.

I could not help but wonder, as Imbohl's eyes had been
used to imprison our country, could Marcus' vision be
used to free it? After Imbohl's slaves had tasted the anger
of my weapon, I described for him the plague of the
Soulprisons.

For these ten long years Marcus has fought from
within the Spirit Realm. He cannot return to you. However, if you wish to join the fight, you may rendezvous
with him.

There is, in the north, one of the mightiest of the
Soulprisons. It is known as Archangel. Countless of our
comrades are held there, awaiting salvation.

This is the place where you may be reunited.

Know this, comrades. To accept this quest is to become champions of truth. And truth is a blade that leaves not its wielder unscathed.

From this moment forward, you will be enemies of the State. Your countrymen will be ordered to destroy you at all costs. Most of them, blinded by their obedience, will have no idea that your cause is their own. Some of them, fully aware of their role in Imbohl's terror, will use all means available to stop you.

Fly your vessel northward. Toward Archangel. Know that I will be guiding you.

Farewell.

She turned her back to them and then was gone. In the blink of an eye. All the five could see was the glare of the rising sun.

Urik looked to Torin to see his reaction. Torin shrugged and lit yet another cigarette.

Urik looked to Kyuzo. Kyuzo scowled and scratched his bald head.

And then to Maya: her complexion was as pale as that of the ancient undead, yet her jaw was set with grim determination. "Do you think that we could actually make it? That we could reach him?"

"I see that you're not questioning her veracity in the slightest!" exclaimed Urik.

"It's a little late for you to worry about her veracity. I notice that when I saw Marcus was still alive, you straightened up awfully fast!"

"Well, for all we know, he could be dead by now. That's an old letter!"

"There is still hope!"

"I know!" Urik slammed his fist into his palm. "Damnit, I know. It's all so much. The problem is..."

"What?" snapped Maya.

"I sense the location of Archangel. It must be what the woman in red meant when she said she would guide us. I know where to go."

"I've been eager to make a suggestion," said Kyuzo, with a wry smile.

"It's still on this plane. The Mortal Realm. But above it, or beyond it, in another dimension, lies the Soulprison. I can do more than sense it. I can feel it, without a doubt!"

"We're going to have to do this fast, aren't we?" said Maya.

"Well, if one were to try," said Urik, attempting to be objective about the problem, "there is only one way. Run like hell, accelerate to transfer speed, and hope you haven't been obliterated by the time you've kast the jumpgate. Torin, how many of the crew would come with us?"

Torin rubbed his chin. "Hmmm. I'd say about two thirds of the crew are loyal enough, thanks to your generous rations of Citadel mead."

"And I was hoping it was because I try to treat them fairly."

"That too. They will follow you, sir, into Hell, if necessary."

"I'm asking them to follow me into Hell literally."

Torin. "They will do that too. The other third is going to think we've lost their minds."

Maya asked, "Urik, what are you going to do?"

He looked her in the eye, as openingly and honestly as he had ever dared. "I know you want to go, come hellfire and damnation, and I want to go too, but I have my crew to consider. The woman in red was addressing me directly for a reason. The ultimate decision is up me."

"I understand that," said Maya firmly. 'However, I believe time is an issue here.

Urik nodded. "I understand. Give me a minute." He turned away from them, walked to the railing, and looked down upon the battered, snowbound city of Bahamut as the rays of the rising sun bestowed upon it a stark and terrible beauty. Such a useless war. A stupid war, or more precisely, a war even more pointless than most wars. Men were at fault, obviously, but if it was indeed true that powerful forces from the Spirit Realm were aggravating mankind's bellicose tendencies, then it was also true that for the last several centuries Russians and Nokgorkans could have been friends and neighbors, rather than conquerors and the conquered.

If he could change that, then it might be worth it to become a traitor.

Curses, he thought. *Why is it I always have to make my biggest decisions while I have a hangover? Oh well, I'm not going to have another drink until Marcus and I can have a toast together. Oh Father! I promised I would never let the State separate Marcus and me. But the State deceived me. I served my entire life, thinking that in doing so, I served our people. How could I have been so naive? At last I see the State for what it is. A machine that forged the past into chains that bind the future.*

No longer.

Marcus is still alive. I can feel it.

I will break those chains, Father. I promise you.

"Maya, Torin, assemble the crew. They've got a decision to make."

"The girl!" Maya exclaimed. "She's gone!"

"Kyuzo, you mug!" said Urik, not unkindly. "That's twice she's lost you."

Kyuzo sneered. "It's the last time. Unless she's grown wings."

A few hours later, at an airfield in Al'istaan, Skymarshall Brusilov, former Commander of the *Konstantinov*, current member of the Military Administrative Committee of Defense, watched as the Transnational skyfurnace, twice as large as the Red model, set down with the ease of a bird.

"Their machines are awesome," said his attaché, Lt. Roza Horowitz, a young redhead with a photographic memory and the projectile aim of a Hailer.

"Don't envy them," said Brusilov.

The rear platform of the skyfurnace opened and three men walked down it. The smaller, dark-skinned man in the middle was flanked by two large guards wearing the thick chemical-resistant suits and the visor-shielded helmets of the Transnational elite fighting units. Officially, the guards carried their weapons because the Red Fleet had granted them the courtesy, but unofficially the Reds could do nothing to prevent them. Save for lodging yet another futile and embarrassing diplomatic protest.

"You're too young to remember when our nation was so bold," continued Brusilov, "but try to imagine the kind of burden it must be to have so vast an empire as the Transnationalists. Now, because of a heinous act of unconventional warfare, they want Al'istaan. And because their enemy happens to be our enemy as well, we must stand by and see if they can do what we could not."

"Do you think they can?" asked Roza. "Subjugate the land, I mean."

"Yes. I wonder how long they'll be able to hold it all."

The Trans soldier flanked by the guards saluted smartly

as he approached them. Though not nearly as large as the guards (whose size was undoubtedly exaggerated by the bulk of their protective gear), he looked very sharp, every inch a soldier. "Marshall Brusilov. It's been a while."

"Since the liberation of the Gulf, Colonel Rogers," said Brusilov, returning the salute. "I see you have fulfilled your early promise and risen rapidly in the ranks. Welcome to the Nistaani borderlands."

Rogers smiled modestly. "I wanted to say hello before the goddamned press arrives and starts the flag-waving."

"It is good to see you. Allow me to express my sorrow at the loss of your father in the attacks on the Imperial City. He was a great soldier, and an even better man. He extended the hand of friendship to me during a time when it was very difficult for Internationalists and Transnationals to see beyond their narrow ideological differences and work together for mutual peace."

"He often spoke highly of you too, sir. He always said—and I must emphasize he always smiled when he said it—that 'If anyone could turn that backwards country around, it'd be Alexei.'"

"I'll do whatever I can to avenge his death, Steven."

"Thank you, sir." He approached the Skymarshall and said conspiratorially, "With all due respect though, and off the record, I'm not sold on the idea that those responsible for the attacks on the Great White Way are even in this country."

Roza raised an eyebrow. There was a contingent in the Red Fleet who believed their government's cooperation with the Trans' "police action" in Al'istaan was either a mistake or a deliberate act of misdirection. It had not occurred to her that a Trans soldier might possess the independence of thought to question authority.

"I don't want to say what gives me reason for such doubt," Colonel Rogers continued. "It's just something in my gut. In the meantime, I'll do my duty."

"You've reminded me of something your father often said to me," said Brusilov. "How does it go exactly? 'History is always written by the powerful, and the powerful always have something to hide...' Your armed forces can take Al'istaan easily enough. We controlled the entire country in a month. Holding it, keeping your grip on it, that's the test, Rogers, the real test."

Colonel Rogers grinned. "Not really. We just want to kick some serious ass. Then, after a serious regime change, we'll be out of here."

Lt. Roza Horowitz tapped Brusilov on the shoulder. "Please excuse me, Colonel."

"What is it, Lieutenant?"

"Excuse me, sir, but there is an urgent communiqué from Central. It was just given to me by a courier."

Brusilov snorted. He hadn't even noticed. "Can't this wait?"

"No, sir. Straight from the top. It's about your former command, sir—the *Konstantinov*."

"Give it to me." He put on his reading glasses and opened the envelope. What he read was very disturbing, to say the least.

COMMUNIQUÉ FROM CENTRAL COMMAND.
TO ALL COMMANDING OFFICERS.
SKYMARSHALL URIK ANTARES, SORCERESS-MAJOR MAYA ANTARES, CHIEF ENGINEER ANDRE TORIN AND A MAJORITY OF THE CREW (EST. TWO-THIRDS) HAVE STAGED A MUTINY AND ABANDONED THEIR DUTIES IN NOKGORKA. REMAINING CREW REFUSED TO JOIN MUTINY,

WERE GIVEN SAFE PASSAGE GROUNDSIDE, AND ARE
CURRENTLY UNDER QUESTIONING.

THE DESTINATION OF THEIR VESSEL THE R.R.S.
KONSTANTINOV IS UNKNOWN AT THIS TIME.

SKYMARSHALL ANTARES HAS REFUSED TO SURRENDER
HIMSELF, HIS CREW, OR HIS VESSEL. THE ONLY RESPONSE
HAS BEEN HOSTILE REACTION: THE KONSTANTINOV HAS
FIRED UPON AND IMMOBILIZED THE R.S.S. FIRIN DURING
A BRIEF ENGAGEMENT.

FOR THIS TREASONOUS INSUBORDINATION, THE
OFFICERS AND CREW OF THE KONSTANTINOV HAVE BEEN
STRIPPED OF RANK AND MILITARY PRIVILEGES AND FROM
THIS DAY FORWARD ARE CONSIDERED TO BE ENEMIES OF
THE STATE.

ORDERS FOLLOW:

MAKE NO FURTHER ATTEMPT AT NEGOTIATION WITH
THE ENEMY VESSEL.

INTERCEPT AND USE ALL FORCE NECESSARY TO SUB-
DUE. IF SUBDUING THE VESSEL IS UNFEASIBLE, ORDERS
ARE TO ENGAGE AND DESTROY.

REPEAT:

ENGAGE AND DESTROY.

Brusilov handed the message to Lt. Horowitz. "What do
you think of this?"

"It's strange, sir," she said, after reading it. "The *Konstantinov*'s top-ranking sorceress registered kasting a
reenact protocol yesterday, which is very unusual—and
then this." She opened a line on her comlink and received
a message into her earphone. "According to Central
Command, the latest update says the *Tantarov* and support ship have them engaged, sir."

Brusilov scowled. Urik Antares was one of the most patriotic men he'd ever had the pleasure to serve with. Granted, the officer had had personal problems since the death of his brother, but they hadn't affected his ability to perform his duties—at least, not so much that Central Command would notice. It was inconceivable that Antares could capriciously turn traitor, and furthermore, that he could persuade so many others to join him. Something extraordinary must be up. Something very extraordinary.

"That information is two hours old, but against Marshall Volkov?" said the lieutenant. "It's probably over by now. Indeed, it was probably over very quickly."

"With all due respect to Marshall Volkov and his crew, Lieutenant, you don't know my old ship. And you don't know Urik Antares..."

Urik Antares had played war games before. He was considered a master of them capable of accessing the limitations of any given set of rules and then breaking them in such a way that he changed the playing field to his advantage. But like certain war gamers during the Great War of half a century earlier, who did not write enemy subfurnace night attacks into their scenarios, thus denying seafurnace captains and crews the experience required to fend off enemy blows, the war gamers had never provided Urik with a scenario that pitted a Red skyfurnace against a concerted attack from Red skyfurnaces with equal firepower and capabilities. The *Konstantinov* was surrounded on all sides, from above and below, and the Red Skymarshalls weren't being shy about ordering their sorceresses to direct devastating blasts at his ship's most vital areas. He avoided most of them—he was famous for his sharp turns, though he had to be careful not to tilt the ship so much that his crew lost their footing—but every one that hit rocked the ship like it was being toyed with by a kid in a bathtub.

Was it the seventh or the eighth blast? He could not be sure, but he decided around then that he'd better cease merely trying to avoid the next blow and find out how the *Konstantinov* was holding up. He double-checked the straps holding him in the captain's chair and punched up his chief engineer on the com line.

"Torin! Full damage report!"

The chief engineer's voice was uncharacteristically tense. "Sector Bravo Six—isolator tanks A to G on fire! Handing it now! Sector Gamma Nine—Furnace 45! Overheating fifty percent past reline! Rear Sector seven two seven—Engine one at critical! Sector De—"

Urik found he could not read the words—Torin's words—appearing simultaneously on the red-lit panel floating before his eyes. Indeed, comprehending the enormity of the damage inflicted thus far was difficult.

"No more damage reports!" he ordered. "If we start to freefall, I'll be the first to know! Maya! How much longer before we can gatekast out of here?"

Maya, much to his dismay, was just as tense, though it was not an unreasonable reaction under the circumstances. "Be aware that with the remaining kasters we have only one Gatekast Protocol! Repeat! We have one chance to gate out!"

Urik was afraid he'd heard that correctly. "In the meantime, order the 21st isolator battery to fire on the *Taktarov*!" Which would mean of course that he was ordering the 21st to fire on his own countrymen. If only he could simply direct the blast at Volkov's head instead...

"The 21st is one of the units that turned down our invitation," Maya reminded him.

Damn! Now he remembered. The whole unit was deserted.

Another blast struck the rear of the ship. This one was so powerful that it shook the skyfurnace with sufficient force to shear two of the bolts holding down his chair. A light broke free and almost smashed him on the cranium. Figuring he'd be just as safe on the open deck, he unstrapped himself and dashed through the postern. He reached outside just in time to see the pulverized pieces of his ship emerging from the yellow ball of flame and dropping toward the ground, where they would join the debris that already comprised the majority of Bahamut.

"5th battery!" he ordered. "Fire at will!"

His men did as ordered, but they missed, whether through simple error or an unconscious desire not to slay their own countrymen, he could not sure. Nor did it matter. He couldn't help but wonder if his aim would have any better.

"If this keeps up," he mumbled to himself, "we'll be rat food in Nokgorka."

A transmission came in to his com line. "Informkast to Skymarshall Antares. The *Taktarov* is moving alongside. They're—"

Urik was on starboard. He looked to port and completed the sentence. "Preparing to board!"

"Yes, sir!"

We're in now, he thought. "Antares to Captain Zubov!"

"Zubov here, sir!"

"Get up here with my command team and prepare to repel boarders. And bring me my goddamned guns!"

Makita feels like she's explored every passage of this flying killing machine, like she's examined every plate and every bolt in her efforts to sneak around undetected.

So far she has avoided being spotted, but she is frustrated because she has not found one parachute, gasbag, or ski-jet. Just breathing the same air as these Reds is making her nauseous, and she cannot wait until she is safely off this ship of zanies and can safely watch it freefall while she stands on solid ground.

Now that she has come upon the fightercraft take-off dock. It is deserted; apparently most of the pilots—of this unit, anyway—had decided Antares' proposition was just a little bit too crazy, even for a Red. She dashes to the closest fightercraft, opens the canopy, and climbs in. Her feet barely reach the floor, but the take-off dock is open, the city lies tantalizingly below. All she has to do is push the right button and the engines will switch on and she will be off.

But the controls are very colorful and complicated. There are no words, only symbols, and she has no idea what they mean. The button with the perpendicular tri-angle on it looks promising. She reaches for it...

Suddenly there's a knock on the canopy. A shadow is looming over her. Through the transparent Plexiglas she sees the giant form of that blasted Hailer, shaking his head in the negative. "No, not that one. Not unless you want to eject at thirty kilometers per hour." He looks to the ceiling. "You would make a darling paste. Let us say that by some ridiculous miracle, you were suddenly able to fly one of these. Then what happens?"

Kyuzo opens the canopy; she'd forgotten to lock it. "First, you'd be confronted with a wall of superheated autofire. If that doesn't tear the fightercraft to burning shreds, and you along with it, eventually you'd have to land. I'd give you ninety to ten against slamming into a building at full throttle."

Makita's lip trembles. She is about to cry.

"You must understand," says Kyuzo. "We are all criminals now—every one of us on this ship. Our own countrymen have been ordered to shoot us out of the sky. We're under attack from all sides. I know you want to go home. But that is impossible for any of us now."

"Then why did you bring me here? Why didn't you leave me where I belong?"

The ship shakes from the impact of yet another blast.

Kyuzo holds onto the fightercraft for stability. "Believe me, if the Major thinks you belong here, then this is where you belong. I do not pretend to understand her reasons—she has not confided in me—and I do not care. But Alexandra Goncharova gave her life for you, and maybe that is reason enough. There is only one way for us to go now. Forward. Only forward. Into what we cannot know. You don't believe me, then I'll give you a choice."

"Really?"

"That button releases the fore and aft stops. Push it and you launch into freefall. From there you have thirty seconds to learn how to fly."

"Okay."

Kyuzo turns his back to her and walks away. "Or you can follow me and kill some Reds. The choice is yours."

Makita huffs and looks out onto the vista of the battered city that was once her home. She realizes that her emotions, rather than her intellect, have already made the decision for her. She climbs out of the fightercraft. "Hey, old man! Did you say 'Kill some Reds?'"

Kyuzo turns and looks her in the eye with such steel in his soul that she comes to a complete stop. "I did, but I want you to think about two things. First, think about your boy friend. Proto. 'Love.'"

"So? What of him?"

"He killed my friend, but I cannot hate him, for he was very brave, he just happened to be fighting on a side other than my own. Do you not think the harvesters of souls will want his? If we have learned anything today, young lady, it is the fact that death is not the end."

"Are you saying this Imbohl has stolen Proto's soul?"

"I am saying it is possible. Kill Reds all you want, for fun and profit, but remember certain Reds are fighting for Proto's soul as well as the souls of those they love. Second, I must tell you, I have a confession."

"You do?"

"See those weights tethered to the wheels of the fightercraft? The weights that keep it in place through every dip and turn the ship has made during this battle? I forgot all about them. If you had decided to leave, you would not have had even thirty seconds before you endured your own personal immolation."

"You bastard!"

Kyuzo smiles and shrugs. "Follow me," is all he says.

It was a relatively easy thing for gatekasters to kast portals a hundred meters or less away, but it was more difficult for them to do so with precision. The gates were too high above the upper deck of the *Konstantinov* for the boarders to come out fighting; instead they came out dropping anywhere from thirty to forty meters and many were in no position to get up and take part in the fighting afterwards.

For that, Urik was grateful, though every time he drew a bead at a Red leveling his weapon to fire, he had to fight his every instinct and reflex. *Kill or be killed*—he was used to that. But killing your own countrymen because a higher principle than national solidarity was at stake—that was something he had never trained for.

Not even the intellectuals in the university had discussed this moral dilemma, at least not in any way meaningful to the man who would one day have to pull the trigger.

But pull the trigger he did. He and Captain Zubov and the command team were hunkered down behind the precious little cover the upper deck provided—the radar, the deck crane, the debris from a hanger that had been by a sorceress blast. Their former countrymen used their dead and in some cases their wounded as cover, exactly what they had been trained to do. Otherwise both sides were fighting in the open, and could only pray the fear and confusion of those on the other side unsteadied their aim. It was the most fragile prayer Urik had ever depended on.

He had just shot a corpse while aiming at the head of a Red when Maya came in on the com link. "Urik, where the hell are you?"

"Top deck, Zone three! How's that goddamn kast coming? I'm trying to save my brother, not butcher our countrymen." He fired several more slugs into the corpse, hoping the soldier he was trying to impress would keep his head down. He didn't have the time or spare attention to see if the rest of the Command team was trying to be as judicious. He thought not. "Now get us out of this!"

"How much longer can you hold on?"

"Depends on how many more siege gates they decide to drop on us!"

"Informkast to Marshall Antares—"

Damn it! He hated being interrupted when he was doing something important. "Save the formalities and report, Lieutenant!"

"We've got a breach in the command decks, sir! Invasion bridge locking to deck block 30:39!"

"Damnit! Anybody in the area?"

"No one but the enemy squad crossing the expanse, sir!"

"Was that supposed to be funny, Lieutenant?" Urik gave both barrels to the man who until a second ago had been keeping his head down. The man, unfortunately, would not be having that problem in the future.

Another communication came in: "Kyuzo here, sir! I'll handle the boarding party on block 39!"

"Kyuzo, where the hell have you been?"

"Had to stop the Gorka from growing wings, sir!"

"What? A few hours of freedom and they're all god-damned comedians! Zubov! Incoming!"

An invasion bridge is simply a metal corridor that extends from one skyfurnace and clamps onto the another. It is strong enough to hold the relative positions of the skyfurnaces in place and as many men who can fit crossing from one side to the other. Looking at the decks of the *Tartarov*, Kyuzo estimates there are about five hundred soldiers waiting their turn in the cue. Luckily the corridor is only wide enough to permit two men to enter at a time. That is the only lucky thing.

Kyuzo darts past an anti-fightercraft gun on a revolving turret.

"Old man!" shouts Makita. "Where are you going? Should you be—?"

"That one's for you. Sit down and start firing at the bridge, and don't stop till I tell you stop. The trigger's on the left."

And he keeps running.

She sits down and stares at a series of controls every bit as complicated as those in the fightercraft. *No wonder Dushka is always getting into trouble with his elders,* she thought. But she didn't have time to miss him. She had work to do.

"Hey, old man! The seat adjust is broken! I can't see!"

"Welcome to the Red Fleet!" Kyuzo shouts, as he reached an anti-fightercraft gun that had been blown off its turret earlier in the battle. He looks down the corridor. The leading man is halfway to boarding the *Konstantinov*, and he is aiming his weapon while on the run. "Forget the adjust!" he calls to the wolf cub. With that gun you don't need to see. Just hold down the trigger!"

"I see a blinking red light! What does that—?"

Kyuzo is in the midst of picking up the gun. He holds it by the turret control rod with one hand, by the trigger with the other, and is attempting to keep it at the proper angle by supporting it on one thigh. The gun weighs nearly as much as he does. The lead man in the corridor is about to take his shot.

"The blinking red light means that if you don't start firing right now, your chances of living would have been much higher as a pilot than a gunner!"

The man in the corridor is firing. The bullets ricochet off Kyuzo's armor, but of course there are parts of his body aren't covered with armor to facilitate movement. The bullets pass directly through those. Fortunately there aren't too many of them.

"This seat adjust is completely useless!" Makita shouts. "Typical!"

"Gorka! Shut up and listen! Pedals control horizontal rotation—"

"What?"

"Pedals! Rotation! Thumb switch! Elevation!"

"What locks the feed?"

Kyuzo fires a few shots into the corridor and the man

goes down. Those right behind him stumble, giving Kyuzo a precious few seconds to put a piece of severed conduit in his mouth to bite down on. He's going to need it to deal with the pain, which is already considerable.

"Bottom lever!" he shouts to the wolf cub. "The one that says 'Ammo Feed.'"

"You're not funny!"

"Gorka, listen now! No more time! Hold down that trigger and do not let go! You're on your own!"

And so is Kyuzo. He bites down on the conduit and holds down the trigger and his weapon and cuts loose with enough lead to poison the Roman Empire.

Standard assault force: fifty men, he thinks. *Dragunov 60mm. Autocannon. At short range can cut them in half. The Gorka. Firing a heavy D.S.H.K. She's blind, untrained. I've got ten at best. And she has twenty seconds to live, if she's lucky. Then they regroup, and coordinate their fire on me. And it's over. Unless we're lucky.*

Meanwhile, Makita is holding down the trigger with both hands. It's a good thing she's blind because the heat, flash and noise of every round causes her to instinctively close her eyes, and the power of every round rattles her like electroshock therapy.

Then there's the matter of the rounds whizzing past her. There is something to be said for not knowing exactly how many Reds are shooting at you.

Suddenly the sounds of men screaming quadruples, and Makita opens her eyes just in time to see Reds falling through a section of the invasion bridge that is coming apart.

The bridge snaps in two. Both sides tilt and the men begin to slip out.

"Hey, old man!" she shouts.

Not realizing that a couple of men are shooting at her while they're on the way down. Bullets rip through the seat's backrest.

"Never mind about the seat adjust!" she says.

Kyuzo drops the weapon, crawls to the edge of the corridor clamps and, pistol in hand, peers down.

There is no one. This part of the invasion strategy has been stymied.

He discovers that he is laughing. He has become a traitor to everything he had ever stood for, save for his personal loyalties, and he cannot stop laughing. She did it! The Gorka did it! "Damn, girl!" he said, tears streaming from his eyes. "You are a pistol!"

"Urik! Come in, it's Maya. Give me status!"

Urik looked at the bloody upper deck. He was still alive, reasonably capable of standing, and supported the wounded Captain Zubov. He felt sick, disgusted at the waste of men's lives, but he knew in his heart there existed creatures in this universe who, far from being disgusted, were delighted.

"One more push and they would have had us," he said, "but they were ordered back! Uh-oh!" He paused. "The *Taktarov* is pulling behind us. Damnit! They're trying to—"

"Slave onto our jump co-ordinates! I know, Uri," said Maya. She sat in the Warkaster administrator chair with her eyes locked on the semi-transparent crimson charts and controls being worked on by a row of busy data processing sorceresses.

"Volkov is too damn good!" said Urik. The looming skyfurnace looked like a military command and control center suddenly released from the constraints of gravity.

"He's trying to kill our jump with the added mass! How do you plan to compensate, Major?"

"Maybe you'd like to come down here and kast it yourself, Skymarshall!" Which was her way of saying she had no idea at the moment.

"Save your tongue for my brother, witch! If you ever want to see him again, then kast that gate!"

His words stung her, she seethed with anger and resentment. How dare he talk to her that way, after all she'd done? If she had the power of a witch of old, she'd turn him into a toad. And he'd have to be kissed on some place other than his lips to be changed back into a man. But perhaps there was a way...

"Torin!" she said. "We'll do this the hard way! Cut all defensive shields on my mark! All power to Gatekast!

Maya knew what she was asking. Red skyfurnaces did not transfer power with the push of a button or the muttering of a protocol, as Transnational ships did. Every move in a Red engine required the vast exertion of physical labor. Immediately upon receiving her orders, Torin and his second-in-command Razin put the huge chains attached to the power storage cells over their shoulders and, unheeding of radiation levels, began dragging the cells to the kast batteries.

"If Volkov figures out we've dropped our shields, he could spit at us knock us out of the sky," Torin com linked to Maya.

"You heard me, Torin! Now!"

"We're doing it, ma'am, we are doing it. Estimated exposure time with zero shields is thirty-six seconds starting... NOW!"

The batteries were in place. The red light that always permeated the engine fortresses intensified.

"Shields at zero!" Torin reported.

"Not long now, Olga," said Razin, speaking to the spirit of his deceased wife, which he had felt very close to him since the revelations of this morning. "I'm on my way to you soon, my darling!"

Torin hefted another chain Razin's way; they needed more power. "Put your back in it, Razin. We'll be in Hell soon enough! Cry to her then!"

While on top of the *Konstantinov*, Urik was hustling the survivors of the skirmish—be they friend or foe—through the hatches, pushing them down below if need be.

"All units," he broadcast, "when we're through the gate—it's going to be hellfire with the slaved pursuit ships. Be prepared for immediate conflict! If they want to follow us, then God help them! For now, get the Hell below! Antares out!"

The Red obeyed without question. Makita was another story. She wondered aloud why she was obligated to listen to that pompous alcoholic popinjay.

"I do not have time for an argument," said Kyuzo. Though still bleeding profusely from the wounds he had sustained, he grabbed and carried her like a bushel of wheat as he leapt through the nearest hatch.

"Put me down, you bald-headed bastard! No good sonuvabitch! What in the name of the Motherland do you think—"

Kyuzo found her gratitude very amusing.

Meanwhile, in the Warkasting room, Maya saw that everything was coming together. She also saw that at least six other skyfurnaces were sticking close, their skymarshals undoubtedly concentrating on coming through the gate with them or causing an etcoplasmic disaster that would preclude a jump; but they probably did not suspect the *Konstantinov* was diverting power and had no shields.

"Major Antares to all kasters! Confirm we are at maximum acceleration!"

They did.

"Coordinates locked. Transferring mass in TEN!

"NINE!"

With gratitude and the faint stirrings of hope, she saw an expanse of pure white opening up in the atmosphere directly above them. Tendrils of ectoplasmic power snaked from the newly forming gate and reached out to the tip of the *Konstantinov*. Another few moments and she would arrive at a place few people who were still alive had ever seen, or else she would face oblivion, and see the place as the dead souls saw it. Either way, Marcus would be there, waiting...

"THREE!

"TWO!

"TRANSFER!"

And she channeled all her power through her. She was no longer the heat of her nation's anger, she was fueled by the great love she had nurtured for ten years. She discovered that love was the more powerful, because it was founded upon a foundation of truth.

Which was more than she could say for her nation.

The *Konstantinov* shot through the gate.

At that moment, of what happened to the other ships, she neither knew, nor cared. She only knew the great ship was ascending through a tunnel of fire, and when it emerged on the other side, guided by the light of the Goddess Pravda, they would make war on a prison of souls.